The End of the World and Other Stories

Mavis Gallant

Introduction by Robert Weaver
General Editor: Malcolm Ross

New Canadian Library No. 91

M&S

ıe Other Paris," "The Picnic," and "About Geneva": Copyright© 1952, 1953, 1954, 1955 by Mavis Gallant. Reprinted by permission of Houghton Mifflin Company. "Acceptance of Their Ways," "My Heart Is Broken," and "An Unmarried Man's Summer": reprinted from *My Heart Is Broken*, published by Random House. Copyright© 1964 by Mavis Gallant. "The End of the World": Copyright© 1967 by Mavis Gallant. Reprinted from *The New Yorker*, June 10, 1967. "The Accident": Copyright© 1967 by Mavis Gallant. Reprinted from *The New Yorker*, October 28, 1967. "Malcolm and Bea": Copyright© 1968 by Mavis Gallant. Reprinted from *The New Yorker*, March 23, 1968. "The Prodigal Parent": Copyright© 1969 by Mavis Gallant. Reprinted from *The New Yorker*, June 7, 1969. "The Wedding Ring": Copyright© 1969 by Mavis Gallant. Reprinted from *The New Yorker*, June 28, 1969. "New Year's Eve": Copyright© 1970 by Mavis Gallant. Reprinted from *The New Yorker*, January 10, 1970. "In the Tunnel": Copyright© 1971 by Mavis Gallant. Reprinted from *The New Yorker*, September 18, 1971.

Introduction© 1974, McClelland and Stewart

Reprinted 1987

Canadian Cataloguing in Publication Data

Gallant, Mavis, 1922–
    The end of the world and other stories

(New Canadian library ; N91)
ISBN 0-7710-9191-5

I. Title. II. Series: New Canadian library ; no. 91.

PS8513.A44E63 1987   C813'.54   C87-095133-5
PR9199.3.G348E63 1987

Manufactured in Canada by Webcom Limited

McClelland and Stewart
The Canadian Publishers
481 University Avenue
Toronto, Ontario
M5G 2E9

Contents

Introduction

Mavis Gallant was born in Montreal and educated in schools in Canada and the United States, but she didn't begin to make her reputation as a writer until after she left this country, in 1950, to live in Europe. In Montreal she worked briefly for the National Film Board and then on the Montreal *Standard*, a weekly newspaper of the *Star Weekly* type that was later killed off to make way for *Weekend*, the supplement that still appears every Saturday in a number of local newspapers across the country. Miss Gallant was married to a musician and divorced from him. Not long before she left Montreal for Paris a friend persuaded Mavis Gallant to send one of her unpublished short stories to *The New Yorker;* it was returned, but with an interested comment. She sent a second story to the magazine, it was accepted, and almost all the stories she has published since that time have first appeared in *The New Yorker*.

Mavis Gallant belongs roughly to the same generation as Margaret Laurence, Mordecai Richler and Norman Levine, all of whom have lived abroad for long periods without forfeiting their identity as Canadian writers, but she has come to seem the complete expatriate. Her books have been distributed in Canada by New York publishers, and not much attention has been paid to them here. She has had admirers in Canada, mostly among her fellow writers, and a few of her stories have been published in Canadian anthologies. Some of her stories have Canadian backgrounds, and, in her fiction that is set in Europe, Canadians have a habit of turning up in what is to me an attractively natural and unforced manner. But now that cultural nationalism is turning us in on ourselves, Mavis Gallant's work may have even less chance than before of attracting much attention in her own country. That would be a pity, because she is simply too fine a writer for us to ignore. And so here at least is this selection of some of her stories for a Canadian reprint series.

Mavis Gallant's fiction includes two novels, *Green Water, Green Sky* (1959) and *A Fairly Good Time* (1970), and three collections of stories, *The Other Paris* (1956), *My Heart Is Broken* (1964), and *The Pegnitz Junction* (1973), which consists of a novella and five short stories all linked together by the fact that they are fictions about "Germany and the Germans, either at home or abroad." In addition she has contributed two remarkable non-fiction examinations of French society to *The New Yorker* in recent years.

7

The first novel, *Green Water, Green Sky*, is a short book –
about 150 pages – with an atmosphere, for me at any rate, of
latter day Scott Fitzgerald and Zelda. Miss Gallant's fictions, so
subtle in their explorations of character, are never easy to para-
phrase, and this book is no exception. In her later novel, *A Fairly
Good Time*, she says at one point that "the correspondence
between mother and daughter ... was an uninterrupted dialogue
of the deaf." What seems to be taking place in *Green Water,
Green Sky*, and indeed in much of her fiction, is just such a
continuing "dialogue of the deaf."

Green Water, Green Sky is a study of alienation, and Mavis
Gallant describes the book's destructive force, the mother, in this
way:

> When Bonnie was still under forty, her husband had caught
> her out in a surpassingly silly affair – she had not in the least
> loved the lover – and had divorced her, so that her concep-
> tion of herself was fragmented, unreconciled. There was Bon-
> nie, sweet-faced, with miniature roses; wicked Mrs. Hauks-
> bee, the stormy petrel of a regimental outpost; and, some-
> thing near the truth, a lost, sallow, frightened Bonnie wan-
> dering from city to city in Europe, clutching her daughter by
> the hand.

Bonnie, of course, survives. Her nephew George, a sometime
observer of the scene, rejects the destructive element in his family,
and survives. The daughter Florence, fragmented in her turn, has
become by the end of the novel a Zelda-figure. And Florence's
husband, Bob Harris, burdened with two women his generous
nature was never designed to cope with, turns into "someone soft
and patient with the empty profile of the blind."

In the early 1960s, when the American man of letters Edmund
Wilson was working in Paris on his book about Canadian writers
and Canadian society, *O Canada*, Mavis Gallant ·assisted him
in his research, and he read her early fiction. "She is more
international than Canadian," Mr. Wilson wrote in *O Canada*,
"... she gets away from the Canadian bleakness and her work
displays a color and wit rather rare among native writers.... But
she has not quite found her form and her stance. [Her early] stories are likely to impress one as being not so much real short stories as episodes from some larger fiction – the projection of a
mixed experience – that she has not yet found out how to manage, and even episodes of the novel itself [*Green Water, Green
Sky*] give something of this impression".

More than ten years separate Mavis Gallant's first novel from
A Fairly Good Time, and the second novel is a larger and more

ambitious work and a clearer evidence of her talent for long fiction. When the book first appeared it was described by the American novelist Elizabeth Janeway as being "very funny and very frightening," and that's an accurate summary of the impression it gives. Shirley Perrigny, who was born Shirley Higgins in Montreal, became a young widow stranded in Europe, and married again. Her second husband Philippe Perrigny is an ambitious and determinedly bourgeois French journalist with an even more determinedly bourgeois French family arrayed behind him. When the novel begins Philippe has left his wife and retreated behind the battlements of his family's respectability, and Shirley with her messy and incoherent life style has been stranded for a second time in Europe.

The trouble with Shirley is that she cannot comprehend Edith Wharton's cool advice, from which the novel takes its title: "There are lots of ways of being miserable, but there's only one way of being comfortable, and that is to stop running round after happiness. If you make up your mind not to be happy there's no reason why you shouldn't have a fairly good time."

Shirley will have none of this, nor is she allowed some detachment from life. If a friend needs an abortion, Shirley is there; if a suicide is attempted, Shirley becomes involved. In more ordinary affairs she blunders, misunderstands, then cannot extricate herself; she is the destructive innocent at large in the world, and like Bonnie and Florence in *Green Water, Green Sky*, fragmented. *A Fairly Good Time* is, as Elizabeth Janeway declared, a very funny book, particularly in its sour view of French middle class life. But it is frightening because while we can't brush off Shirley's sympathy and involvement with others – she is only too human – we end up praying that we may never have the misfortune to be entangled with her.

The two issues of *The New Yorker* for September 14 and 21, 1968 included Mavis Gallant's diary kept during the student rebellion in Paris in May of that year. The diary covers the month from May 3 to June 4, and it compresses into that month a sort of profile-in-small of revolution. On May 3 it notes the ironic beginnings of the affair. Members of a right wing student group were waiting that day outside the Sorbonne to beat up left wing students. But they began fighting with the police when they saw that the left wing students were being arrested. The two radical student groups suddenly found that they had more in common with one another than either had with the police force hired to protect the bourgeois French Republic.

Soon the normal life of the city had been disrupted, and the students were cheerfully helping to direct traffic. Their revolution was in its springtime, and there was a buoyancy about the early days of May, 1968 in Paris that sounds a minor echo of the Anarchist take-over of Barcelona during the Spanish Civil War. But of course the Paris students had too little sense of history to know anything about that.

It didn't take long, however, for the forces of order and tradition, among them the official Communist Party, to begin re-establishing old methods of bargaining to preserve the state. Within a month Mavis Gallant is able to describe the Revolution Betrayed: "No one speaks of students now," her diary tells us. "They are forgotton, except as pests. Talk is of salaries, elections. . . . News is of death on the roads."

It would be inaccurate to suggest that Mavis Gallant recorded with great sympathy the uprising of the students and their defeat. Her diary is often quite testy, and it gives the reader the impression that after twenty years of living with them, she looks on Frenchmen of all ages and classes with a cool eye. The diary is the personal record of a political incident written by someone who finds politics distasteful: "I loathe slogans; I hate shouting." No one would be advised to look on the diary as a complete or objective document, but in her distaste for politics Mavis Gallant is freed to come up with this kind of sharp observation:

> When workers are asked, in interviews, what they think of the students, they invariably refer to them as "our future bosses" and say they hope this experience will make better *chefs* of them than their fathers have been.

Mavis Gallant's second essay in non-fiction was also published in *The New Yorker* and later as the introduction to a book called *The Affair of Gabrielle Russier* (1971). Gabrielle Russier was a thirty-year-old teacher of languages in Marseilles, divorced and the mother of nine-year-old twins, who committed the fatal error of falling in love with one of her students, Christian Rossi, who was sixteen when their affair began.

Rossi's parents were teachers, intellectuals, and Communists (supporters of the official Communist Party; their son seems to have been attracted by Maoism), but they made every frantic effort to break up the affair, at one time committing their son to a private sanitarium where he endured an extreme treatment known as the "sleep cure." Then they turned to the legal authorities, and Gabrielle Russier was arrested and kept waiting six months for her trial. The case was tried in closed court, but even so Gabrielle Russier got off with a suspended sentence. At this point her case was reopened by the public prosecutor, who was evidently determined to get a sentence that would make it impossible for her ever to teach again. Faced with the loss of her profession, fragmented we might say like some character in a Mavis Gallant fiction, Gabrielle Russier killed herself, and with her suicide the affair became a scandal throughout France.

The Affair of Gabrielle Russier contains, in addition to Mavis Gallant's superb long essay about the case, letters that Gabrielle wrote from prison while she was waiting for her trial. The letters are pathetic more than profound. Gabrielle Russier was an intellectual of a very narrow and traditional kind, she was emotionally immature, and she suffered through the whole case perhaps not really comprehending what was happening to her. She was that kind of fated innocent who would immediately be recognized by novelists like Graham Greene or Morley Callaghan.

Mavis Gallant's essay about Gabrielle Russier, more detached but also much more unrelenting than her diary of the Paris student rebellion, is an indictment of French society. It is also, if anyone cares to make use of it in that way, a document for Women's Liberation. What was at the core of Gabrielle Russier's personal disaster, Miss Gallant writes, was "the Latin attitude towards men and women. A Don Juan is admired; perhaps God punishes him, but that is God's affair. Whereas anyone who publicly defended Gabrielle Russier was apt to receive a deluge of letters reminding her defender that Gabrielle was a disgrace to womanhood, as well as a whore, a pervert and a nymphomaniac. Gabrielle Russier was nine before women were allowed to vote, twenty-eight when married women could have bank accounts, and thirty before she could legally get advice from a doctor about contraception. She died before women were allowed to enroll their children in kindergarten without the husband's written consent, or have a say in where the family would live." In this world of double standards an innocent of Gabrielle Russier's kind had no chance.

The thirteen stories in *The End of the World and Other Stories* represent about a quarter of the short stories that Mavis Gallant has published in the past twenty years. Three stories have been reprinted here from each of her first two collections of short fiction, *The Other Paris* and *My Heart Is Broken*. The remaining stories all appeared in *The New Yorker* between 1967 and 1971, and are uncollected. The author herself wishes it to be mentioned that the stories from *The Other Paris* and *My Heart Is Broken* were all written during the 1950s and the early 1960s, and belong to their time. About the story "The Other Paris," for example, Miss Gallant wrote in a letter to me that it "would simply be mystifying to a young foreigner in Paris today, but that *was* the city five years after the last war."

And yet surely, even to a young reader today, this story could be seen to possess qualities that are not mystifying because they are associated with that unreachable immediate past but are tantalizing because they still seem relevant and are so sharply observed. Mavis Gallant has been an expatriate for twenty years, and she writes often about the world of the expatriate, and with a degree of ambivalence. In "The Other Paris" Carol Frazier finds herself living as an expatriate in Paris trapped in a boring, middle class existence and preparing to marry her dull, conventional fiancé Howard Mitchell. This isn't really what Carol expected to find in Paris, and through her only French friend Odile she tries at the last moment to discover some fragments of the legendary and romantic city. But Odile's Paris – the other Paris to Carol – turns out to be a terrible, grubby failure.

In "Acceptance of Their Ways" there is a portrait of another kind of expatriate: here three English ladies squabble together in a *pension* on the unfashionable Italian Riviera. In the superb "An Unmarried Man's Summer" the living is several cuts above a *pension*, but here too squabbling and envy serve as forms of communication. In "The Picnic" and "Malcolm and Bea" we meet those unique expatriates of the immediate postwar years who lead artificial and fleeting lives in the American army bases of Western Europe.

There are two or three more stories in *The End of the World and Other Stories* that I would like to mention briefly. Anyone who has read Mavis Gallant's novel, *A Fairly Good Time*, will find an intriguing prologue to this book in the short story called "The Accident." Anyone curious to see how she has treated Canada directly in her fiction should look at "My Heart Is Broken," a beautifully crafted exploration of character done in a small space; its setting is a road construction camp in Northern Quebec. The title story for this book, "The End of the World," is perhaps a curious choice for that purpose because it may seem untypical of Miss Gallant's fiction. Its setting is a French provincial hospital; its theme, desertion and betrayal; and it has a remarkable emotional weight and a wrenching harshness of tone that seem to me entirely arresting.

There is a great deal of intelligence at work in Mavis Gallant's fiction, and it gains substance from her curiosity about social detail. But in the forefront are those human figures, fragmented by life, so often expatriated in one way or another, that she observes with amusement and affection, with pity and sadness, and frequently with a kind of bitchy impatience that seems to me to be peculiarly her trademark. The "uninterrupted dialogue of the deaf" that we seem continually to be overhearing in such brilliant and subtle detail in her fiction becomes fascinating, irritating, and frighteningly human.

The Other Paris

By the time they decided what Carol would wear for her wedding (white with white flowers), it was the end of the afternoon. Madame Germaine removed the sketchbooks, the scraps of net and satin, the stacks of *Vogue*; she had, already, a professional look of anxiety, as if it could not possibly come out well. One foresaw seams ripped open, extra fittings, even Carol's tears.

Odile, Carol's friend, seemed disappointed. "White isn't *original*," she said. "If it were me, I would certainly not be married in all that rubbish of lace, like a First Communion." She picked threads from her skirt fastidiously, as if to remove herself completely from Carol and her unoriginal plans.

I wonder if anyone has ever asked Odile to marry him, Carol thought, placidly looking out the window. As her wedding approached, she had more and more the engaged girl's air of dissociation: nothing mattered until the wedding, and she could not see clearly beyond it. She was sorry for all the single girls of the world, particularly those who were, like Odile, past thirty. Odile looked sallow and pathetic, huddled into a sweater and coat, turning over samples of lace with a disapproving air. She seemed all of a piece with the day's weather and the chilly air of the dressmaker's flat. Outside, the street was still damp from a rain earlier in the day. There were no trees in sight, no flowers, no comforting glimpse of park. No one in this part of Paris would have known it was spring.

"Even *blue*," said Odile. But there was evidently no conversation to be had with Carol, who had begun to hum, so she said to the dressmaker, "Just imagine! Miss Frazier came to Paris to work last autumn, and fell in love with the head of her department."

"*Non!*" Madame Germaine recoiled, as if no other client had ever brought off such an extraordinary thing.

"Fell in love with Mr. Mitchell," said Odile, nodding. "At first sight, *le coup de foudre*."

"At first sight?" said the dressmaker. She looked fondly at Carol.

"Something no one would have expected," said Odile. "Although Mr. Mitchell is charming. *Charming*."

"I think we ought to go," said Carol.

Odile looked regretfully, as if she had more to say. Carol made

15

an appointment for the following day, and the two left the flat together, Odile's sturdy heels making a clatter as they went down the staircase.

"Why were you so funny just then?" Odile said. "I didn't say anything that wasn't true, and you know how women like that love to hear about weddings and love and everything. And it's such a wonderful story about you and Mr. Mitchell. I tell it to everyone."

This, Carol thought, could not be true, for Odile was rarely interested in anyone but herself, and had never shown the least curiosity about Carol's plans, other than offering to find a dressmaker.

"It was terribly romantic," Odile said, "whether you admit it or not. You and Mr. Mitchell. Our Mr. Mitchell."

It penetrated at last that Odile was making fun of her.

People had assured Carol so often that her engagement was romantic, and she had become so accustomed to the word, that Odile's slight irony was perplexing. If anyone had asked Carol at what precise moment she fell in love, or where Howard Mitchell proposed to her, she would have imagined, quite sincerely, a scene that involved all at once the Seine, moonlight, barrows of violets, acacias in flower, and a confused, misty background of the Eiffel Tower and little crooked streets. This was what everyone expected, and she had nearly come to believe it herself.

Actually, he had proposed at lunch, over a tuna-fish salad. He and Carol had known each other less than three weeks, and their conversation, until then, had been limited to their office – an American government agency – and the people in it. Carol was twenty-two; no one had proposed to her before, except an unsuitable medical student with no money and eight years' training still to go. She was under the illusion that in a short time she would be so old no one would ask her again. She accepted at once, and Howard celebrated by ordering an extra bottle of wine. Both would have liked champagne, as a more emphatic symbol of the unusual, but each was too diffident to suggest it.

The fact that Carol was not in love with Howard Mitchell did not dismay her in the least. From a series of helpful college lectures on marriage she had learned that a common interest, such as a liking for Irish setters, was the true basis for happiness, and that the illusion of love was a blight imposed by the film industry, and almost entirely responsible for the high rate of divorce. Similar economic backgrounds, financial security, belonging to the same church – these were the pillars of the married union. By an astonishing coincidence, the fathers of Carol and Howard were both attorneys and both had been defeated in their one attempt to get elected a judge. Carol and Howard were both vaguely Protestant, although a serious discussion of religious beliefs would have gravely embarrassed them. And Howard, best of all, was sober, old enough to know his own mind, and absolutely reliable. He was an economist who had had sense enough to attach himself to a corporation that continued to pay his salary during his loan to the government. There was no reason for the engagement or the marriage to fail.

Carol, with great efficiency, nearly at once set about the business of falling in love. Love required only the right conditions, like a geranium. It would wither exposed to bad weather or in dismal surroundings; indeed, Carol rated the chances of love in a cottage or a furnished room at zero. Given a good climate, enough money, and a pair of good-natured, *intelligent* (her college lectures had stressed this) people, one had only to sit back and watch it grow. All winter, then, she looked for these right conditions in Paris. When, at first, nothing happened, she blamed it on the weather. She was often convinced she would fall deeply in love with Howard if only it would stop raining. Undaunted, she waited for better times.

Howard had no notion of any of this. His sudden proposal to Carol had been quite out of character – he was uncommonly cautious – and he alternated between a state of numbness and a state of self-congratulation. Before his engagement he had sometimes been lonely, a malaise he put down to overwork, and he was discontented with his bachelor households, for he did not enjoy collecting old pottery or making little casserole dishes. Unless he stumbled on a competent housemaid, nothing ever got done. This in itself would not have spurred him into marriage had he not been seriously unsettled by the visit of one of his sisters, who advised him to marry some nice girl before it was too late. "Soon," she told him, "you'll just be a person who fills in at dinner."

Howard saw the picture at once, and was deeply moved by it. Retreating by inches, he said he knew of no one who would do.

Nonsense, his sister said. There were plenty of nice girls everywhere. She then warned him not to marry a French girl, who might cause trouble once he got her home to Chicago, or a Catholic, because of the children, and to avoid anyone fast, nervous, divorced, or over twenty-four. Howard knew a number of girls in Paris, most of whom worked in his office or similar agencies. They struck him as cheerful and eager, but aggressive – not at all what he fancied around the house. Just as he was becoming seriously baffled by this gap in his life, Carol Frazier arrived.

He was touched by her shy good manners, her earnest college French. His friends liked her, and, more important, so did the wives of his friends. He had been seriously in love on earlier occasions, and did not consider it a reliable emotion. He and Carol got on well, which seemed to him a satisfactory beginning. His friends, however, told him that she was obviously in love with him and that it was pretty to see. This he expected, not because he was vain but because one took it for granted that love, like a harmless familiar, always attended young women in friendships of this nature. Certainly he was fond of Carol and concerned for her comfort. Had she complained of a toothache, he would have seen to it that she got to a dentist. Carol was moved to another department, but they met every day for lunch and dinner, and talked without discord of any kind. They talked about the job Howard was returning to in Chicago; about their wedding, which was to take place in the spring; and about the movies they saw together. They often went to parties, and then they talked about everyone who had been there, even though they would see most of them next day, at work.

It was a busy life, yet Carol could not help feeling that something had been missed. The weather continued unimproved. She shared an apartment in Passy with two American girls, a temporary ménage that might have existed anywhere. When she rode the Métro, people pushed and were just as rude as in New York. Restaurant food was dull, and the cafés were full of Coca-Cola signs. No wonder she was not in love, she would think. Where was the Paris she had read about? Where were the elegant and expensive-looking women? Where, above all, were the men, those men with their gay good looks and snatches of merry song, the delight of English lady novelists? Traveling through Paris to and from work, she saw only shabby girls bundled into raincoats, hurrying along in the rain, or men who needed a haircut. In the famous parks, under the drizzly trees, children whined peevishly and were slapped. She sometimes thought that perhaps if she and Howard had French friends . . . She suggested it to him.

"You have a French friend," said Howard. "How about Odile?"

But that was not what Carol meant. Odile Pontmoret was Howard's secretary, a thin, dark woman who was (people said) the niece of a count who had gone broke. She seldom smiled and, because her English was at once precise and inaccurate, often sounded sarcastic. All winter she wore the same dark skirt and purple pullover to work. It never occurred to anyone to include her in parties made up of office people, and it was not certain that she would have come anyway. Odile and Carol were friendly in an impersonal way. Sometimes, if Howard was busy, they lunched together. Carol was always careful not to complain about Paris, having been warned that the foreign policy of her country hinged on chance remarks. But her restraint met with no answering delicacy in Odile, whose chief memory of her single trip to New York, before the war, was that her father had been charged twenty-four dollars for a taxi fare that, they later reasoned, must have been two dollars and forty cents. Repeating this, Odile would look indignantly at Carol, as if Carol had been driving the taxi. "And there was no service in the hotel, no service at all," Odile would say. "You could drop your nightgown on the floor and they would sweep around it. And still expect a tip."

These, her sole observations of America, she repeated until Carol's good nature was strained to the limit. Odile never spoke of her life outside the office, which Carol longed to hear about, and she touched on the present only to complain in terms of the past. "Before the war, we traveled, we went everywhere," she would say. "Now, with our poor little franc, everything is finished. I work to help my family. My brother publicizes wines – *Spanish* wines. We work and work so that our parents won't feel the change and so that Martine, our sister, can study music."

Saying this, she would look bewildered and angry, and Carol would have the feeling that Odile was somehow blaming her. They usually ate in a restaurant of Odile's choice – Carol was tactful about this, for Odile earned less than she did – where the food was lumpy and inadequate and the fluorescent lighting made everyone look ill. Carol would glance around at the neighboring tables, at which sat glum and noisy Parisian office workers and shop clerks, and observe that everyone's coat was too long or too short, that the furs were tacky.

There must be more to it than this, she would think. Was it possible that these badly groomed girls liked living in Paris? Surely the sentimental songs about the city had no meaning for them. Were many of them in love, or – still less likely – could any man be in love with any of them?

Every evening, leaving the building in which she and Howard worked, she would pause on the stair landing between the first and second floors to look through the window at the dark winter twilight, thinking that an evening, a special kind of evening, was forming all over the city, and that she had no part in it. At the same hour, people streamed out of an old house across the street that was now a museum, and Carol would watch them hurrying off under their umbrellas. She wondered where they were going and where they lived and what they were having for dinner. Her interest in them was not specific; she had no urge to run into the street and introduce herself. It was simply that she believed they knew a secret, and if she spoke to the right person, or opened the right door, or turned down an unexpected street, the city would reveal itself and she would fall in love. After this pause at the landing, she would forget all her disappointments (the Parma violets she had bought that were fraudulently cut and bound, so that they died in a minute) and run the rest of the way down the stairs, meaning to tell Howard and see if he shared her brief optimism.

On one of these evenings, soon after the start of the cold weather, she noticed a young man sitting on one of the chairs put out in an inhospitable row in the lobby of the building, for job seekers. He looked pale and ill, and the sleeves of his coat were short, as if he were still growing. He stared at her with the expression of a clever child, at once bold and withdrawn. She had the impression that he had seen her stop at the window on the landing and that he was, for some reason, amused. He did not look at all as if he belonged there. She mentioned him to Howard.

"That must have been Felix," Howard said. "Odile's friend." He put so much weight on the word "friend" that Carol felt there was more, a great deal more, and that, although he liked gossip as well as anyone else, he did not find Odile's affairs interesting enough to discuss. "He used to wait for her outside every night. Now I guess he comes in out of the rain."

"But she's never mentioned him," Carol protested. "And he must be younger than she is, and so pale and funny-looking! Where does he come from?"

Howard didn't know. Felix was Austrian, he thought, or Czech. There was something odd about him, for although he obviously hadn't enough to eat, he always had plenty of American cigarettes. That was a bad sign. "Why are you so interested?" he said. But Carol was not interested at all.

After that, Carol saw Felix every evening. He was always polite and sometimes murmured a perfunctory greeting as she passed his chair. He continued to look tired and ill, and Carol wondered if it was true that he hadn't enough to eat. She mentioned him to Odile, who was surprisingly willing to discuss her friend. He was twenty-one, she said, and without relatives. They had all been killed at the end of the war, in the final bombings. He was in Paris illegally, without a proper passport or working papers. The police were taking a long time to straighten it out, and meanwhile, not permitted to work, Felix "did other things." Odile did not say what the other things were, and Carol was rather shocked.

That night, before going to sleep, she thought about Felix, and about how he was only twenty-one. She and Felix, then, were closer in age than he was to Odile or she herself was to Howard. When I was in school, he was in school, she thought. When the war stopped, we were fourteen and fifteen . . . But here she lost track, for where Carol had had a holiday, Felix's parents had been killed. Their closeness in age gave her unexpected comfort, as if someone in this disappointing city had some tie with her. In the morning she was ashamed of her disloyal thoughts – her closest tie in Paris was, after all, with Howard – and decided to ignore Felix when she saw him again. That night, when she passed his chair, he said "Good evening," and she was suddenly acutely conscious of every bit of her clothing: the press of the belt at her waist, the pinch of her earrings, the weight of her dress, even her gloves, which felt as scratchy as sacking. It was a disturbing feeling; she was not sure that she liked it.

"I don't see why Felix should just sit in that hall all the time," she complained to Howard. "Can't he wait for Odile somewhere else?"

Howard was too busy to worry about Felix. It occurred to him that Carol was being tiresome, and that this whining over who sat in the hall was only one instance of her new manner. She had taken to complaining about their friends, and saying she wanted to meet new people and see more of Paris. Sometimes she looked at him helplessly and eagerly, as if there were something he ought to be saying or doing. He was genuinely perplexed; it seemed to him they got along well and were reasonably happy together. But Carol was changing. She hunted up odd, cheap restaurants. She made him walk in the rain. She said that they ought to see the sun come up from the steps of the Sacré-Coeur, and actually succeeded in dragging him there, nearly dead of cold. And, as he might have foreseen, the expedition came to nothing, for it was a rainy dawn and a suspicious gendarme sent them both home.

At Christmas, Carol begged him to take her to the carol singing in the Place Vendôme. Here, she imagined, with the gentle fall of snow and the small, rosy choirboys singing between lighted Christmas trees, she would find something – a warm memory that would, later, bring her closer to Howard, a glimpse of the Paris other people liked. But, of course, there was no snow. Howard and Carol stood under her umbrella as a fine, misty rain fell on the choristers, who sang over and over the opening bars of "Il est né, le Divin Enfant," testing voice levels for a broadcast. Newspaper photographers drifted on the rim of the crowd, and the flares that lit the scene for a newsreel camera blew acrid smoke in their faces. Howard began to cough. Around the square, the tenants of the Place emerged on their small balconies. Some of them had champagne glasses in their hands, as if they had interrupted an agreeable party to step outside for a moment. Carol looked up at the lighted open doorways, through which she could see a painted ceiling, a lighted chandelier. But nothing happened. None of the people seemed beautiful or extraordinary. No one said, "Who *is* that charming girl down there? Let's ask her up!"

Howard blew his nose and said that his feet were cold; they drifted over the square to a couturier's window, where the Infant Jesus wore a rhinestone pin, and a worshipping plaster angel extended a famous brand of perfume. "It just looks like New York or something," Carol said, plaintive with disappointment. As she stopped to close her umbrella, the wind carried to her feet a piece of mistletoe and, glancing up, she saw that cheap tinsel icicles and bunches of mistletoe had been tied on the street lamps of the square. It looked pretty, and rather poor, and she thought of the giant tree in Rockefeller Center. She suddenly felt sorry for Paris, just as she had felt sorry for Felix because he looked hungry and was only twenty-one. Her throat went warm, like the prelude to a rush of tears. Stooping, she picked up the sprig of mistletoe and put it in her pocket.

"Is this all?" Howard said. "Was this what you wanted to see?" He was cold and uncomfortable, but because it was Christmas, he said nothing impatient, and tried to remember, instead, that she was only twenty-one.

"I suppose so."

They found a taxi and went on to finish the evening with some friends from their office. Howard made an amusing story of their adventure in the Place Vendôme. She realized for the first time that something could be perfectly accurate but untruthful – they had not found any part of that evening funny – and that this might cover more areas of experience than the occasional amusing story. She looked at Howard thoughtfully, as if she had learned something of value.

The day after Christmas, Howard came down with a bad cold, the result of standing in the rain. He did not shake it off for the rest of the winter, and Carol, feeling guiltily that it was her fault, suggested no more excursions. Temporarily, she put the question of falling in love to one side. Paris was not the place, she thought; perhaps it had been, fifty years ago, or whenever it was that people wrote all the songs. It did not occur to her to break her engagement.

She wore out the winter working, nursing Howard's cold, toying with office gossip, and, now and again, lunching with Odile, who was just as unsatisfactory as ever. It was nearly spring when Odile, stopping by Carol's desk, said that Martine was making a concert début the following Sunday. It was a private gathering, a subscription concert. Odile sounded vague. She dropped two tickets on Carol's desk and said, walking away, "If you want to come."

"If I *want* to!"

Carol flew away to tell Howard at once. "It's a sort of private musical thing," she said. "There should be important musicians there, since it's a début, and all Odile's family. The old count — everyone." She half expected Odile's impoverished uncle to turn up in eighteenth-century costume, his hands clasped on the head of a cane.

Howard said it was all right with him, provided they needn't stand out in the rain.

"Of course not! It's a *concert*." She looked at the tickets; they were handwritten slips bearing mimeographed numbers. "It's probably in someone's house," she said. "In one of those lovely old drawing rooms. Or in a little painted theatre. There are supposed to be little theatres all over Paris that belong to families and that foreigners never see."

She was beside herself with excitement. What if Paris had taken all winter to come to life? Some foreigners lived there forever and never broke in at all. She spent nearly all of one week's salary on a white feather hat, and practiced a few graceful phrases in French. "*Oui, elle est charmante*," she said to her mirror. "*La petite Martine est tout à fait ravissante. Je connais très bien Odile. Une coupe de champagne? Mais oui, merci bien. Ah, voici mon fiancé! Monsieur Mitchell, le Baron de . . .*" and so forth.

She felt close to Odile, as if they had been great friends for a long time. When, two days before the concert, Odile remarked, yawning, that Martine was crying night and day because she hadn't a suitable dress, Carol said, "Would you let me lend her a dress?"

Odile suddenly stopped yawning and turned back the cuffs of her pullover as if it were a task that required all her attention. "That would be very kind of you," she said, at last.

"I mean," said Carol, feeling gauche, "would it be all right? I have a lovely pale green tulle that I brought from New York. I've only worn it twice."

"It sounds very nice," said Odile.

Carol shook the dress out of its tissue paper and brought it to work the next day. Odile thanked her without fervor, but Carol knew by now that that was simply her manner.

"We're going to a private musical début," she wrote to her mother and father. "The youngest niece of the Count de Quel-quechose . . . I've lent her my green tulle." She said no more than that, so that it would sound properly casual. So far, her letters had not contained much of interest.

The address Odile had given Carol turned out to be an ordinary, shabby theatre in the Second Arrondissement. It was on an obscure street, and the taxi driver had to stop and consult his street guide so often that they were half an hour late. Music came out to meet them in the empty lobby, where a poster said only "J. S. Bach." An usher tiptoed them into place with ill grace and asked Carol please to have some thought for the people behind her and remove her hat. Carol did so while Howard groped for change for the usher's tip. She peered around: the theatre was less than half filled, and the music coming from the small orchestra on the stage had a thin, echoing quality, as if it were traveling around an empty vault. Odile was nowhere in sight. After a moment, Carol saw Felix sitting alone a few rows away. He smiled – much too familiarly, Carol thought. He looked paler than usual, and almost deliberately untidy. He might at least have taken pains for the concert. She felt a spasm of annoyance, and at the same time her heart began to beat so quickly that she felt its movement must surely be visible.

What ever is the matter with me, she thought. If one could believe all the arch stories on the subject, this was traditional for brides-to-be. Perhaps, at this unpromising moment, she had begun to fall in love. She turned in her seat and stared at Howard; he looked much as always. She settled back and began furnishing in her mind the apartment they would have in Chicago. Sometimes the theatre lights went on, startling her out of some problem involving draperies and Venetian blinds; once Howard went out to smoke. Carol had just finished papering a bedroom green and white when Martine walked onstage, with her violin. At the same moment, a piece of plaster bearing the painted plump foot of a nymph detached itself from the ceiling and crashed into the aisle, just missing Howard's head. Everyone stood up to look, and Martine and the conductor stared at Howard and Carol furiously, as if it were their fault. The commotion was horrifying. Carol slid down in her seat, her hands over her eyes. She retained, in all her distress, an impression of Martine, who wore an ill-fitting blue dress with a little jacket. She had not worn Carol's pretty tulle; probably she had never intended to.

Carol wondered, miserably, why they had come. For the first time, she noticed that all the people around them were odd and shabby. The smell of stale winter coats filled the unaired theatre; her head began to ache, and Martine's violin shrilled on her ear like a penny whistle. At last the music stopped and the lights went on. The concert was over. There was some applause, but people were busy pulling on coats and screaming at one another from aisle to aisle. Martine shook hands with the conductor and, after looking vaguely around the hall, wandered away.

"Is this all?" said Howard. He stood up and stretched.

Carol did not reply. She had just seen Felix and Odile together. Odile was speaking rapidly and looked unhappy. She wore the same skirt and pullover Carol had seen all winter, and she was carrying her coat.

"Odile!" Carol called. But Odile waved and threaded her way through the row of seats to the other side of the theatre, where she joined some elderly people and a young man. They went off together backstage.

Her family, Carol thought, sickening under the snub. And she didn't introduce me, or even come over and speak. She was positive now that Odile had invited her only to help fill the hall, or because she had a pair of tickets she didn't know what to do with.

"Let's go," Howard said. Their seats were near the front. By the time they reached the lobby, it was nearly empty. Under the indifferent eyes of the usher, Howard guided Carol into her coat. "They sure didn't put on much of a show for Martine," he said.

"No, they didn't."

"No flowers," he said. "It didn't even have her name on the program. No one would have known."

It had grown dark, and rain poured from the edge of the roof in an unbroken sheet. "You stay here," said Howard. "I'll get a taxi."

"No," said Carol. "Stay with me. This won't last." She could not bring herself to tell him how hurt and humiliated she was, what a ruin the afternoon had been. Howard led her behind the shelter of a billboard.

"That dress," he went on. "I thought you'd lent her something."

"I had. She didn't wear it. I don't know why."

"Ask Odile."

"I don't care. I'd rather let it drop."

He agreed. He felt that Carol had almost knowingly exposed herself to an indignity over the dress, and pride of that nature he understood. To distract her, he spoke of the job waiting for him in Chicago, of his friends, of his brother's sailboat.

Against a background of rain and Carol's disappointment, he sounded, without meaning to, faintly homesick. Carol picked up his mood. She looked at the white feather hat the usher had made her remove and said suddenly, "I wish I were home. I wish

I were in my own country, with my own friends."

"You will be," he said, "in a couple of months." He hoped she would not begin to cry.

"I'm tired of the way everything is here – old and rotten and falling down."

"You mean that chunk of ceiling?"

She turned from him, exasperated at his persistently missing the point, and saw Felix not far away. He was leaning against the ticket booth, looking resignedly at the rain. When he noticed Carol looking at him, he said, ignoring Howard, "Odile's backstage with her family." He made a face and went on, "No admission for us foreigners."

Odile's family did not accept Felix; Carol had barely absorbed this thought, which gave her an unexpected and indignant shock, when she realized what he had meant by "us foreigners." It was rude of Odile to let her family hurt her friend; at the same time, it was even less kind of them to include Carol in a single category of foreigners. Surely Odile could see the difference between Carol and this pale young man who "did other things." She felt that she and Felix had been linked together in a disagreeable way, and that she was floating away from everything familiar and safe. Without replying, she bent her head and turned away, politely but unmistakably.

"Funny kid," Howard remarked as Felix walked slowly out into the rain, his hands in his pockets.

"He's horrible," said Carol, so violently that he stared at her. "He's not funny. He's a parasite. He lives on Odile. He doesn't work or anything, he just hangs around and stares at people. Odile says he has no passport. Well, why doesn't he *get* one? Any man can work if he wants to. Why are there people like that? All the boys I ever knew at home were well brought up and manly. I never knew anyone like Felix."

She stopped, breathless, and Howard said, "Well, let Odile worry."

"Odile!" Carol cried. "Odile must be crazy. What is she thinking of? Her family ought to put a stop to it. The whole thing is terrible. It's bad for the office. It ought to be stopped. Why, he'll never marry her! Why should he? He's only a boy, an orphan. He needs friends, and connections, and somebody his own age. Why should he marry Odile? What does he want with an old maid from an old, broken-down family? He needs a good meal, and – and help." She stopped, bewildered. She had been about to say "and love."

Howard, now beyond surprise, felt only a growing wave of annoyance. He did not like hysterical women. His sisters never behaved like that.

"I want to go *home*," said Carol, nearly wailing.

He ran off to find a taxi, glad to get away. By "home" he thought she meant the apartment she shared with the two American girls in Passy.

For Carol, the concert was the end, the final *clou*. She stopped caring about Paris, or Odile, or her feelings for Howard. When Odile returned her green dress, nicely pressed and folded in a cardboard box, she said only, "Just leave it on my desk." Everyone seemed to think it normal that now her only preoccupation should be the cut of her wedding dress. People began giving parties for her. The wash of attention soothed her fears. She was good-tempered, and did not ask Howard to take her to tiresome places. Once again he felt he had made the right decision, and put her temporary waywardness down to nerves. After a while, Carol began lunching with Odile again, but she did not mention the concert.

As for Felix, Carol now avoided him entirely. Sometimes she waited until Odile had left the office before leaving herself. Again, she braced herself and walked briskly past him, ignoring his "Good evening." She no longer stopped on the staircase to watch the twilight; her mood was different. She believed that something fortunate had happened to her spirit, and that she had become invulnerable. Soon she was able to walk by Felix without a tremor, and after a while she stopped noticing him at all.

"Have you noticed winter is over?" Odile said. She and Carol had left the dressmaker's street and turned off on a broad, oblique avenue. "It hasn't rained for hours. This was the longest winter I remember, although I think one says this every year."

"It was long for me, too," Carol said. It was true that it was over. The spindly trees of the avenue were covered with green, like a wrapping of tissue. A few people sat out in front of shops, sunning themselves. It was, suddenly, like coming out of a tunnel.

Odile turned to Carol and smiled, a rare expression for her. "I'm sorry I was rude at Madame Germaine's just now," she said. "I don't know what the matter is nowadays – I am dreadful to everyone. But I shouldn't have been to you."

"Never mind," said Carol. She flushed a little, for Howard had taught her to be embarrassed over anything as direct as an apology. "I'd forgotten it. In fact, I didn't even notice."

"Now you are being nice," said Odile unhappily. "Really, there is something wrong with me. I worry all the time, over money, over Martine, over Felix. I think it isn't healthy." Carol murmured something comforting but indistinct. Glancing at her, Odile said, "Where are you off to now?"

"Nowhere. Home, I suppose. There's always something to do these days."

"Why don't you come along with me?" Odile stopped on the street and took her arm. "I'm going to see Felix. He lives near here. Oh, he would be so surprised!"

"Felix?" Automatically Carol glanced at her watch. Surely she had something to do, some appointment? But Odile was hurrying her along. Carol thought, Now, this is all wrong. But they had reached the Boulevard de Grenelle, where the Métro ran overhead, encased in a tube of red brick. Light fell in patterns underneath; the boulevard was lined with ugly shops and dark, buff-painted cafés. It was a far cry from the prim street a block or so away where the dressmaker's flat was. "Is it far?" said Carol nervously. She did not like the look of the neighborhood. Odile shook her head. They crossed the boulevard and a few crooked, narrow streets filled with curbside barrows and marketing crowds. It was a section of Paris Carol had not seen; although it was on the Left Bank, it was not pretty, not picturesque. There were no little restaurants, no students' hotels. It was simply down-and-out and dirty, and everyone looked ill-tempered. Arabs lounging in doorways looked at the two girls and called out, laughing.

"Look straight ahead," said Odile. "If you look at them, they come up and take your arm. It's worse when I come alone."

How dreadful of Felix to let Odile walk alone through streets like this, Carol thought.

"Here," said Odile. She stopped in front of a building on which the painted word "Hôtel" was almost effaced. They climbed a musty-smelling staircase, Carol taking care not to let her skirt brush the walls. She wondered nervously what Howard would say when he heard she had visited Felix in his hotel room. On a stair landing, Odile knocked at one of the doors. Felix let them in. It took a few moments, for he had been asleep. He did not look at all surprised but with a slight bow invited them in, as if he frequently entertained in his room.

The room was so cluttered, the bed so untidy, that Carol stood bewildered, wondering where one could sit. Odile at once flung herself down on the bed, dropping her handbag on the floor, which was cement and gritty with dirt.

"I'm tired," she said. "We've been choosing Carol's wedding dress. White, and *very* pretty."

Felix's shirt was unbuttoned, his face without any color. He glanced sidelong at Carol, smiling. On a table stood an alcohol stove, some gaudy plastic bowls, and a paper container of sugar. In the tiny washbasin, over which hung a cold-water faucet, were a plate and a spoon, and, here and there on the perimeter, Felix's shaving things and a battered toothbrush.

"Do sit on that chair," he said to Carol, but he made no move to take away the shirt and sweater and raincoat that were bundled on it. Everything else he owned appeared to be on the floor. The room faced a court and was quite dark. "I'll heat up this coffee," Felix said, as if casting about for something to do as a host. "Miss Frazier, sit down." He put a match to the stove and a blue flame leaped along the wall. He stared into a saucepan of coffee, sniffed it, and added a quantity of cold water. "A new PX has just been opened," he said to Odile. He put the saucepan over the flame, apparently satisfied. "I went around to see what was up," he said. "Nothing much. It is really sad. Everything is organized on such a big scale now that there is no room for little people like me. I waited outside and finally picked up some cigarettes – only two cartons – from a soldier."

He talked on, and Carol, who was not accustomed to his conversation, could not tell if he was joking or serious. She had finally decided to sit down on top of the raincoat. She frowned at her hands, wondering why Odile didn't teach him to make coffee properly and why he talked like a criminal. For Carol, the idea that one might not be permitted to work was preposterous. She harbored a rigid belief that anyone could work who sincerely wanted to. Picking apples, she thought vaguely, or down in a mine, where people were always needed.

Odile looked at Carol, as if she knew what she was thinking. "Poor Felix doesn't belong in this world," she said. "He should have been killed at the end of the war. Instead of that, every year he gets older. In a month, he will be twenty-two."

But Odile was over thirty. Carol found the gap between their ages distasteful, and thought it indelicate of Odile to stress it. Felix, who had been ineffectively rinsing the plastic bowls in cold water, now poured the coffee out. He pushed one of the bowls toward Odile; then he suddenly took her hand and, turning it over, kissed the palm. "*Why* should I have been killed?" he said.

Carol, breathless with embarrassment, looked at the brick wall of the court. She twisted her fingers together until they hurt. How can they act like this in front of me, she thought, and in such a dirty room? The thought that they might be in love entered her head for the first time, and it made her ill. Felix, smiling, gave her a bowl of coffee, and she took it without meeting his eyes. He sat down on the bed beside Odile and said happily, "I'm glad you came. You both look beautiful."

Carol glanced at Odile, thinking, Not beautiful, not by any stretch of good manners. "French girls are all attractive," she said politely.

"Most of them are frights," said Felix. No one disputed it, and no one but Carol appeared distressed by the abrupt termination of the conversation. She cast about for something to say, but Odile put her bowl on the floor, said again that she was tired, lay back, and seemed all at once to fall asleep.

Felix looked at her. "She really can shut out the world whenever she wants to," he said, suggesting to Carol's startled ears that he was quite accustomed to see her fall asleep. Of course, she might have guessed, but why should Felix make it so obvious? She felt ashamed of the way she had worried about Felix, and the way she had run after Odile, wanting to know her family. This was all it had come to, this dirty room. Howard was right, she thought. It doesn't pay.

At the same time, she was perplexed at the intimacy in which she and Felix now found themselves. She would have been more at ease alone in a room with him than with Odile beside him asleep on his bed.

"I must go," she said nervously.

"Oh, yes," said Felix, not stopping her.

"But I can't find my way back alone." She felt as if she might cry.

"There are taxis," he said vaguely. "But I can take you to the Métro, if you like." He buttoned his shirt and looked around for a jacket, making no move to waken Odile.

"Should we leave her here?" said Carol. "Shouldn't I say goodbye?"

He looked surprised. "I wouldn't think of disturbing her," he said. "If she's asleep, then she must be tired." And to this Carol could think of nothing to say.

He followed her down the staircase and into the street, dark now, with stripes of neon to mark the cafés. They said little, and because she was afraid of the dark and the Arabs, Carol walked close beside him. On the Boulevard de Grenelle, Felix stopped at the entrance to the Métro.

"Here," he said. "Up those steps. It takes you right over to Passy."

She looked at him, feeling this parting was not enough. She had criticized him to Howard and taught herself to ignore him, but here, in a neighborhood where she could not so much as find her way, she felt more than ever imprisoned in the walls of her shyness, unable to say, "Thank you," or "Thanks for the coffee," or anything perfunctory and reasonable. She had an inexplicable and uneasy feeling that something had ended for her, and that she would never see Felix, or even Odile, again.

Felix caught her look, or seemed to. He looked around, distressed, at the Bar des Sportifs, and the *sportifs* inside it, and said, "If you would lend me a little money, I could buy you a drink before you go."

His unabashed cadging restored her at once. "I haven't time for a drink," she said, all briskness now, as if he had with a little click dropped into the right slot. "But if you'll promise to take Odile to dinner, I'll lend you two thousand francs."

"Fine," said Felix. He watched her take the money from her purse, accepted it without embarrassment, and put it in the pocket of his jacket.

"Take her for a nice dinner somewhere," Carol repeated.

"Of course."

"Oh!" He exasperated her. "Why don't you act like other people?" she cried. "You can't live like this all the time. You could go to America. Mr. Mitchell would help you. I know he would. He'd vouch for you, for a visa, if I asked him to."

"And Odile? Would Mr. Mitchell vouch for Odile too?"

She glanced at him, startled. When Felix was twenty-five, Odile would be nearly forty. Surely he had thought of this? "She could go, too," she said, and added, "I suppose."

"And what would we do in America?" He rocked back and forth on his heels, smiling.

"You could work," she said sharply. She could not help adding, like a scold, "For once in your life."

"As cook and butler," said Felix thoughtfully, and began to laugh. "No, don't be angry," he said, putting out his hand. "One has to wait so long for American papers. I know, I used to do it. To sit there all day and wait, or stand in the queue – how could Odile do it? She has her job to attend to. She has to help her family."

"In America," said Carol, "she would make more money, she could help them even more." But she could not see clearly the picture of Felix and Odile combining their salaries in a neat little apartment and faithfully remitting a portion to France. She could not imagine what on earth Felix would do for a living. Perhaps he and Odile would get married; something told her they would not. "I'm sorry," she said. "It's really your own business. I shouldn't have said anything at all." She moved away, but Felix took her hand and held it.

"You mean so well," he said. "Odile is right, you know. I ought to have been killed, or at least disappeared. No one knows what to do with me or where I fit. As for Odile, her whole family is overdue. But we're not – how does it go in American papers, under the photographs? – 'Happy Europeans find new life away from old cares.' We're not that, either."

"I suppose not. I don't know." She realized all at once how absurd they must look, standing under the Métro tracks, holding hands. Passersby looked at them, sympathetic.

"You shouldn't go this way, looking so hurt and serious," he said. "You're so nice. You mean so well. Odile loves you."

Her heart leaped as if he, Felix, had said he loved her. But no, she corrected herself. Not Felix but some other man, some wonderful person who did not exist.

Odile loved her. Her hand in his, she remembered how he had kissed Odile's palm, and she felt on her own palm the pressure of a kiss; but not from Felix. Perhaps, she thought, what she felt was the weight of his love for Odile, from which she was excluded, and to which Felix now politely and kindly wished to draw her, as if his and Odile's ability to love was their only hospitality, their only way of paying debts. For a moment, standing under the noisy trains on the dark, dusty boulevard, she felt that she had at last opened the right door, turned down the right street, glimpsed the vision toward which she had struggled on winter evenings when, standing on the staircase, she had wanted to be enchanted with Paris and to be in love with Howard.

But that such a vision could come from Felix and Odile was impossible. For a moment she had been close to tears, like the Christmas evening when she found the mistletoe. But she remembered in time what Felix was – a hopeless parasite. And Odile was silly and immoral and old enough to know better. And they were not married and never would be, and they spent heaven only knew how many hours in that terrible room in a slummy quarter of Paris.

No, she thought. What she and Howard had was better. No one could point to them, or criticize them, or humiliate them by offering to help.

She withdrew her hand and said with cold shyness, "Thank you for the coffee, Felix."

"Oh that." He watched her go up the steps to the Métro, and then he walked away.

Upstairs, she passed a flower seller and stopped to buy a bunch of violets, even though they would be dead before she reached home. She wanted something pretty in her hand to take away the memory of the room and the Arabs and the dreary cafés and the messy affairs of Felix and Odile. She paid for the violets and noticed as she did so that the little scene – accepting the flowers, paying for them – had the gentle, nostalgic air of something past.

Soon, she sensed, the comforting vision of Paris as she had once imagined it would overlap the reality. To have met and married Howard there would sound romantic and interesting, more and more so as time passed. She would forget the rain and her unshared confusion and loneliness, and remember instead the Paris of films, the street lamps with their tinsel icicles, the funny concert hall where the ceiling collapsed, and there would be, at last, a coherent picture, accurate but untrue. The memory of Felix and Odile and all their distasteful strangeness would slip away; for "love" she would think, once more, "Paris," and, after a while, happily married, mercifully removed in time, she would remember it and describe it and finally believe it as it had never been at all.

The Picnic

The three Marshall children were dressed and ready for the picnic before their father was awake. Their mother had been up since dawn, for the coming day of pleasure weighed heavily on her mind. She had laid out the children's clothes, so that they could dress without asking questions – clean blue denims for John and dresses sprigged with flowers for the girls. Their shoes, chalky with whitening, stood in a row on the bathroom window sill.

John, stubbornly, dressed himself, but the girls helped each other, standing and preening before the long looking glass. Margaret fastened the chain of Ellen's heart-shaped locket while Ellen held up her hair with both hands. Margaret never wore her own locket. Old Madame Pégurin, in whose house in France the Marshalls were living, had given her something she liked better – a brooch containing a miniature portrait of a poodle called Youckie, who had died of influenza shortly before the war. The brooch was edged with seed pearls, and Margaret had worn it all summer, pinned to her navy blue shorts.

"How very pretty it is!" the children's mother had said when the brooch was shown to her. "How nice of Madame Pégurin to think of a little girl. It will look much nicer later on, when you're a little older." She had been trained in the school of indirect suggestion, and so skillful had she become that her children sometimes had no idea what she was driving at.

"I guess so," Margaret had replied on this occasion, firmly fastening the brooch to her shorts.

She now attached it to the front of the picnic frock, where, too heavy for the thin material, it hung like a stone. "It looks lovely," Ellen said with serious admiration. She peered through their bedroom window across the garden, and over the tiled roofs of the small town of Virolun, to the blooming summer fields that rose and fell toward Grenoble and the Alps. Across the town, partly hidden by somebody's orchard, were the neat rows of gray-painted barracks that housed American troops. Into this tidy settlement their father disappeared each day, driven in a jeep. On a morning as clear as this, the girls could see the first shining peaks of the mountains and the thin blue smoke from the neighboring village, some miles away. They were too young to care about the view, but their mother appreciated it for them, often reminding them that nothing in her own childhood had been half as agreeable. "You youngsters are very lucky," she would say. "Your father might just as easily as not have been stationed in the middle of Arkansas." The children would listen without comment, although it depressed them inordinately to be told of their good fortune. If they liked this house better than any other they had lived in, it was because it contained Madame Pégurin, her cat, Olivette, and her cook, Louise.

Olivette now entered the girls' bedroom soundlessly, pushing the door open with one paw. "Look at her. She's priceless," Margaret said, trying out the word.

Ellen nodded. "I wish one of us could go to the picnic with *her*," she said. Margaret knew that she meant not the cat but Madame Pégurin, who was driving to the picnic grounds with General Wirtworth, commander of the post.

"One of us might," Margaret said. "Sitting on the General's lap."

Ellen's shriek at the thought woke their father, Major Marshall, who, remembering that this was the day of the picnic, said, "Oh, God!"

The picnic, which had somehow become an Army responsibility, had been suggested by an American magazine of such grandeur that the Major was staggered to learn that Madame Pégurin had never heard of it. Two research workers, vestal maidens in dirndl skirts, had spent weeks combing France to find the most typically French town. They had found no more than half a dozen; and since it was essential to the story that the town be near an American Army post, they had finally, like a pair of exhausted doves, fluttered to rest in Virolun. The picnic, they had explained to General Wirtworth, would be a symbol of unity between two nations – between the troops at the post and the residents of the town. The General had repeated this to Colonel Baring, who had passed it on to Major Marshall, who had brought it to rest with his wife. "Oh, really?" Paula Marshall had said, and if there was any reserve – any bitterness – in her voice, the Major had failed to notice. The mammoth job of organizing the picnic had fallen just where he knew it would – on his own shoulders.

The Major was the post's recreation officer, and he was beset by many difficulties. His status was not clear; sometimes he had to act as public relations officer – there being none, through an extraordinary oversight on the part of the General. The Major's staff was inadequate. It was composed of but two men: a lieutenant, who had developed measles a week before the picnic, and a glowering young sergeant who, the Major feared, would someday write a novel depicting him in an unfavorable manner. The Major had sent Colonel Baring a long memo on the subject of his status, and the Colonel had replied in person, saying, with a comic, rueful smile, "Just see us through the picnic, old man!"

The Major had said he would try. But it was far from easy. The research workers from the American magazine had been joined by a photographer who wore openwork sandals and had so far not emerged from the Hotel Bristol. Messages in his languid handwriting had been carried to Major Marshall's office by the research workers, and answers returned by the Major's sergeant. The messages were grossly interfering and never helpful. Only yesterday, the day before the picnic, the sergeant had placed before the Major a note on Hotel Bristol stationery: "Suggest folk dances as further symbol of unity. French wives teaching American wives, and so on. Object: Color shot." Annoyed, the Major had sent a message pointing out that baseball had already been agreed on as an easily recognized symbol, and the afternoon brought a reply: "Feel that French should make contribution. Anything colorful or indigenous will do."

"Baseball is as far as I'll go," the Major had said in his reply to this.

On their straggling promenade to breakfast, the children halted outside Madame Pégurin's door. Sometimes from behind the white-and-gold painted panels came the sound of breakfast – china on china, glass against silver. Then Louise would emerge with the tray, and Madame Pégurin, seeing the children, would tell them to come in. She would be sitting up, propped with a pillow and bolster. Her hair, which changed color after every visit to Paris, would be wrapped in a scarf and Madame herself enveloped in a trailing dressing gown streaked with the ash of her cigarette. When the children came in, she would feed them sugared almonds and pistachio creams and sponge cakes soaked in rum, which she kept in a tin box by her bedside, and as they stood lined up rather comically, she would tell them about little dead Youckie, and about her own children, all of whom had married worthless, ordinary, social-climbing men and women. "In the end," she would say, sighing, "there is nothing to replace the love one can bear a cat or a poodle."

The children's mother did not approve of these morning visits, and the children were frequently told not to bother poor Madame Pégurin, who needed her rest. This morning, they could hear the rustle of paper as Madame Pégurin turned the pages of *Le Figaro*, which came to Virolun every day from Paris. Madame Pégurin looked at only one section of it, the *Carnet du Jour* – the daily account of marriages, births and deaths – even though, as she told the children, one found in it nowadays names that no one had heard of, families who sounded foreign or commonplace. The children admired this single-minded reading, and they thought it "commonplace" of their mother to read books.

"Should we knock?" Margaret said. They debated this until their mother's low, reproachful "Children!" fetched them out of the upstairs hall and down a shallow staircase, the wall of which was papered with the repeated person of a shepherdess. Where a railing should have been were jars of trailing ivy they had been warned not to touch. The wall was stained at the level of their hands; once a week Louise went over the marks with a piece of white bread. But nothing could efface the fact that there were boarders, American Army tenants, in old Madame Pégurin's house.

During the winter, before the arrival of the Marshalls, the damage had been more pronounced; the tenants had been a Sergeant and Mrs. Gould, whose children, little Henry and Joey, had tracked mud up and down the stairs and shot at each other with water pistols all over the drawing room. The Goulds had departed on bad terms with Madame Pégurin, and it often worried Major Marshall that his wife permitted the Gould children to visit the Marshall children and play in the garden. Madame Pégurin closed her bedroom shutters at the sound of their voices, which, it seemed to the Major, was suggestion enough.

The Gould and Marshall children were to attend the picnic together; it was perhaps for this reason that Madame Pégurin rattled the pages of *Le Figaro* behind her closed door. She disliked foreigners; she had told the Marshall children so. But they, fortunately, did not consider themselves foreign, and had pictured instead dark men with curling beards. Madame Pégurin had tried, as well as she could, to ignore the presence of the Americans in Virolun, just as, long ago, when she traveled, she had overlooked the natives of whichever country she happened to be in. She had ignored the Italians in Italy and the Swiss in Switzerland, and she had explained this to Margaret and Ellen, who, agreeing it was the only way to live, feared that their mother would never achieve this restraint. For she *would* speak French, and she carried with her, even to market, a book of useful phrases.

Madame Pégurin had had many troubles with the Americans; she had even had troubles with the General. It had fallen to her, as the highest-ranking resident of Virolun, to entertain the highest-ranking American officer. She had asked General Wirtworth to tea, and he had finished off a bottle of whiskey she had been saving for eleven years. He had then been moved to kiss her hand, but this could not make up for her sense of loss. There had been other difficulties – the tenancy of the Goulds, and a row with Colonel Baring, whose idea it had been to board the Goulds and their hoodlum children with Madame Pégurin. Madame Pégurin had, indeed, talked of legal action, but nothing had come of it. Because of all this, no one believed she would attend the picnic, and it was considered a triumph for Major Marshall that she had consented to go, and to drive with the General, and to be photographed.

"I hope they take her picture eating a hot dog," Paula Marshall said when she heard of it.

"It was essential," the Major said reprovingly. "I made her see that. She's a symbol of something in this town. We couldn't do the thing properly without her."

"Maybe she just likes to have her picture taken, like anyone else," Paula said. This was, for her, an uncommonly catty remark.

The Major said nothing. He had convinced Madame Pégurin that she was a symbol only after a prolonged teatime wordplay that bordered on flirtation. This was second nature to Madame Pégurin, but the Major had bogged down quickly. He kept coming around to the point, and Madame Pégurin found the point uninteresting. She wanted to talk about little Youckie, and the difference between French and American officers, and how well Major Marshall looked in his uniform, and what a good idea it was for Mrs. Marshall not to bother about her appearance, running as she did all day after the children. But the Major talked about the picnic and by the weight of blind obduracy won.

The little Marshalls, thinking of the sugared almonds and pistachio creams in Madame Pégurin's room, slid into their places at the breakfast table and sulked over their prunes. Before each plate was a motto, in their mother's up-and-down hand: "I will be good at the picnic," said John's. This was read aloud to him, to circumvent the happy excuse that he could not yet read writing. "I will not simper. I will help Mother and be an example. I will not ask the photographer to take my picture," said Ellen's. Margaret's said, "I will mind my own business and not bother Madame Pégurin."

"What's simper?" Ellen asked.

"It's what you do all day," said her sister. To their mother she remarked, "Madame is reading the *Figaro* in her bed." There was, in her voice, a reproach that Paula Marshall did not spend her mornings in so elegant a manner, but Paula, her mind on the picnic, the eggs to be hard-boiled, scarcely took it in.

"You might, just this once, have come straight to breakfast," she said, "when you know I have this picnic to think of, and it means so much to your father to have it go well." She looked, as if for sympathy, at the portrait of Madame Pégurin's dead husband, who each day surveyed with a melancholy face these strangers around his table.

"It means a lot to Madame, too," Margaret said. "Riding there with the General! Perhaps one of us might go in the same car?"

There was no reply.

Undisturbed, Margaret said, "She told me what she is wearing. A lovely gray thing, and a big lovely hat, and diamonds." She looked thoughtfully at her mother, who, in her sensible cotton dress, seemed this morning more than ever composed of starch and soap and Apple Blossom cologne. She wore only the rings that marked her engagement and her wedding. At her throat, holding her collar, was the fraternity pin Major Marshall had given her fifteen years before. "Diamonds," Margaret repeated, as if their mother might take the hint.

"Ellen, *dear*," said Paula Marshall. "There is, really, a way to eat prunes. Do you children see *me* spitting?" The children loudly applauded this witticism, and Paula went on, "Do be careful of the table. Try to remember it isn't ours." But this the Army children had heard so often it scarcely had a meaning. "It isn't ours," they were told. "It doesn't belong to us." They had lived so much in hotels and sublet apartments and all-alike semi-detached houses that Madame Pégurin's table, at which minor nobility had once been entertained, meant no more to them than the cross-legged picnic tables at that moment being erected in Virolun community soccer field.

"You're so fond of poor Madame," said Paula, "and all her little diamonds and trinkets. I should think you would have more respect for her furniture. Jewels are only a commodity, like tins of soup. Remember that. They're bought to be sold." She wondered why Madame Pégurin did not sell them – why she kept her little trinkets but had to rent three bedrooms and a drawing room to a strange American family.

"Baseball is as far as I'll go," said the Major to himself as he was dressing, and he noted with satisfaction that it was a fine day. Outside in the garden sat the children's friends Henry and Joey Gould. The sight of these fair-haired little boys, waiting patiently on a pair of swings, caused a cloud to drift across the Major's day, obscuring the garden, the picnic, the morning's fine beginning, for the Gould children, all unwittingly, were the cause of a prolonged disagreement between the Major and his wife.

"It's not that I'm a snob," the Major had explained. "God

knows, no one could call me that!" But was it the fault of the Major that the Goulds had parted with Madame Pégurin on bad terms? Could the Major be blamed for the fact that the father of Henry and Joey was a sergeant? The Major personally thought that Sergeant Gould was a fine fellow, but the children of officers and the children of sergeants were not often invited to the same parties, and the children might, painfully, discover this for themselves. To the Major, it was clear and indisputable that the friendship should be stopped, or at least tapered. But Paula, unwisely, encouraged the children to play together. She had even asked Mrs. Gould to lunch on the lawn, which was considered by the other officers' wives in Virolun an act of great indelicacy.

Having the Gould children underfoot in the garden was particularly trying for Madame Pégurin, whose window overlooked their antics in her lily pond. She had borne with much; from her own lips the Major had heard about the final quarrel of the previous winter. It had been over a head of cauliflower – only slightly bad, said Madam Pégurin – that Mrs. Gould had dropped, unwrapped, into the garbage can. It had been retrieved by Louise, Madame Pégurin's cook, who had suggested to Mrs. Gould that it be used in soup. "I don't give my children rotten food," Mrs. Gould had replied, on which Louise, greatly distressed, had carried the slimy cauliflower in a clean towel up to Madame Pégurin's bedroom. Madame Pégurin, considering both sides, had then composed a message to be read aloud, in English, by Louise: "Is Mrs. Gould aware that many people in France have not enough to eat? Does she know that wasted food is saved for the poor by the garbage collector? Will she please in future wrap the things she wastes so that they will not spoil?" The message seemed to Madame Pégurin so fair, so unanswerable, that she could not understand why Mrs. Gould, after a moment of horrified silence, burst into tears and quite irrationally called Louise a Communist. This political quarrel had reached the ears of the General, who, insisting he could not have that sort of thing, asked Colonel Baring to straighten the difficulty out, since it was the Colonel's fault the Goulds had been sent there in the first place.

All this had given Virolun a winter of gossip, much of which was still repeated. One of the research workers had, quite recently, asked Major Marshall whether it was true that when young Mrs. Gould asked Madame Pégurin if she had a vacuum cleaner, she had been told, "No, I have a servant." Was this attitude widespread, the research worker had wanted to know. Or was the Army helping break down the feudal social barriers of the little town. Oh, yes, the Major had replied. Oh, yes, indeed.

Passing Louise on the staircase with Madame Pégurin's breakfast tray, the Major smiled, thinking of Madame Pégurin and of how fond she was of his children. Often, on his way to breakfast, he saw the children through the half-open door, watching her as she skimmed from her coffee a web of warm milk; Madame Pégurin's levees, his wife called them. Paula said that Madame Pégurin was so feminine it made her teeth ache, and that her influence on the children was deplorable. But the Major could not take this remark seriously. He admired Madame Pégurin, confusing her, because she was old and French and had once been rich, with courts and courtesans and the eighteenth century. In her presence, his mind took a literary turn, and he thought of vanished glories, something fine that would never return, gallant fluttering banners, and the rest of it.

He found his wife in the dining room, staring moodily at the disorder left by the children. "They've vanished," she said at once. "I sent them to wait in the garden with Joey and Henry, but they're not out there now. They must have crept in again by the front door. I think they were simply waiting for you to come down so that they could go up to her room." She was flushed with annoyance and the unexpected heat of the morning. "These red walls," she said, looking around the room. "They've made me so uncomfortable all summer I haven't enjoyed a single meal." She longed to furnish a house of her own once more, full of chintz and robin's-egg blue, and pictures of the children in frames.

In the red dining room, Madame Pégurin had hung yellow curtains. On a side table was a vase of yellow late summer flowers. The Major looked around the room, but with an almost guilty enjoyment, for, just as the Methodist child is seduced by the Roman service, the Major had succumbed in Madame Pégurin's house to something warm and rich, composed of red and yellow, and branching candelabra.

"If they would only stay in the garden," Paula said. "I hate it, always having to call them and fetch them. The girls, at least, could help with the sandwiches." She began to pile the plates one on another, drawing the crumbs on the tablecloth toward her with a knife. "And they're probably eating things. Glacéed pineapple. Cherries in something – something *alcoholic*. Really, it's too much. And you don't help."

She seemed close to tears, and the Major, looking down at his cornflakes, wondered exactly how to compose his face so that it would be most comforting. Paula was suspicious of extravagant tastes or pleasures. She enjoyed the nursery fare she gave the children, sharing without question their peas and lamb chops, their bland and innocent desserts. Once, long ago, she had broken off an engagement only because she had detected in the young man's eyes a look of sensuous bliss as he ate strawberries and cream. And now her own children came to the table full of rum-soaked sponge cake and looked with condescension at their lemon jello.

"You exaggerate," the Major said, kindly. "Madame Pégurin takes a lot of trouble with the children. She's giving them a taste of life they might never have had."

"I know," Paula said. "And while she's at it, she's ruining all my good work." She often used this expression of the children, as if they were a length of Red Cross knitting. As the Major drank his coffee, he made marks in a notebook on the table. She sighed and, rising with the plates in her hands, said, "We'll leave it for now, because of the picnic. But tomorrow you and I must have a long talk. About everything."

"Of course," the Major said. "We'll talk about everything – the little Goulds, too. And you might try, just this once, to be nice to Mrs. Baring."

"I'll try," said Paula, "but I can't promise." There were tears in her eyes, of annoyance at having to be nice to Colonel Baring's wife.

Madame Pégurin, in the interim, descended from the shuttered gloom of her room and went out to the garden, trailing wings of gray chiffon, and followed by the children and Louise, who were bearing iced tea, a folding chair, a parasol, a hassock, and a blanket. Under the brim of her hat her hair was drawn into tangerine-colored scallops. She sat down on the chair and put her feet on the hassock. On the grass at her feet, Margaret and Ellen lay prone, propped on their elbows. John sat beside them, eating something. The little Goulds, identical in striped jerseys, stood apart, holding a ball and bat.

"And how is your mother?" Madame Pégurin asked Joey and Henry. "Does she still have so very much trouble with the vegetables?"

"I don't know," Henry said innocently. "Where we live now, the maid does everything."

"Ah, of course," Madame Pégurin said, settling back in her chair. Her voice was warm and reserved – royalty at a bazaar. Between her and the two girls passed a long look of feminine understanding.

In the kitchen, attacking the sandwiches, Paula Marshall wondered what, if anything, Mrs. Baring would say to Madame

Pégurin, for the Barings had been snubbed by her so severely that, thinking of it, Paula was instantly cheered. The Barings had wanted to live with Madame Pégurin. They had been impressed by the tidy garden, the house crowded with the salvage of something better, the portrait of Monsieur Pégurin, who had been, they understood, if not an ambassador, something just as nice. But they had offended Madame Pégurin, first by giving her a Christmas present, a subscription to the *Reader's Digest* in French, and then by calling one afternoon without an invitation. Mrs. Baring had darted about the drawing room like a fish, remarking, in the sort of voice reserved for the whims of the elderly, "*My* mother collects milk glass." And the Colonel had confided to Madame Pégurin that his wife spoke excellent French and would, if pressed, say a few words in that language – a confidence that was for Madame Pégurin the depth of the afternoon. "I wouldn't think of taking into my house anyone but the General," she was reported to have said. "Or someone on his immediate staff." The Barings had exchanged paralyzed looks and then the Colonel, rising to it, had said that he would see, and the following week he had sent Sergeant Gould, who was the General's driver, and his wife, and the terrible children. The Barings had never mentioned the incident, but they often, with little smiles and movements of their eyebrows, implied that by remaining in a cramped room at the Hotel Bristol and avoiding Madame Pégurin's big house they had narrowly escaped a season in Hell.

Now they were all going to the picnic, that symbol of unity, Sergeant Gould driving the General and Madame Pégurin, the Barings following with the mayor of Virolun, and the Marshalls and the little Goulds somewhere behind.

The Major came into the kitchen, carrying his notebook, and Paula said to him, "It will be queer, this thing today."

"Queer?" he said absently. "I don't see why. Look," he said. "I may have to make a speech. I put everyone on the agenda but myself, but I may be asked." He frowned at his notes. "I could start with 'We are gathered together.' Or is that stuffy?"

"I don't know," Paula said. With care, and also with a certain suggestion of martyrdom, she rolled bread around watercress. "Actually, I think it's a quote."

"It could be." The Major looked depressed. He ate an egg sandwich from Paula's hamper. The basket lunch had been his idea; every family was bringing one. The Major had declared the basket lunch to be typically American, although he had never in his life attended such a function. "You should see them all in the garden," he said, cheering up. "Madame Pégurin and the kids. What a picture! The photographer should have been there. He's never around when you want him."

Describing this scene, which he had watched from the dining-room windows, the Major was careful to leave out any phrases that might annoy his wife, omitting with regret the filtered sunlight, the golden summer garden, and the blue shade of the parasol. It had pleased him to observe, although he did not repeat this either, that even a stranger could have detected which children were the little Goulds and which the little Marshalls. "I closed the dining-room shutters," he added. "The sun seems to have moved around." He had become protective of Madame Pégurin's house, extending his care to the carpets.

"That's fine," Paula said. In a few minutes, the cars would arrive to carry them all away, and she had a sudden prophetic vision of the day ahead. She saw the tiny cavalcade of motorcars creeping, within the speed limit, through the main street and stopping at the 1914 war memorial so that General Wirtworth could place a wreath. She foresaw the failure of the Coca-Cola to arrive at the picnic grounds, and the breakdown of the movie projector. On the periphery, scowling and eating nothing, would be the members of the Virolun Football Club, which had been forced to postpone a match with the St. Etienne Devils because of the picnic. The Major would be everywhere at once, driving his sergeant before him like a hen. Then the baseball, with the mothers of Virolun taking good care to keep their pinafored children away from the wayward ball and the terrible waving bat. Her imagination sought the photographer, found him on a picnic table, one sandaled foot next to a plate of doughnuts, as he recorded Mrs. Baring fetching a cushion for General Wirtworth and Madame Pégurin receiving from the little Goulds a cucumber sandwich.

Paula closed the picnic hamper and looked at her husband with compassion. She suddenly felt terribly sorry for him, because of all that was in store for him this day, and because the picnic was not likely to clarify his status, as he so earnestly hoped. There would be fresh misunderstandings and further scandals. She laid her hand over his. "I'm sorry," she said. "I should have been listening more carefully. Read me your speech, and start with 'We are gathered together.' I think it's quite appropriate and very lovely."

"Do you?" said the Major. His eyes hung on her face, trusting. "But then suppose I have to give it in French? How the hell do you say 'gathered together' in French?"

"You won't have to give it in French," Paula said, in just such a voice as she used to her children when they had a fever or nightmares. "Because, you see, the mayor will speak in French, and that's quite enough."

"That's right," said the Major, "I can say, in French, 'Our good French friends will excuse this little talk in English.' "

"That's right," Paula said.

Reassured, the Major thrust his notes in his pocket and strode from the kitchen to the garden, where, squaring his shoulders, he rallied his forces for the coming battle.

About Geneva

Granny was waiting at the door of the apartment. She looked small, lonely, and patient, and at the sight of her the children and their mother felt instantly guilty. Instead of driving straight home from the airport, they had stopped outside Nice for ice cream. They might have known how much those extra twenty minutes would mean to Granny. Colin, too young to know what he felt, or why, began instinctively to misbehave, dragging his feet, scratching the waxed parquet. Ursula bit her nails, taking refuge in a dream, while the children's mother, Granny's only daughter, felt compelled to cry in a high, cheery voice, "Well, Granny, here they are, safe and sound!"

"Darlings," said Granny, very low. "Home again." She stretched out her arms to Ursula, but then, seeing the taxi driver, who had carried the children's bags up the stairs, she drew back. After he had gone she repeated the gesture, turning this time to Colin, as if Ursula's cue had been irrevocably missed. Colin was wearing a beret. "Wherever did that come from?" Granny said. She pulled it off and stood still, stricken. "My darling little boy," she said, at last. "What have they done to you? They have cut your hair. Your lovely golden hair. I cannot believe it. I don't want to believe it."

"It was high time," the children's mother said. She stood in the outer corridor, waiting for Granny's welcome to subside. "It was high time someone cut Colin's hair. The curls made such a baby of him. We should have seen that. Two women can't really bring up a boy."

Granny didn't look at all as if she agreed. "Who cut your hair?" she said, holding Colin.

"Barber," he said, struggling away.

"Less said the better," said Colin's mother. She came in at last, drew off her gloves, looked around, as if she, and not the children, had been away.

"He's not my child, of course," said Granny, releasing Colin. "If he were, I can just imagine the letter I should write. Of all the impudence! When you send a child off for a visit you expect at the very least to have him returned exactly as he left. And you," she said, extending to Ursula a plump, liver-spotted hand, "what changes am I to expect in you?"

"Oh, Granny, for Heaven's sake, it was only two weeks." She permitted her grandmother to kiss her, then went straight to the

46

sitting room and hurled herself into a chair. The room was hung with dark engravings of cathedrals. There were flowers, red carnations, on the rickety painted tables, poked into stiff arrangements by a maid. It was the standard seasonal Nice *meublé*. Granny spent every winter in rented flats more or less like this one, and her daughter, since her divorce, shared them with her.

Granny followed Ursula into the room and sat down, erect, on an uncomfortable chair, while her daughter, trailing behind, finally chose a footstool near the empty fireplace. She gave Granny a gentle, neutral look. Before starting out for the airport, earlier, she had repeated her warning: There were to be no direct questions, no remarks. It was all to appear as natural and normal as possible. What, indeed, could be more natural for the children than a visit with their father?

"What, indeed," said Granny in a voice rich with meaning.

It was only fair, said the children's mother. A belief in fair play was so embedded in her nature that she could say the words without coloring deeply. Besides, it was the first time he had asked.

"And won't be the last," Granny said. "But, of course, it is up to you."

Ursula lay rather than sat in her chair. Her face was narrow and freckled: She resembled her mother who, at thirty-four, had settled into a permanent, anxious-looking, semi-youthfulness. Colin, blond and fat, rolled on the floor. He pulled his mouth out at the corners, then pulled down his eyes to show the hideous red underlids. He looked at his grandmother and growled like a lion.

"Colin has come back sillier than ever," Granny said. He lay prone, noisily snuffing the carpet. The others ignored him.

"Did you go boating, Ursula?" said Granny, not counting this as a direct question. "When I visited Geneva, as a girl, we went boating on the lake." She went on about white water birds, a parasol, a boat heaped with colored cushions.

"Oh, Granny, no," said Ursula. "There weren't even any big boats, let alone little ones. It was cold."

"I hope the house, at least, was warm."

But evidently Ursula had failed to notice the temperature of her father's house. She slumped on her spine (a habit Granny had just nicely caused her to get over before the departure for Geneva) and then said, unexpectedly, "She's not a good manager."

Granny and her daughter exchanged a look, eyebrows up.

"Oh?" said Ursula's mother, pink. She forgot about the direct questions and said, "Why?"

"It's not terribly polite to speak that way of one's hostess," said Granny, unable to resist the reproof but threatening Ursula's revelation at the source. Her daughter looked at her, murderous.

"Well," said Ursula, slowly, "once the laundry didn't come back. It was her fault, he said. Our sheets had to be changed, he said. So she said Oh, all right. She took the sheets off Colin's bed and put them on my bed, and took the sheets off my bed and put them on Colin's. To make the change, she said."

"Dear God," said Granny.

"Colin's sheets were a mess. He had his supper in bed sometimes. They were just a mess."

"Not true," said Colin.

"Another time . . . ," said Ursula, and stopped, as if Granny had been right, after all, about criticizing one's hostess.

"Gave us chocolate," came from Colin, his face muffled in carpet.

"Not every day, I trust," Granny said.

"For the plane."

"It might very well have made you both airsick," said Granny.

"Well," said Ursula, "it didn't." Her eyes went often to the luggage in the hall. She squirmed upright, stood up, and sat down again. She rubbed her nose with the back of her hand.

"Ursula, do you want a handkerchief?" said Granny.

"No," said Ursula. "Only it so happens I'm writing a play. It's in the suitcase."

Granny and the children's mother looked at each other again. "I *am* pleased," Granny said, and her daughter nodded, agreeing, for, if impertinence and slumping on one's spine were unfortunate inherited tendencies, this was something else. It was only fair that Ursula's father should have bequeathed her *something* to compensate for the rest. "What is it about?" said Granny.

Ursula looked at her feet. After a short silence she said, "Russia. That's all I want to tell. It was her idea. She lived there once."

Quietly, controlled, the children's mother took a cigarette from the box on the table. Granny looked brave.

"Would you tell us the title, at least?" said Granny.

"No," said Ursula. But then, as if the desire to share the splendid thing she had created were too strong, she said, "I'll tell you one line, because they said it was the best thing they'd ever heard anywhere." She took a breath. Her audience was gratifyingly attentive, straining, nearly, with attention and control. "It goes like this," Ursula said. " 'The Grand Duke enters and sees Tatiana all in gold.' "

"Well?" said Granny.

"Well, what?" said Ursula. "That's it. That's the line." She looked at her mother and grandmother and said, "*They* liked it. They want me to send it to them, and everything else, too. She even told me the name Tatiana."

"It's lovely, dear," said Ursula's mother. She put the cigarette back in the box. "It sounds like a lovely play. Just when did she live in Russia?"

"I don't know. Ages ago. She's pretty old."

"Perhaps one day we shall see the play after all," said Granny. "Particularly if it is to be sent all over the Continent."

"You mean they might act in it?" said Ursula. Thinking of this, she felt sorry for herself. Ever since she had started "The Grand Duke" she could not think of her own person without being sorry. For no reason at all, now, her eyes filled with tears of self-pity. Drooping, she looked out at the darkening street, to the leafless trees and the stone facade of a public library.

But the children's mother, as if Granny's remark had for her an entirely different meaning, not nearly so generous, said, "I shall give you the writing desk from my bedroom, Ursula. It has a key."

"Where will you keep your things?" said Granny, protesting. She could not very well say that the desk was her own, not to be moved. Like everything else – the dark cathedrals, the shaky painted tables – it had come with the flat.

"I don't need a key," said the children's mother, lacing her fingers tightly around her knees. "I'm not writing a play, or anything else I want kept secret. Not any more."

"They used to take Colin for walks," said Ursula, yawning, only vaguely taking in the importance of the desk. "That was when I started to write this thing. Once they stayed out the whole afternoon. They never said where they'd been."

"I wonder," said her mother, thoughtful. She started to say something to Ursula, something not quite a question, but the child was too preoccupied with herself. Everything about the trip, in the end, would crystallize around Tatiana and the Grand Duke. Already, Ursula was Tatiana. The children's mother looked at Ursula's long bare legs, her heavy shoes, her pleated skirt, and she thought, I must do something about her clothes, something to make her pretty.

"Colin, dear," said Granny in her special inner-meaning voice, "do you remember your walks?"

"No."

"I wonder why they wanted to take him alone," said Colin's mother. "It seems odd, all the same."

"Under seven," said Granny, cryptic. "Couldn't influence girl.

Too old. Boy different. Give me first seven years, you can have rest."

"But it wasn't seven years. He hasn't been alive that long. It was only two weeks."

"Two very impressionable weeks," Granny said.

"I understand everything you're saying," Ursula said, "even when you talk that way. They spoke French when they didn't want us to hear, but we understood that, too."

"I fed the swans," Colin suddenly shouted.

There, he had told about Geneva. He sat up and kicked his heels on the carpet as if the noise would drown out the consequence of what he had revealed. As he said it, the image became static; a gray sky, a gray lake, and a swan wonderfully turning upside down with the black rubber feet showing above the water. His father was not in the picture at all; neither was *she*. But Geneva was fixed for the rest of his life: gray, lake, swan.

Having delivered his secret he had nothing more to tell. He began to invent. "I was sick on the plane," he said, but Ursula at once said that this was a lie, and he lay down again, humiliated. At last, feeling sleepy, he began to cry.

"He never once cried in Geneva," Ursula said. But by the one simple act of creating Tatiana and the Grand Duke, she had removed herself from the ranks of reliable witnesses.

"How would you know?" said Granny bitterly. "You weren't always with him. If you had paid more attention, if you had taken care of your little brother, he wouldn't have come back to us with his hair cut."

"Never mind," said the children's mother. Rising, she helped Colin to his feet and led him away to bed.

She stood behind him as he cleaned his teeth. He looked male and self-assured with his newly cropped head, and she thought of her husband, and how odd it was that only a few hours before Colin had been with him. She touched the tender back of his neck. "Don't," he said. Frowning, concentrating, he hung up his toothbrush. "I told about Geneva."

"Yes, you did." He had fed swans. She saw sunshine, a blue lake, and the boats Granny had described, heaped with colored cushions. She saw her husband and someone else (probably in white, she thought, ridiculously bouffant, the origin of Tatiana) and Colin with his curls shorn, revealing ears surprisingly large. There was nothing to be had from Ursula – not, at least, until the Grand Duke had died down. But Colin seemed to carry the story of the visit with him, and she felt the faintest stirrings of envy, the resentfulness of the spectator, the loved one left behind.

"Were you really sick on the plane?" she said.

"Yes," said Colin.

"Were they lovely, the swans?"

But the question bore no relation to anything he had seen. He said nothing. He played with toothpaste, dawdling.

"Isn't that child in bed yet?" called Granny. "Does he want his supper?"

"No," said Colin.

"No," said his mother. "He was sick on the plane."

"I thought so," Granny said. "That, at least, is a fact."

They heard the voice of Ursula, protesting.

But how can they be trusted, the children's mother thought. Which of them can one believe? "Perhaps," she said to Colin, "one day, you can tell me more about Geneva?"

"Yes," he said perplexed.

But, really, she doubted it; nothing had come back from the trip but her own feelings of longing and envy, the longing and envy she felt at night, seeing, at a crossroad or over a bridge, the lighted windows of a train sweep by. Her children had nothing to tell her. Perhaps, as she had said, one day Colin would say something, produce the image of Geneva, tell her about the lake, the boats, the swans, and why her husband had left her. Perhaps he could tell her, but, really, she doubted it. And, already, so did he.

Acceptance of Their Ways

Prodded by a remark from Mrs. Freeport, Lily Littel got up and fetched the plate of cheese. It was in her to say, "Go get it yourself," but a reputation for coolness held her still. Only the paucity of her income, at which the *Sunday Express* horoscope jeered with its smart talk of pleasure and gain, kept her at Mrs. Freeport's, on the Italian side of the frontier. The coarse and grubby gaiety of the French Riviera would have suited her better, and was not far away; unfortunately it came high. At Mrs. Freeport's, which was cheaper, there was a whiff of infirm nicety to be breathed, a suggestion of regularly aired decay; weakly, because it was respectable, Lily craved that, too. "We seem to have finished with the pudding," said Mrs. Freeport once again, as though she hadn't noticed that Lily was on her feet.

Lily was not Mrs. Freeport's servant, she was her paying guest, but it was a distinction her hostess rarely observed. In imagination, Lily became a punishing statue and raised a heavy marble arm; but then she remembered that this was the New Year. The next day, or the day after that, her dividends would arrive. That meant she could disappear, emerging as a gay holiday Lily up in Nice. Then, Lily thought, turning away from the table, then watch the old tiger! For Mrs. Freeport couldn't live without Lily, not more than a day. She could not stand Italy without the sound of an English voice in the house. In the hush of the dead season, Mrs. Freeport preferred Lily's ironed-out Bayswater to no English at all.

In the time it took her to pick up the cheese and face the table again, Lily had added to her expression a permanent-looking smile. Her eyes, which were a washy blue, were tolerably kind when she was plotting mischief. The week in Nice, desired, became a necessity; Mrs. Freeport needed a scare. She would fear, and then believe, that her most docile boarder, her most pliant errand girl, had gone forever. Stealing into Lily's darkened room, she would count the dresses with trembling hands. She would touch Lily's red with the white dots, her white with the poppies, her green wool with the scarf of mink tails. Mrs. Freeport would also discover – if she carried her snooping that far – the tooled-leather box with Lily's daisy-shaped earrings, and the brooch in which a mother-of-pearl pigeon sat on a nest made of Lily's own hair. But Mrs. Freeport would not find the diary, in which Lily had recorded her opinion of so many interesting things, nor would she come upon a single empty bottle. Lily kept her drinking to Nice, where, anonymous in a large hotel, friendly and lavish in a bar, she let herself drown. "Your visits to your sister seem to do you so much good," was Mrs. Freeport's unvarying comment when Lily returned from these excursions, which always followed the arrival of her income. "But you spend far too much money on your sister. You are much too kind." But Lily had no regrets. Illiberal by circumstance, grudging only because she imitated the behavior of other women, she became, drunk, an old forgotten Lily-girl, tender and warm, able to shed a happy tear and open a closed fist. She had been cold sober since September.

"Well, there you are," she said, and slapped down the plate of cheese. There was another person at the table, a Mrs. Garnett, who was returning to England the next day. Lily's manner toward the two women combined bullying with servility. Mrs. Freeport, large, in brown chiffon, wearing a hat with a water lily upon it to cover her thinning hair, liked to *feel* served. Lily had been a paid companion once; she had never seen a paradox in the joining of those two words. She simply looked on Mrs. Freeport and Mrs. Garnett as more of that race of ailing, peevish elderly children whose fancies and delusions must be humored by the sane.

Mrs. Freeport pursed her lips in acknowledgement of the cheese. Mrs. Garnett, who was reading a book, did nothing at all. Mrs. Garnett had been with them four months. Her blued curls, her laugh, her moist baby's mouth, had the effect on Lily of a stone in the shoe. Mrs. Garnett's husband, dead but often mentioned, had evidently liked them saucy and dim in the brain. Now that William Henry was no longer there to protect his wife, she was the victim of the effect of her worrying beauty – a torment to shoe clerks and bus conductors. Italians were dreadful; Mrs. Garnett hardly dared put her wee nose outside the house. "You are a little monkey, Edith!" Mrs. Freeport would sometimes say, bringing her head upward with a jerk, waking out of a sweet dream in time to applaud. Mrs. Garnett would go on telling how she had been jostled on the pavement or offended on a bus. And Lily Littel, who knew – but truly knew – about being followed and hounded and pleaded with, brought down her thick eyelids and smiled. Talk leads to overconfidence and errors. Lily had guided her life to this quiet shore by knowing when to open her mouth and when to keep it closed.

Mrs. Freeport was not deluded but simply poor. Thirteen years of pension-keeping on a tawdry stretch of Mediterranean coast had done nothing to improve her fortunes and had probably diminished them. Sentiment kept her near Bordighera, where someone precious to her had been buried in the Protestant part of the cemetery. In Lily's opinion, Mrs. Freeport ought to have cleared out long ago cutting her losses, leaving the servants out of pocket and the grocer unpaid. Lily looked soft; she was round and pink and yellow-haired. The imitation pearls screwed on to her doughy little ears seemed to devour the flesh. But Lily could have bitten a real pearl in two and enjoyed the pieces. Her nature was generous, but an admiration for superior women had led her to cherish herself. An excellent cook, she had dreamed of being a poisoner, but decided to leave that for the loonies; it was no real way to get on. She had a moral program of a sort – thought it wicked to set a poor table, until she learned that the sort of woman she yearned to become was often picky. After that she tried to put it out of her mind. At Mrs. Freeport's she was enrolled in a useful school, for the creed of the house was this: It is pointless to think about anything so temporary as food; coffee grounds can be used many times, and moldy bread, revived in the oven, mashed with raisins and milk, makes a delicious pudding. If Lily had settled for this bleached existence, it was explained by a sentence scrawled over a page of her locked diary: "I live with gentlewomen now." And there was a finality about the statement that implied acceptance of their ways.

Lily removed the fly netting from the cheese. There was her bit left over from luncheon. It was the end of a portion of Dutch so dry it had split. Mrs. Freeport would have the cream cheese, possibly still highly pleasing under its coat of pale fur, while Mrs. Garnett, who was a yoghurt fancier, would require none at all.

"Cheese, Edith," said Mrs. Freeport loudly, and little Mrs. Garnett blinked her doll eyes and smiled: No, thank you. Let others thicken their figures and damage their souls.

The cheese was pushed along to Mrs. Freeport, then back to Lily, passing twice under Mrs. Garnett's nose. She did not look up again. She was moving her lips over a particularly absorbing passage in her book. For the last four months, she had been reading the same volume, which was called "Optimism Unlimited." So as not to stain the pretty dust jacket, she had covered it with brown paper, but now even that was becoming soiled. When Mrs. Freeport asked what the book was about, Mrs. Garnett smiled a timid apology and said, "I'm *afraid* it is philosophy." It was, indeed, a new philosophy, counseling restraint in all things, but recommending smiles. Four months of smiles and restraint had left Mrs. Garnett hungry, and, to mark her last evening at Mrs. Freeport's, she had asked for an Italian meal. Mrs. Freeport thought it extravagant – after all, they were still digesting an English Christmas. But little Edith was so sweet when she begged, putting her head to one side, wrinkling her face, that Mrs. Freeport, muttering about monkeys, had given in. The dinner was prepared and served, and Mrs. Garnett, suddenly remembering about restraint, brought her book to the table and decided not to eat a thing.

It seemed that the late William Henry had found this capriciousness adorable, but Mrs. Freeport's eyes were stones. Lily supposed this was how murders came about – not the hasty, soon regretted sort but the plan that is sown from an insult, a slight, and comes to flower at temperate speed. Mrs. Garnett deserved a reprimand. Lily saw her, without any emotion, doubled in two and shoved in a sack. But did Mrs. Freeport like her friend enough to bother teaching her lessons? Castigation, to Lily, suggested love. Mrs. Garnett and Mrs. Freeport were old friends, and vaguely related. Mrs. Garnett had been coming to Mrs. Freeport's every winter for years, but she left unfinished letters lying about, from which Lily – a greater reader – could learn that dear Vanessa was becoming meaner and queerer by the minute. Thinking of Mrs. Freeport as "dear Vanessa" took flexibility, but Lily had that. She was not "Miss" and not "Littel;" she was, or, rather, had been, a Mrs. Cliff Little, who had taken advantage of the disorders of war to get rid of Cliff. He vanished, and his memory grew smaller and faded from the sky. In the bright new day strolled Miss Lily Littel, ready for anything. Then a lonely, fretful widow had taken a fancy to her and, as soon as travel was possible, had taken Lily abroad. There followed eight glorious years of trains and bars and discreet afternoon gambling, of eating éclairs in English-style tearooms, and discovering cafés where bacon and eggs were fried. Oh, the discovery of that sign in Monte Carlo: "Every Friday Sausages and Mashed"! That was the joy of being in foreign lands. One hot afternoon, Lily's employer, hooked by Lily into her stays not an hour before, dropped dead in a cinema lobby in Rome. Her will revealed she had provided for "Miss Littel," for a fox terrier, and for an invalid niece. The provision for the niece prevented the family from coming down on Lily's head; all the same, Lily kept out of England. She had not inspired the death of her employer, but she had nightmares for some time after, as though she had taken the wish for the deed. Her letters were so ambiguous that there was talk in England of an inquest. Lily accompanied the coffin as far as the frontier, for a letter of instructions specified cremation, which Lily understood could take place only in France. The coffin was held up rather a long time at customs, documents went back and forth, and in the end the relatives were glad to hear the last of it. Shortly after that, the fox terrier died, and Lily appropriated his share, feeling that she deserved it. Her employer had been living on overdrafts; there was next to nothing for dog, companion, or niece. Lily stopped having nightmares. She continued to live abroad.

With delicate nibbles, eyes down, Lily ate her cheese. Glancing sidewise, she noticed that Mrs. Garnett had closed the book. She wanted to annoy; she had planned the whole business of the Italian meal, had thought it out beforehand. Their manners were still strange to Lily, although she was a quick pupil. Why not clear the air, have it out? Once again she wondered what the two friends meant to each other. "Like" and "hate" were possibilities she had nearly forgotten when she stopped being Mrs. Cliff and became this curious, two-faced Lily Littel.

Mrs. Freeport's pebbly stare was focussed on her friend's jar of yoghurt. "Sugar?" she cried, giving the cracked basin a shove along the table. Mrs. Garnett pulled it toward her, defiantly. She spoke in a soft, martyred voice, as though Lily weren't there. She said that it was her last evening and it no longer mattered. Mrs. Freeport had made a charge for extra sugar – yes, she had seen it on her bill. Mrs. Garnett asked only to pay and go. She was never coming again.

"I look upon you as essentially greedy." Mrs. Freeport leaned forward, enunciating with care. "You pretend to eat nothing, but I cannot look at a dish after you have served yourself. The *wreck* of the lettuce. The *destruction* of the pudding."

A bottle of wine, adrift and forgotten, stood by Lily's plate. She had not seen it until now. Mrs. Garnett, who was fearless, covered her yoghurt thickly with sugar.

"Like most people who pretend to eat like birds, you manage to keep your strength up," Mrs. Freeport said. "That sugar is the equivalent of a banquet, and you also eat between meals. Your drawers are stuffed with biscuits, and cheese, and chocolate, and heaven knows what."

"Dear Vanessa," Mrs. Garnett said.

"People who make a pretense of eating nothing always stuff furtively," said Mrs. Freeport smoothly. "Secret eating is exactly the same thing as secret drinking."

Lily's years abroad had immunized her to the conversation of gentlewomen, their absorption with money, their deliberate over- or underfeeding, their sudden animal quarrels. She wondered if there remained a great deal more to learn before she could wear their cast-off manners as her own. At the reference to secret drinking she looked calm and melancholy. Mrs. Garnett said, "That is most unkind." The yoghurt remained uneaten. Lily sighed, and wondered what would happen if she picked her teeth.

"My change man stopped by today," said Mrs. Garnett, all at once smiling and widening her eyes. How Lily admired that shift of territory – that carrying of banners to another field. She had not learned everything yet. "I *wish* you could have seen his face when he heard I was leaving! There really was no need for his coming, because I'd been in to his office only the week before, and changed all the money I need, and we'd had a lovely chat."

"The odious little money merchant in the bright-yellow automobile?" said Mrs. Freeport.

Mrs. Garnett, who often took up farfetched and untenable arguments, said, "William Henry wanted me to be happy."

"Edith!"

Lily hooked her middle finger around the bottle of wine and pulled it gently toward her. The day after tomorrow was years away. But she did not take her eyes from Mrs. Freeport, whose blazing eyes perfectly matched the small sapphires hanging from her ears. Lily could have matched the expression if she had cared to, but she hadn't arrived at the sapphires yet. Addressing herself, Lily said, "Thanks," softly, and upended the bottle.

"I meant it in a general way," said Mrs. Garnett. "William Henry wanted me to be happy. It was nearly the last thing he said."

"At the time of William Henry's death, he was unable to say anything," said Mrs. Freeport. "William Henry was my first cousin. Don't use him as a platform for your escapades."

Lily took a sip from her glass. Shock! It hadn't been watered – probably in honor of Mrs. Garnett's last meal. But it was sour, thick, and full of silt. "I have always thought a little sugar would improve it," said Lily chattily, but nobody heard.

Mrs. Freeport suddenly conceded that William Henry might have wanted his future widow to be happy. "It was because he spoiled you," she said. "You were vain and silly when he married you, and he made you conceited and foolish. I don't wonder poor William Henry went off his head."

"Off his head?" Mrs. Garnett looked at Lily; calm, courteous Miss Littel was giving herself wine. "We might have general conversation," said Mrs. Garnett, with a significant twitch of face. "Miss Littel has hardly said a word."

"Why?" shouted Mrs. Freeport, throwing her table napkin down. "The meal is over. You refused it. There is no need for conversation of any kind."

She was marvelous, blazing, with that water lily on her head.

Ah, Lily thought, but you should have seen me, in the old days. How I could let fly . . . poor old Cliff.

They moved in single file down the passage and into the sitting room, where, for reasons of economy, the hanging lustre contained one bulb. Lily and Mrs. Freeport settled down directly under it, on a sofa; each had her own newspaper to read, tucked down the side of the cushions. Mrs. Garnett walked about the room. "To think that I shall never see this room again," she said.

"I should hope not," said Mrs. Freeport. She held the paper before her face, but as far as Lily could tell she was not reading it.

"The trouble is" – for Mrs. Garnett could never help giving herself away – "I don't know where to *go* in the autumn."

"Ask your change man."

"Egypt," said Mrs. Garnett, still walking about. "I had friends who went to Egypt every winter for years and years, and now they have nowhere to go, either."

"Let them stay home," said Mrs. Freeport. "I am trying to read."

"If Egypt continues to carry on, I'm sure I don't know where we shall all be," said Lily. Neither lady took the slightest notice.

"They were perfectly charming people," said Mrs. Garnett, in a complaining way.

"Why don't you do the *Times* crossword, Edith?" said Mrs. Freeport.

From behind them, Mrs. Garnett said, "You know that I can't, and you said that only to make me feel small. But William Henry did it until the very end, which proves, I think, that he was not o.h.h. By o.h.h. I mean *off his head*."

The break in her voice was scarcely more than a quaver, but to the two women on the sofa it was a signal, and they got to their feet. By the time they reached her, Mrs. Garnett was sitting on the floor in hysterics. They helped her up, as they had often done before. She tried to scratch their faces and said they would be sorry when she had died.

Between them, they got her to bed. "Where is her hot-water bottle?" said Mrs. Freeport. "No, not that one. She must have her own – the bottle with the bunny head."

"My yoghurt," said Mrs. Garnett, sobbing. Without her make-up she looked shrunken, as though padding had been removed from her skin.

"Fetch the yoghurt," Mrs. Freeport commanded. She stood over the old friend while she ate the yoghurt, one tiny spoonful at a time. "Now go to sleep," she said.

In the morning, Mrs. Garnett was taken by taxi to the early train. She seemed entirely composed and carried her book. Mrs. Freeport hoped that her journey would be comfortable. She and Lily watched the taxi until it was out of sight on the road, and then, in the bare wintry garden, Mrs. Freeport wept into her hands.

"I've said goodbye to her," she said at last, blowing her nose. "It is the last goodbye. I shall never see her again. I was so horrid to her. And she is so tiny and frail. She might die. I'm convinced of it. She won't survive the summer."

"She has survived every other," said Lily reasonably.

"Next year, she must have the large room with the balcony. I don't know what I was thinking, not to have given it to her. We must begin planning now for next year. She will want a good reading light. Her eyes are so bad. And, you know, we should have chopped her vegetables. She doesn't chew. I'm sure that's at the bottom of the yoghurt affair."

"I'm off to Nice tomorrow," said Lily, the stray. "My sister is expecting me."

"You are so devoted," said Mrs. Freeport, looking wildly for her handkerchief, which had fallen on the gravel path. Her hat was askew. The house was empty. "So devoted . . . I suppose that one day you will want to live in Nice, to be near her. I suppose that day will come."

Instead of answering, Lily set Mrs. Freeport's water lily straight, which was familiar of her; but they were both in such a state, for different reasons, that neither of them thought it strange.

My Heart Is Broken

"When that Jean Harlow died," Mrs. Thompson said to Jeannie, "I was on the 83 streetcar with a big, heavy paper parcel in my arms. I hadn't been married for very long, and when I used to visit my mother she'd give me a lot of canned stuff and preserves. I was standing up in the streetcar because nobody'd given me a seat. All the men were unemployed in those days, and they just sat down wherever they happened to be. You wouldn't remember what Montreal was like then. *You* weren't even on earth. To resume what I was saying to you, one of these men sitting down had an American paper – the *Daily News*, I guess it was – and I was sort of leaning over him, and I saw in big print 'JEAN HARLOW DEAD.' You can believe me or not, just as you want to, but that was the most terrible shock I ever had in my life. I never got over it."

Jeannie had nothing to say to that. She lay flat on her back across the bed, with her head toward Mrs. Thompson and her heels just touching the crate that did as a bedside table. Balanced on her flat stomach was an open bottle of coral-pink Cutex nail polish. She held her hands up over her head and with some difficulty applied the brush to the nails of her right hand. Her legs were brown and thin. She wore nothing but shorts and one of her husband's shirts. Her feet were bare.

Mrs. Thompson was the wife of the paymaster in a road-construction camp in northern Quebec. Jeannie's husband was an engineer working on the same project. The road was being pushed through country where nothing had existed until now except rocks and lakes and muskeg. The camp was established between a wild lake and the line of raw dirt that was the road. There were no towns between the camp and the railway spur, sixty miles distant.

Mrs. Thompson, a good deal older than Jeannie, had become her best friend. She was a nice, plain, fat, consoling sort of person, with varicosed legs, shoes unlaced and slit for comfort, blue flannel dressing gown worn at all hours, pudding-bowl haircut, and coarse gray hair. She might have been Jeannie's own mother, or her Auntie Pearl. She rocked her fat self in the rocking chair and went on with what she had to say: "What I was starting off to tell you is you remind me of her, of Jean Harlow. You've got the same teeny mouth, Jeannie, and I think your hair was a whole lot prettier before you started fooling around with it. That peroxide's no good. It splits the ends. I

60

know you're going to tell me it isn't peroxide but something more modern, but the result is the same."

Vern's shirt was spotted with coral-pink that had dropped off the brush. Vern wouldn't mind; at least, he wouldn't say that he minded. If he hadn't objected to anything Jeannie did until now, he wouldn't start off by complaining about a shirt. The campsite outside the uncurtained window was silent and dark. The waning moon would not appear until dawn. A passage of thought made Mrs. Thompson say, "Winter soon."

Jeannie moved sharply and caught the bottle of polish before it spilled. Mrs. Thompson was crazy; it wasn't even September.

"Pretty soon," Mrs. Thompson admitted. "Pretty soon. That's a long season up here, but I'm one person doesn't complain. I've been up here or around here every winter of my married life, except for that one winter Pops was occupying Germany."

"I've been up here seventy-two days," said Jeannie, in her soft voice. "Tomorrow makes seventy-three."

"Is that right?" said Mrs. Thompson, jerking the rocker forward, suddenly snappish. "Is that a fact? Well who asked you to come up here? Who asked you to come and start counting days like you was in some kind of jail? When you got married to Vern, you must of known where he'd be taking you. He told you, didn't he, that he liked road jobs, construction jobs, and that? Did he tell you, or didn't he?"

"Oh, he told me," said Jeannie.

"You know what, Jeannie?" said Mrs. Thompson. "If you'd of just listened to me, none of this would have happened. I told you that first day, the day you arrived here in your high-heeled shoes, I said, 'I know this cabin doesn't look much, but all the married men have the same sort of place.' You remember I said that? I said, 'You just get some curtains up and some carpets down and it'll be home! I took you over and showed you my place, and you said you'd never seen anything so lovely."

"I meant it," said Jeannie. "Your cabin is just lovely. I don't know why, but I never managed to make this place look like yours."

Mrs. Thompson said, "That's plain enough." She looked at the cold grease spattered behind the stove, and the rag of towel over by the sink. "It's partly the experience," she said kindly. She and her husband knew exactly what to take with them when they went on a job, they had been doing it for so many years. They brought boxes for artificial flowers, a brass door knocker, a portable bar decorated with sea shells, a cardboard fireplace that looked real, and an electric fire that sent waves of light rippling over the ceiling and walls. A concealed gramophone played the records they loved and cherished – the good old tunes. They had comic records that dated back to the year I, and sad soprano records about shipwrecks and broken promises and babies' graves. The first time Jeannie heard one of the funny records, she was scared to death. She was paying a formal call, sitting straight in her chair, with her skirt pulled around her knees. Vern and Pops Thompson were talking about the Army.

"I wish to God I was back," said old Pops.

"Don't I?" said Vern. He was fifteen years older than Jeannie and had been through a lot.

At first there were only scratching and whispering noises, and then a mosquito orchestra started to play, and a dwarf's voice came into the room. "Little Johnnie Green, little Sallie Brown," squealed the dwarf, higher and faster than any human ever could. "Spooning in the park with the grass all around."

"Where is he?" Jeannie cried, while the Thompsons screamed with laughter and Vern smiled. The dwarf sang on: "And each little bird in the treetop high/Sang 'Oh you kid!' and winked his eye."

It was a record that had belonged to Pops Thompson's mother. He had been laughing at it all his life. The Thompsons loved living up north and didn't miss cities or company. Their cabin smelled of cocoa and toast. Over their beds were oval photographs of each other as children, and they had some Teddy bears and about a dozen dolls.

Jeannie capped the bottle of polish, taking care not to press it against her wet nails. She sat up with a single movement and set the bottle down on the bedside crate. Then she turned to face Mrs. Thompson. She sat cross-legged, with her hands outspread before her. Her face was serene.

"Not an ounce of fat on you," said Mrs. Thompson. "You know something? I'm sorry you're going. I really am. Tomorrow you'll be gone. You know that, don't you? You've been counting days, but you won't have to any more. I guess Vern'll take you back to Montreal. What do you think?"

Jeannie dropped her gaze, and began smoothing wrinkles on the bedspread. She muttered something Mrs. Thompson could not understand.

"Tomorrow you'll be gone," Mrs. Thompson continued. "I know it for a fact. Vern is at this moment getting his pay, and borrowing a jeep from Mr. Sherman, and a Polack driver to take you to the train. He sure is loyal to you. You know what I heard Mr. Sherman say? He said to Vern, 'If you want to send her off,

Vern, you can always stay,' and Vern said, 'I can't very well do that, Mr. Sherman.' And Mr. Sherman said, 'This is the second time you've had to leave a job on account of her, isn't it?,' and then Mr. Sherman said, 'In my opinion, no man by his own self can rape a girl, so there were either two men or else she's invented the whole story.' Then he said, 'Vern, you're either a saint or a damn fool.' That was all I heard. I came straight over here, Jeannie, because I thought you might be needing me.'' Mrs. Thompson waited to hear she was needed. She stopped rocking and sat with her feet flat and wide apart. She struck her knees with her open palms and cried, "I *told* you to keep away from the men. I told you it would make trouble, all that being cute and dancing around, I said to you, I remember saying it, I said nothing makes trouble faster in a place like this than a grown woman behaving like a little girl. Don't you remember?"

"I only went out for a walk," said Jeannie. "Nobody'll believe me, but that's all. I went down the road for a walk."

"In high heels?" said Mrs. Thompson. "With a purse in your arm, and a hat on your head? You don't go taking a walk in the bush that way. There's no place to walk to. Where'd you think you were going? I could smell Evening in Paris a quarter mile away."

"There's no place to go," said Jeannie, "but what else is there to do? I just felt like dressing up and going out."

"You could have cleaned up your home a bit," said Mrs. Thompson. "There was always that to do. Just look at that sink. That basket of ironing's been under the bed since July. I know it gets boring around here, but you had the best of it. You had the summer. In winter it gets dark around three o'clock. Then the wives have a right to go crazy. I knew one used to sleep the clock around. When her Nembutal ran out, she took about a hundred aspirin. I knew another learned to distill her own liquor, just to kill time. Sometimes the men get so's they don't like the life, and that's death for the wives. But here you had a nice summer, and Vern liked the life."

"He likes it better than anything," said Jeannie. "He liked the Army, but this was his favorite life after that."

"There," said Mrs. Thompson. "You had every reason to be happy. What'd you do if he sent you off alone, now, like Mr. Sherman advised? You'd be alone and you'd have to work. Women don't know when they're well off. Here you've got a good, sensible husband working for you and you don't appreciate it. You have to go and do a terrible thing."

"I only went for a walk," said Jeannie. "That's all I did."

"It's possible," said Mrs. Thompson, "but it's a terrible thing.

It's about the worst thing that's ever happened around here. I don't know why you let it happen. A woman can always defend what's precious, even if she's attacked. I hope you remembered to think about bacteria."

"What d'you mean?"

"I mean Javel, or something."

Jeannie looked uncomprehending and then shook her head.

"I wonder what it must be like," said Mrs. Thompson after a time, looking at the dark window. "I mean, think of Berlin and them Russians and all. Think of some disgusting fellow you don't know. Never said hello to, even. Some girls ask for it, though. You can't always blame the man. The man loses his job, his wife if he's got one, everything, all because of a silly girl."

Jeannie frowned, absently. She pressed her nails together, testing the polish. She licked her lips and said, "I was more beaten up, Mrs. Thompson. It wasn't exactly what you think. It was only afterwards I thought to myself, Why, I was raped and everything."

Mrs. Thompson gasped, hearing the word from Jeannie. She said, "Have you got any marks?"

"On my arms. That's why I'm wearing this shirt. The first thing I did was change my clothes."

Mrs. Thompson thought this over, and went on to another thing: "Do you ever think about your mother?"

"Sure."

"Do you pray? If this goes on at nineteen – "

"I'm twenty."

" – what'll you be by the time you're thirty? You've already got a terrible, terrible memory to haunt you all your life."

"I already can't remember it," said Jeannie. "Afterwards I started walking back to camp, but I was walking the wrong way. I met Mr. Sherman. The back of his car was full of coffee, flour, all that. I guess he'd been picking up supplies. He said, 'Well, get in.' He didn't ask any questions at first. I couldn't talk anyway."

"Shock," said Mrs. Thompson wisely.

"You know, I'd have to see it happening to know what happened. All I remember is that first we were only talking . . . "

"You and Mr. Sherman?"

"No, no, before. When I was taking my walk."

"Don't say who it was," said Mrs. Thompson. "We don't any of us need to know."

"We were just talking, and he got sore all of a sudden and grabbed my arm."

"Don't say the name!" Mrs. Thompson cried.

"Like when I was little, there was this Lana Turner movie. She had two twins. She was just there and then a nurse brought her in the two twins. I hadn't been married or anything, and I didn't know anything, and I used to think if I just kept on seeing the movie I'd know how she got the two twins, you know, and I went, oh, I must have seen it six times, the movie, but in the end I never knew any more. They just brought her the two twins."

Mrs. Thompson sat quite still, trying to make sense of this. "Taking advantage of a woman is a criminal offense," she observed. "I heard Mr. Sherman say another thing, Jeannie. He said, "If your wife wants to press a charge and talk to some lawyer, let me tell you,' he said, 'you'll never work again anywhere,' he said. Vern said, 'I know that, Mr. Sherman.' And Mr. Sherman said, 'Let me tell you, if any reporters or any investigators start coming around here, they'll get their...they'll never...' Oh, he was mad. And Vern said, 'I came over to tell you I was quitting, Mr. Sherman.' " Mrs. Thompson had been acting this with spirit, using a quiet voice when she spoke for Vern and a blustering tone for Mr. Sherman. In her own voice, she said, "If you're wondering how I came to hear all this, I was strolling by Mr. Sherman's office window – his bungalow, that is. I had Maureen out in her pram." Maureen was the Thompsons' youngest doll.

Jeannie might not have been listening. She started to tell something else: "You know, where we were before, on Vern's last job, we weren't in a camp. He was away a lot, and he left me in Amos, in a hotel. I liked it. Amos isn't all that big, but it's better than here. There was this German in the hotel. He was selling cars. He'd drive me around if I wanted to go to a movie or anything. Vern didn't like him, so we left. It wasn't anybody's fault."

"So he's given up two jobs," said Mrs. Thompson, "One because he couldn't leave you alone, and now this one. Two jobs, and you haven't been married five months. Why should another man be thrown out of work? We don't need to know a thing. I'll be sorry if it was Jimmy Quinn," she went on slowly. "I like that boy. Don't say the name, dear. There's Evans. Susini. Palmer. But it might have been anybody, because you had them all on the boil. So it might have been Jimmy Quinn – let's say – and it could have been anyone else, too. Well, now let's hope they can get their minds back on the job."

"I thought they all liked me," said Jeannie sadly. "I get along with people. Vern never fights with me."

"Vern never fights with anyone. But he ought to have thrashed *you*."

"If he . . . you know. I won't say the name. If he'd liked me, I wouldn't have minded. If he'd been friendly. I really mean that. I wouldn't have gone wandering up the road, making all this fuss."

"Jeannie," said Mrs. Thompson, "you don't even know what you're saying."

"He could at least have liked me," said Jeannie. "He wasn't even friendly. It's the first time in my life somebody hasn't liked me. My heart is broken, Mrs. Thompson. My heart is just broken."

She has to cry, Mrs. Thompson thought. She has to have it out. She rocked slowly, tapping her foot, trying to remember how she'd felt about things when she was twenty, wondering if her heart had ever been broken, too.

An Unmarried Man's Summer

The great age of the winter society Walter Henderson frequents on the French Riviera makes him seem young to himself and a stripling to his friends. In a world of elderly widows his relative youth appears a virtue, his existence as a bachelor a precious state. All winter long he drives his sporty little Singer over empty roads, on his way to parties at Beaulieu, or Roquebrune, or Cap Ferrat. From the sea he and his car must look like a drawing of insects: a firefly and a flea. He drives gaily, as if it were summer. He is often late. He has a disarming gesture of smoothing his hair as he makes his apologies. Sometimes his excuse has to do with Angelo, his hilarious and unpredictable manservant. Or else it is Mme. Rossi, the *femme de ménage,* who has been having a moody day. William of Orange, Walter's big old ginger tomcat, comes into the account. As Walter describes his household, he is the victim of servants and pet animals, he is chief player in an endless imbroglio of intrigue, swindle, cuckoldry – all of it funny, of course; haven't we laughed at Molière?

"*Darling* Walter," his great friend Mrs. Wiggott has often said to him. *This* could only happen to *you.*"

He tells his stories in peaceful dining rooms, to a circle of loving, attentive faces. He is surrounded by the faces of women. Their eyes are fixed on his dotingly, but in homage to another man: a young lover killed in the 1914 war; an adored but faithless son. "Naughty Walter," murmurs Mrs. Wiggott. "*Wicked* boy." Walter must be wicked, for part of the memory of every vanished husband or lover or son is the print of his cruelty. Walter's old friends are nursing bruised hearts. Mrs. Wiggott's injuries span four husbands, counted on four arthritic fingers – the gambler, the dipsomaniac, the dago, and poor Wiggott, who ate a good breakfast one morning and walked straight in front of a train. "None of my husbands was from my own walk of life," Mrs. Wiggott has said to Walter. "I made such mistakes with men, trying to bring them up to my level. I've often thought, Walter, if only I had met *you* forty years ago!"

"Yes, indeed," says Walter heartily, smoothing his hair.

They have lost their time sense in this easy climate; when Mrs. Wiggott was on the lookout for a second husband forty years ago, Walter was five.

"If your life isn't exactly the way you want it to be by the time you are forty-five," said Walter's father, whom he admired, "not much point in continuing. You might as well hang yourself." He also said, "Parenthood is sacred. Don't go about creating children right and left"; this when Walter was twelve. Walter's Irish grandmother said, "Don't touch the maids," which at least was practical. "I stick to the women who respect and admire me," declared his godfather. He was a bachelor, a great diner-out. "What good is beauty to a boy?" Walter's mother lamented. "I have such a plain little girl, poor little Eve. Couldn't it have been shared?" "Nothing fades faster than the beauty of a boy." Walter has read that, but cannot remember where.

A mosaic picture of Walter's life early in the summer of his forty-fifth year would have shown him dead center, where nothing can seem more upsetting than a punctured tire or more thrilling than a sunny day. On his right is Angelo, the comic valet. Years ago, Angelo followed Walter through the streets of a shadeless, hideous town. He was begging for coins; that was their introduction. Now he is seventeen, and quick as a knife. In the mosaic image, Walter's creation, he is indolent, capricious, more trouble than he is worth. Mme. Rossi, the *femme de ménage,* is made to smile. She is slovenly but good-tempered, she sings, her feet are at ease in decaying shoes. Walter puts it about that she is in love with a driver on the Monte Carlo bus. That is the role he has given her in his dinner-party stories. He has to say something about her to bring her to life. His cat, William of Orange, is in Angelo's arms. As a cat he is film star, prize fighter, and stubbornness itself; as a personality, he lives in a cloud of black thoughts. The figures make a balanced and nearly perfect design, supported by a frieze of pallida iris in mauve, purple, and white.

The house in the background, the stucco façade with yellow shutters, three brick steps, and Venetian door is called Les Anémones. It belongs to two spinsters, Miss Cooper and Miss Le Chaine. They let Walter live here rent-free, with the understanding that he pay the property taxes, which are small, and keep the garden alive and the roof in repair. Miss Cooper is headmistress of a school in England; Miss Le Chaine is her oldest friend. When Miss Cooper retires from her post fifteen years from now, she and Miss Le Chaine plan to come down to the Riviera and live in Les Anémones forever. Walter will then be sixty years of age and homeless. He supposes he ought to be doing something about it; he ought to start looking around for another place. He sees himself, aged sixty, Mrs. Wiggott's permanent guest, pushing her in a Bath chair along the Promenade des Anglais at Nice. It is such a disgusting prospect that he hates Mrs. Wiggott because of the imaginary chair.

Walter knows that pushing a Bath chair would be small return for everything Mrs. Wiggott has done for him: it was Mrs. Wiggott who persuaded Miss Cooper and Miss Le Chaine there might be a revolution here – nothing to do with politics, just a wild upheaval of some kind. (Among Walter's hostesses, chaos is expected from week to week, and in some seasons almost hourly.) With revolution a certain future, is it not wise to have someone like Walter in charge of one's house? Someone who will die on the brick doorstep, if need be, in the interests of Miss Cooper and Miss Le Chaine? Having had a free house for many years, and desiring the arrangement to continue, Walter will feel he has something to defend. So runs Mrs. Wiggott's reasoning, and it does sound sane. It sounded sane to the two ladies in England, luckily for him. He does not expect a revolution, because he does not expect anything; he would probably defend Les Anémones because he couldn't imagine where else he might go. This house is a godsend, because Walter is hard up. In spite of the total appearance of the mosaic, he has to live very carefully indeed, never wanting anything beyond the moment. He has a pension from the last war, and he shares the income of a small trust fund with his sister Eve, married and farming in South Africa. When anyone asks Walter why he has never married, he smiles and says he cannot support a wife. No argument there.

This picture belongs to the winter months. Summer is something else. In all seasons the sea is blocked from his view by a large hotel. From May to October, this hotel is festooned with drying bathing suits. Its kitchen sends the steam of tons of boiled potatoes over Walter's hedge. His hostesses have fled the heat; his telephone is still. He lolls on a garden chair, rereading his boyhood books – the Kipling, the bound albums of *Chums*. He tries to give Angelo lessons in English literature, using his old schoolbooks, but Angelo is silly, laughs; and if Walter persists in trying to teach him anything, he says he feels sick. Mme. Rossi carries ice up from the shop in a string bag. It is half melted when she arrives, and it leaves its trail along the path and over the terrace and through the house to the kitchen. In August, even she goes to the mountains, leaving Walter, Angelo, and the cat to get on as best they can. Walter wraps a sliver of ice in a handkerchief and presses the handkerchief to his wrists. He is deafened by cicadas and nauseated by the smell of jasmine. His skin does not sweat; most of his body is covered with puckered scars. Twenty years ago, he was badly burned. He reads, but does not quite know what he is reading. Fortunately, his old books were committed to memory years before.

At last the good weather fades, the crowds go away. The hotel closes its shutters. His hostesses return. They have survived the season in Scotland and Switzerland – somewhere rainy and cold. They are back now, in time for the winter rain. All at once Walter's garden seems handsome, with the great fig tree over the terrace, and the Judas tree waiting for its late-winter flowering. After Christmas the iris will bloom, and Walter will show his tottering visitors around. "I put in the iris," he explains, "but, of course, Miss Cooper shall have them when I go." This sounds as though he means to die on the stroke of sixty, leaving the iris as a mauve-and-white memorial along the path. "Naughty Walter," Mrs. Wiggott chides him. "Morbid boy." Yet the only morbid remark he has ever made in her presence went unheard, or at least unanswered: "I wish it had been finished off for me in the last war." That last war, recalled by fragments of shell dug up in Riviera gardens, was for many of his present friends the last commerce with life, if life means discomfort, bad news. They still see, without reading them, the slogans praising Mussolini, relics of the Italian occupation of the coast. Walter has a faded old *Viva* on the door to his garage. He thought he might paint over it one day, but Mrs. Wiggott asked him not to. Her third husband was a high-up Fascist, close to Mussolini. Twenty years ago, she wore a smart black uniform, tailored for her in Paris, and she had a jaunty tasseled hat. She was the first foreign woman to give her wedding ring to the great Italian gold collection; at least she says she was. But Walter has met two other women, one Belgian and one American, who claim the same thing.

He lay in a garden chair that summer – the summer he had not hanged himself, having arranged life exactly as he wanted it – unshaven, surviving, when a letter arrived that contained disagreeable news. His sister and brother-in-law had sold their African farm, were flying to England, and intended to stop off and have a short holiday with him on the way. His eyes were bloodshot. He did not read the letter more than twice. He had loved his sister, but she had married a farmer, a Punch squire, blunt, ignorant, Anglo-Irish. Walter, who had the same mixture in his blood, liked to think that Frank Osborn had "the worst of both." Frank was a countryman. He despised city life, yet the country got the better of him every time. In twelve years in Africa, he and Eve had started over twice. He attracted bad luck. Once, Eve wrote Walter asking if he would let some of the capital out of the trust whose income they shared. She and Frank wanted to buy new equipment, expand. They had two children now, a girl and a boy. She hinted that halving the income was no longer quite fair. Walter answered the letter without making any mention of her request, and was thankful to hear no more about it.

Now, dead center of summer, she was making a new claim: she was demanding a holiday. Walter saw pretty clearly what had happened. Although Frank and Eve had not yet been dispossessed in South Africa, they were leaving while the going was good. Eve wrote that no decent person could stand the situation down there, and Walter thought that might well be the truth, but only part of it; the rest of the truth was they had failed. They kept trying, which was possibly to their credit; but they had failed. Five days after the arrival of this letter came a second letter, giving the date of their arrival – August fifteenth.

On the fifteenth of August, Walter stood upon his terrace in an attitude of welcome. A little behind him was Angelo, excited as only an Italian can be by the idea of "family." William of Orange sat on the doorstep, between two tubs, each holding an orange tree. Walter had not met the family at the airport, because there was not room for them all in the Singer, and because Eve had written a third letter, telling him not to meet them. The Osborns were to be looked after by a man from Cook's, who was bringing to the airport a Citroën Frank had hired. In the Citroën they proposed to get from the airport to Walter, a distance of only thirty-odd miles, but through summer traffic and over unfamiliar roads. Walter thought of them hanging out the car windows, shouting questions. He knew there were two children, but pictured six. He thought of them lost, and the six children in tears.

Toward the end of the afternoon, when Walter had been pacing the terrace, or nervously listening, for the better part of the day, Angelo shouted that he heard children's voices on the other side of the hedge. Walter instantly took up a new position. He seemed to be protecting the house against the expected revolution. Then – there was no mistaking it – he heard car doors slammed, and the whole family calling out. He stared down the path to the gate, between the clumps of iris Angelo had cut back after the last flowering. The soil was dry and hard and clay. He was still thinking of that, of the terrible soil he had to contend with here, when Eve rushed at him. She was a giantess, around his neck almost before he saw her face. He had her damp cheek, her unsophisticated talcum smell. She was crying, but that was probably due to fatigue. She drew back and said to him, "Your're not a minute older, darling, except where you've gone gray." What remarkable eyes she must have, Walter thought, and what gifts of second sight; for his hair was *slightly* gray, but only at the back. Eve was jolly and loud. It had been said in their childhood that she should have been a boy. Frank came along with a suitcase in each hand. He put the cases down. "Well, old Frank," said Walter. Frank replied with astonishment, "Why, it's Walter!"

The two children stared at their uncle and then at Angelo. They were not timid, but seemed to Walter without manners or charm. Eve had written that Mary, the elder, was the image of Walter in appearance and in character. He saw a girl of about eleven with lank yellow hair, and long feet in heavy sandals. Her face was brown, her lashes rabbit white. The boy was half his sister's size, and entirely Osborn; that is, he had his father's round red face. He showed Walter a box he was holding. "There's a hamster in it," he said, and explained in a piping voice that he had bought it from a boy at the airport.

"They don't waste any time when it comes to complicating life," said Frank proudly.

Angelo stood by, smiling, waiting to be presented. Keeping Angelo as a friend and yet not a social friend was a great problem for Walter. Angelo lacked the sophistication required to make the change easily. Walter decided he would not introduce him, but the little Osborn boy suddenly turned to the valet and smiled. The two, Johnny and Angelo, seemed to be struck shy. Until then, Walter had always considered Angelo someone partly unreal, part of his personal mosaic. Once, Angelo had been a figure on the wall of a baroque church; from the wall he came toward Walter, with his hand out, cupped for coins. The church had been intended from its beginnings to blister and crack, to set off black hair, appraising black eyes. The four elements of Angelo's childhood were southern baroque, malaria, idleness, and hunger. They were what he would go back to if Walter were to tire of him, or if he should decide to leave. Now the wall of the church disappeared, and so did a pretty, wheedling boy. Angelo was seventeen, dumpy, nearly coarse. "Nothing fades faster than the beauty of a boy." Angelo looked shrewd; he looked as if he might have a certain amount of common sense – that most defeating of qualities, that destroyer.

The family settled on the terrace, in the wicker chairs that belonged with the house, around the chipped garden table that was a loan from Mrs. Wiggott. They were sprawling, much at ease, like an old-fashioned *Chums* picture of colonials. They praised Angelo, who carried in the luggage and then gave them tea, and the children smiled at him, shyly still.

"They've fallen for him," Eve said.

"What?" It seemed to Walter such an extraordinary way to

talk. The children slid down from their chairs (without permission, the bachelor uncle observed) and followed Angelo around the side of the house.

"They don't love *us* much at the moment," Eve said. "We've taken them away from their home. They don't think anything of the idea. They'll get over it. But it's natural for them to turn to someone else, don't you think? Tell Angelo to watch himself with Mary. She's a seething mass of feminine wiles. She's always after something."

"She doesn't get anything out of *me*," said Mary's father.

"You don't even notice when she does, that's how clever she is," said Eve.

"I told her I'd buy her something at the airport, because Johnny had the hamster," said Frank. "She said she didn't want anything."

"She doesn't want just anything you offer," said Eve. "That's where she's wily. She thinks about what she wants and then she goes after it without saying anything. It's a game. I tell you, she's feminine. More power to her. I'm glad."

"Angelo hasn't much to worry about," said Walter. "I don't think she could get much out of him, because he hasn't got anything. Although I do pay him; I'm a stickler about that. He has his food and lodging and clothes, and although many people would think that enough, I give him pocket money as well." This had an effect he had not expected. His sister and brother-in-law stared as if he had said something puzzling and incomplete. Walter felt socially obliged to go on speaking. In the dry afternoon he inspected their tired faces. They had come thousands of miles by plane, and then driven here in an unknown car. They were still polite enough to listen and to talk. He remembered one of his most amusing stories, which Mrs. Wiggott frequently asked him to repeat. It was about how he had sent Angelo and William of Orange to Calabria one summer so that Angelo could visit his people and William of Orange have a change of air. Halfway through the journey, Angelo had to give it up and come back to Les Anémones. William of Orange hadn't stopped howling from the time the train started to move. "You understand," said Walter, "he couldn't leave William of Orange shut up *in* his basket. It seemed too cruel. William of Orange *wouldn't* keep still, Angelo daren't let him *out,* because he was in such a fury he would have attacked the other passengers. Also, William of Orange was being desperately sick. It was an Italian train, third class. You can imagine the counsel, the good advice! Angelo tried leaving the basket partly open, so that William of Orange could see what was going on but not jump out, but he only screamed all the more. Finally Angelo bundled up all his things, the present he'd been taking his family and William of Orange in his basket, and he got down at some stop and simply took the next train going the other direction. I shall never forget how they arrived early in the morning, having traveled the whole night and walked from the . . ."

"This is a dreadful story," said Eve, slowly turning her head. "It's sad."

Frank said nothing, but seemed to agree with his wife. Walter supposed they thought the cat and the valet should not have been traveling at all; they had come up from South Africa, where they had spent twelve years bullying blacks. He said, "They were traveling third class."

Mary, his niece, sauntered back to the table, as if she had just learned a new way of walking. She flung herself in a chair and picked up her father's cigarettes. She began playing with them, waiting to be told not to. Neither parent said a word.

"And how was your journey?" said Walter gravely.

The girl looked away from the cigarettes and said, "In a way, I've forgotten it."

"No showing off, please," said Eve.

"There's a kind of holiday tonight," said the girl. "There'll be fireworks, all that, Angelo says we can see them from here. He's making Johnny sleep now, on two chairs in the kitchen. He wanted me to sleep, too, but I wouldn't, of course. He's fixing a basket for the hamster up where the cat can't get it. We're going to have the fireworks at dinner, and then he'll take us down to the harbor, he says, to see the people throwing confetti and all that."

"The fireworks won't be seen from our dining room, I fear," said Walter.

"We're having our dinner out here, on the terrace," said the girl. "He says the mosquitoes are awful and you people will have to smoke."

"Do the children always dine with you?" said Walter.

There was no answer, because William of Orange came by, taking their attention. Mary put out her hand, but the cat avoided it. Walter looked at the determined child who was said to resemble him. She bent toward the cat, idly calling. Her hair divided, revealing a delicate ear. The angle of her head lent her expression something thoughtful and sad; it was almost an exaggerated posture of wistfulness. Her arms and hands were thin, but with no suggestion of fragility. She smiled at the cat and said, "*He* doesn't care. He doesn't care what we say." Her bones were made of something tough and precious. She was not pretty, no, but quite lovely, in spite of the straight yellow hair, the plain way she was dressed. Walter knew instantly what he would have given her to wear. He thought, Ballet lessons . . . beautiful French, and saw himself the father of a daughter. The mosaic expanded; there was room for another figure, surely? Yes – but to have a daughter one needed a wife. That brought everything down to normal size again. He smiled to himself, thinking how grateful he was that clods like Frank Osborn could cause enchanting girls to appear, all for the enjoyment of vicarious fathers. It was a new idea, one he would discuss next winter with Mrs. Wiggott. He could develop it into a story. It would keep the old dears laughing for weeks.

Angelo strung paper lanterns on wires between branches of the fig tree. The children were fogged with sleep, but bravely kept their heads up, waiting for the fireworks he had said would be set off over the sea. Neither of them remarked that the sea was hidden by the hotel; they trusted Angelo to produce the sea as he produced their dinner. Walter's nephew slept with his eyes wide. Angelo's lanterns were reflected in his eyes – pinpoints of cobalt blue.

From the table they heard the crowd at the harbor, cheering every burst. Colored smoke floated across the dark sky. The smell of jasmine, which ordinarily made Walter sick, was part of the children's night.

"Do you know my name?" said the little boy, as Angelo moved around the table collecting plates. "It's Johnny." He sighed, and put his head down where the plate had been. Presently Angelo came out of the house wearing a clean white pullover and with his hair well oiled. Johnny woke up as if he had heard a bell. "Are you taking us to the harbor?" he said. "Now?"

Mary, Johnny, and Angelo looked at Eve. It was plain to Walter that these children should not be anywhere except in bed. He was furious with Angelo.

"Is there polio or anything here?" said Eve lazily. Now it was Walter's turn. The children – all three – looked at him with something like terror. He was about to deny them the only pleasure they had ever been allowed; that was what their looks said. Without waiting for his answer about polio, Eve said the children could go.

The candles inside the paper lanterns guttered and had to be blown out. The Osborns smoked conscientiously to keep mosquitoes away. In the light of a struck match, Walter saw his sister's face, her short graying hair. "That's a nice lad," she said.

"The kids are mad about him," said Frank.

"They are besotted," said Eve. "I'm glad. You couldn't have

planned a better welcome, Walter dear," and in the dark she briefly covered his hand with hers.

The family lived in Miss Cooper's house as if it were a normal place to be. They were more at home than Walter had ever been. Mornings, he heard them chattering on the terrace or laughing in the kitchen with Angelo. Eve and Angelo planned the meals, and sometimes they went to the market together. The Osborns took over the household food expenses, and Walter, tactfully, made no mention of it. Sometimes the children had their meals in the kitchen with Angelo and the hamster and the cat. But there was no order, no system, to their upbringing. They often dined with the adults. The parents rose late, but not so late as Walter. They seemed to feel it would be impolite to go off to the beach or the market until Walter's breakfast was over. He was not accustomed to eating breakfast, particularly during the hot weather, but he managed to eat an egg and some cold toast, only because they appeared to expect it.

"Change has got to come in South Africa," said Eve one morning as Walter sat down to a boiled egg. The family had eaten. The table was covered with ashes, eggshells, and crumbs.

"Why at our expense?" said Frank.

"Frank is an anarchist, although you wouldn't think it at times," said Eve, with pride.

Married twelve years and still talking, Walter thought. Frank and Eve were in accord on one thing – that there was bad faith on all sides in South Africa. They interrupted each other, explaining *apartheid* to Walter, who did not want to hear anything about it. Frank repeated that no decent person could stand by and accept the situation, and Eve agreed; but she made no bones about the real reason for their having left. They had failed, failed. The word rolled around the table like a wooden ball.

So Frank was an anarchist, was he, Walter thought, snipping at his egg. Well, he could afford to be an anarchist, living down there, paying next to no income tax. He said, "You will find things different in England."

"An English farm, aha," said Frank, and looked at Eve.

"Just so long as it isn't a poultry farm," said Walter, getting on with his revolting breakfast. The egg had given him something to say. "I have seen people try that."

"As a matter of fact, it *is* a poultry farm," said Eve. Frank's face was earnest and red; this farm had a history of arguments about it. Eve went on, "You see, we try one thing after the other. We're obliged to try things, aren't we? We have two children to educate."

"I wouldn't want to live without doing something," said Frank. "Even if I could afford to. I mean to say that I'm not brainy and it's better for me if I have something to do."

"Walter used to think it better," said Eve. She went on very lightly, "I did envy Walter once. Walter, think of the money that was spent educating you. They wouldn't do it for a girl. Ah, how I used to wish we could have exchanged, then." Having said this, she rounded on her husband, as if it were Frank who had failed to give Walter credit, had underestimated him, dragging schoolroom jealousy across the lovely day. Frank must be told: Walter in Hong Kong in a bank. Walter in amateur theatricals, the image of Douglas Fairbanks. He was marvelous in the war; he was burned from head to foot. He was hours swimming in flames in the North Sea. He should have had the Victoria Cross. Everyone said so.

The two children, sitting nearby sorting colored pebbles they had brought up from the beach, scarcely glanced at their courageous uncle. The impossibility of his ever having done anything splendid was as clear to them as it was to Walter. He agreed with the children – for it had all of it gone, and he wanted nothing but the oasis of peace, the admiration of undemanding old women, the winter months. If he was irritated, it was only by his sister's puritanical insistence on working. Would the world have been a happier place if Walter had remained in Hong Kong in a bank? Luckily, there was William of Orange to talk about. There was William of Orange now, stalking an invisible victim along the terrace wall. Up in the fig tree he went, with his killer's face, his marigold eyes. "Oh, the poor birds!" Eve cried. "He's after birds!" She saw him stretch out his paw, spread like a hand, and then she saw him detach ripe figs and let them fall on the paved terrace. She had never seen a cat do that before. She said that William of Orange was perfectly sweet.

"He doesn't care what you think about him," said Mary, looking up from her heap of stones.

"You know, darling," said Eve, laughing at Walter, "if you aren't careful, you'll become an old spinster with a pussycat."

Frank sat on the terrace wall wearing a cotton shirt and oversized Army shorts. He was burned reddish brown. His arms and legs were covered with a coating of thick fair hair. "What is the appeal about cats?" he said kindly. "I've always wanted to know. I can understand having them on a farm, if they're good mousers." He wore a look of great sincerity most of the time, as if he wanted to say, Please tell me what you are thinking. I so much want to know.

"I like them because they are independent," said Walter.

"They don't care what you think, just as Mary says. They don't care if you like them. They haven't the slightest notion of gratitude, and they never pretend. They take what you have to offer, and away they go."

"That's what all cat fanciers say," said Frank. "But it's hard for someone like me to understand. That isn't the way you feel about people, is it? Do you like people who just take what you can give them and go off?"

Angelo came out of the house with a shopping basket over one arm and a straw sun hat on his head. He took all his orders from Eve now. There had never been a discussion about it; she was the woman of the house, the mother.

"It would be interesting to see what role the cat fancier is trying on," said Walter, looking at Angelo. "He says he likes cats because they don't like anyone. I suppose he is proving he is so tough he can exist without affection."

"I couldn't," said Frank, "and I wouldn't want to try. Without Eve and the children and . . ."

The children jumped to their feet and begged to go to market with Angelo. They snatched at his basket, arguing whose turn it was to carry it. How Angelo strutted; how he grew tall! All this affection, this admiration, Walter thought – it was as bad as over-tipping.

The family stayed two weeks, and then a fortnight more. They were brown, drowsy, and seemed reluctant to face England and the poultry farm. They were enjoying their holiday, no doubt about that. On the beach they met a professor of history who spoke a little English, and a retired consul who asked them to tea. They saw, without knowing what to make of it, a monument to Queen Victoria. They heard people being comic and noisy, they bought rice-and-spinach pies to eat on the beach, and ice cream that melted down to powder and water. They ate melons and peaches nearly as good as the fruit back in Africa, and they buried the peach stones and the melon skins and the ice-cream sticks and the greasy piecrusts in the sand. They drove along the coast as far as Cannes, in the Parma-violet Citroën Frank had hired, sight unseen, from South Africa. He had bought his new farm in the same way. Walter was glad his friends were away, for he was ashamed to be seen in the Citroën. It was a vulgar automobile. He told Frank that the DS was considered exclusively the property of concierges' sons and successful grocers.

"I'm not even that," said Frank.

The seats were covered with plastic leopard skin. At every stop, the car gave a great sigh and sank down like a tired dog. The children loved this. They sat behind, with Eve between them, telling riddles, singing songs. They quarreled across their mother as if she were a hedge. "Silly old sow," Walter heard his nephew saying. He realized the boy was saying it to Eve. His back stiffened. Eve saw.

"Why shouldn't he say it, if he wants to?" she said. "He doesn't know what it means. Do you want me to treat them the way we were treated? Would you like to see some of that?"

"No," said Walter, after a moment.

"Well, then. I'm trying another way."

Walter said, "I don't believe one person should call another a silly old sow." He spoke without turning his head. The children were still as mice; then the little boy began to cry.

They drove home in the dark. The children slept, and the three adults looked at neon lights and floodlit palm trees without saying much. Suddenly Eve said, "Oh, I like *that*." Walter looked at a casino; at the sea; at the Anglican church, which was thirty years old, Riviera Gothic. "That church," she said. "It's like home."

"Alas," said Walter.

"Terrible, is it?" said his brother-in-law, who had not bothered to look.

"I think I'll make up my own mind," said Eve. So she had sat, with her face set, when Walter tried to introduce her to some of his friends and his ideas, fifteen years before. She had never wanted to be anything except a mother, and she would protect anyone who wanted protection – Walter as well. But nothing would persuade her that a church was ugly if it was familiar and reminded her of home.

Walter did not desire Eve's protection. He did not think he could use anything Eve had to give. Sometimes she persuaded him to come to the beach with the family, and then she fussed over him, seeing that the parasol was fixed so that he had full shade. He knew he did not expose his arms and legs to the sun, because of his scars. She made him sit on an arrangement of damp, sandy towels and said, "There. Isn't that nice?" In an odd way, she still admired him; he saw it, and was pleased. He answered her remarks (about Riviera people, French politics, the Mediterranean climate, and the cost of things) with his habitual social fluency, but it was the children who took his attention. He marveled at their singleness of purpose, the energy they could release just in tearing off their clothes. They flung into the water and had to be bullied out. Mauve-lipped, chattering, they said, "What's there to do now?"

"Have you ever wanted to be a ballet dancer?" Walter asked his niece.

"No," she said, with scorn.

One day Angelo spent the morning with them. Frank had taken the car to the Citroën garage and looked forward to half a day with the mechanics there. In a curious way Angelo seemed to replace the children's father. He organized a series of canals and waterways and kept the children digging for more than an hour. Walter noticed that Angelo was doing none of the work himself. He stood over them with his hand on one hip – peacock lad, cock of the walk. When an Italian marries, you see this change, Walter thought. He treats his servants that way, and then his wife. He said, "Angelo, put your clothes on and run up to the bar and bring us all some cold drinks."

"Oh, Uncle Walter," his niece complained.

"I'll go, Uncle Walter," said the little boy.

Angelo pulled his shorts over his bathing suit and stood, waiting for Walter to drop money in his hand.

"Don't walk about naked," Walter said. "Put on your shirt."

Eve was knitting furiously. She sat with her cotton skirt hitched up above her knees and a cotton bolero thrown over her head to keep off the sun. From this shelter her sunglasses gleamed at him, and she said in her plain, loud voice, "I don't like this, Walter, and I haven't been liking it for some time. It's not the kind of world I want my children to see."

"I'm not responsible for the Riviera," said Walter.

"I mean that I don't like your bullying Angelo in front of them. They admire him so. I don't like any of it. I mean to say, the master-servant idea. I think it's bad taste, if you want my opinion."

"Are you trying to tell me you didn't have a servant in South Africa?"

"You know perfectly well what I mean. Walter, what *are* you up to? That sad, crumbling house. Nothing has been changed or painted or made pretty in it for years. You don't seem to have any friends here. Your telephone never rings. It hasn't rung once since I've been here. And that poor boy."

"Poor?" said Walter. "Is that what he's been telling you? You should have seen the house I rescued him from. You should just see what he's left behind him. Twelve starving sisters and brothers, an old harridan of a mother – and a grandmother. He's so frightened of her even at this distance that he sends her every penny I give him. Twelve sisters and brothers . . . "

"He must miss them," said Eve.

"I've sent him home," Walter said. "I sent him for a visit with a first-class ticket. He sold the first-class ticket and traveled third. If I hadn't been certain he wanted to give the difference to his people, I should never have had him back. I hate deceit. If he didn't get home that time it was because the cat was worrying him. I've told you the story. You said it was sad. But it was his idea, taking the cat."

"He eyes the girls in the market," said Eve. "But he never speaks."

"Let him," said Walter. "He is free to do as he likes."

"Perhaps he doesn't think he is."

"I can assure you he is, and knows it. If he is devoted to me because I've been kind to him, it's his own affair."

"It's probably too subtle for me," she said. She pulled her skirts a little higher and stroked her veined, stretched legs. She was beyond vanity. "But I still think it's all wrong. He's sweet with the children, but he's a little afraid of me."

"Perhaps you think he should be familiar with women and call them silly old sows."

"No, not at his age," she said mildly. "Johnny is still a baby, you know. I don't expect much from him." She was veering away from a row.

"My telephone never rings because my friends are away for the summer," he said. "This summer crowd has nothing to do with my normal life." He had to go on with that; her remark about the telephone had annoyed him more than anything else.

Yet he wanted her to approve of him; he wanted even Frank to approve of him, too. He was pushed into seeing himself through their eyes. He preferred his own images, his own creations. Once, he had loved a woman much older than himself. He saw her, by chance, after many years, when she was sixty. What will happen when I am sixty, he wanted to say. He wondered if Eve, with her boundless concern for other people, had any answer to that. What will happen fifteen years from now, when Miss Cooper claims the house?

That night, William of Orange, who lost no love on anyone, pulled himself onto the terrace table, having first attained a chair, and allowed Walter to scratch his throat. When he had had enough, he slipped away and dropped off the table and prowled along the wall. Eve was upstairs, putting the children to bed. It was a task she usually left to Angelo. Walter understood he and Frank had been deliberately left together alone. He knew he was about to be asked a favor. Frank leaned over the table. His stupid, friendly face wore its habitual expression of deep attention: *I am so interested in you. I am trying to get the point of everything you say.* He was easy enough; he never suggested Walter should be married, or working at something. He began to say that he missed South Africa. They had sold their property at a loss. He said he was starting over again for the last time, or so he hoped. He was thirty-seven. He had two children to educate. His face was red as a balloon. Walter let him talk, thinking it was good for him.

"We can always use another person on a farm – another man, that is," said Frank.

"I wouldn't be much use to you, I'm afraid," said Walter.

"No. Well, I meant to say . . . We shall have to pack up soon. I think next week."

"We shall miss you," said Walter. "Angelo will be shattered."

"We're going to drive the Citroën up to Paris," said Frank, suddenly lively, "and turn it in to Cook's there. We may never have a chance to do that trip again. Wonderful for the kids." He went off on one of his favorite topics – motors and mileage – and was diverted from whatever request he had been prodded by Eve to make. Walter was thankful it had been so easy.

Unloved, neglected, the hamster chewed newspaper in its cage. The cage hung from the kitchen ceiling, and rocked with every draft. Angelo remembered to feed the hamster, but as far as the children were concerned it might have been dead. William of Orange claimed them now; he threw up hair balls and string, and behaved as if he were poisoned. Angelo covered his coat with olive oil and pushed mashed garlic down his throat. He grew worse; Angelo found him on the steps one morning, dying, unable to move his legs. He sat with the cat on his knees and roared, as William of Orange had howled on the train in his basket. The cat was dying of old age. Walter assured everyone it was nothing more serious than that. "He came with the house," he repeated again and again. "He must be the equivalent of a hundred and two."

Angelo's grief terrified the children. Walter was frightened as well, but only because too much was taking place. The charming boy against the baroque wall had become this uncontrolled, bellowing adolescent. The sight of his niece's delicate ear, the lamps reflected in his nephew's eyes, his sister's disapproval of him on the beach, his brother-in-law's soulless exposition of his personal disaster – each was an event. Any would have been a stone to mark the season. Any would have been enough. He wanted nothing more distressing than a spoiled dinner, nothing more lively than a drive along the shore. He thought, In three days, four at the most, they will disappear. William of Orange is old and dying, but everything else will be as before. Angelo will be amusing and young. Mrs. Wiggott will invite me to dine. The telephone will ring.

The children recovered quickly, for they saw that William of

Orange was wretched but not quite dead. They were prepared to leave him and go to the beach as usual, but Angelo said he would stay with the cat. The children were sorry for Angelo now. Johnny sat next to Angelo on the step, frowning in a grown-up way, rubbing his brown knees. "Tell me one thing," he said to Angelo from under his sun hat. "Is William of Orange your father or something like that?" That night the little boy wet his bed, and Walter had a new horror. It was the sight of a bedsheet with a great stain flapping on the line.

Fortunately for Walter, the family could no longer put off going away. "There is so much to do," said Eve. "We got the Citroën delivered, but we didn't do a thing about the children's schools. I wonder if the trunks have got to London? I expect there hasn't been time. I hope they get there before the cold weather. All the children's clothes are in them."

"You are preposterous parents," Walter said. "I suppose you know that."

"We are, aren't we?" said Eve cheerfully. "You don't understand how much one has to *do*. If only we could leave the children somewhere, even for a week, while we look at schools and everything."

"You had your children because you wanted them," said Walter. "I suppose."

"Yes, we did," said Frank. It was the only time Walter ever saw his easy manner outdistanced. "We wanted them. So let's hear no more about leaving them. Even for a week."

Only one rainy day marred the holiday, and as it was the last day, it scarcely counted. It was over – the breather between South Africa and England, between home for the children and a new home for Eve. They crowded into the sitting room, waiting for lunch. They had delayed leaving since early that morning, expecting, in their scatterbrained way, that the sky would clear. The room smelled of musty paper and of mice. Walter suddenly remembered what it was like in winter here, and how Angelo was often bored. His undisciplined relations began pulling books off the shelves and leaving them anywhere.

"Are all these yours?" Mary asked him. "Are they old?"

"These shelves hold every book I have ever bought or had given me since I was born," said Walter. And the children looked again at the dark-green and dark-wine covers.

"I know *Kim*," said Mary, and she opened it and began to read in a monotonous voice, "'He sat, in defiance of municipal orders, astride the gun Zam-Zammeh on her brick platform opposite the old Ajaibgher.'"

"I can still see him," said Eve. "I can see Kim."

"I can't see him as I saw him," said Walter.

"Never could bear Kipling, personally," Frank said. "He's at the bottom of all the trouble we're having now. You only have to read something like 'Wee Willie Winkie' to understand that."

"Why is the gun 'her'?" Mary asked.

"Because in an English education it's the only thing allowed to be female," said Frank. "That and boats." He hadn't wanted the change; that was plain. For Eve's sake, Walter hoped it was a change for the good.

"This book is all scribbled in," Mary complained. She began to turn at random, reading the neat hand that had been Walter's at twelve: " 'Shows foresight,' " she read. "Local color. More color. Building up the color. Does not wish to let women interfere with his career.' That's underlined, Uncle Walter," she said, breaking off. " 'A deceiver. Kim's strong will – or white blood? Generous renunciation. Sympathetic. Shows off. Sly. Easily imposed on. Devout. Persistent. Enterprising.' "

"That will do," said Frank. " 'Shows off' is the chief expression where you're concerned."

"Those notes were how Kipling was introduced to me, and I used them when I was teaching Angelo," said Walter. "Angelo doesn't like Kipling, either. You can keep the book, if you want it."

"Thank you very much," said Mary automatically. She placed the book more or less where it had been, as if she recognized that this was a bogus gesture.

"Thank you, darling Walter," said Eve, and she picked up the book and stroked the cover, dirtying her hand. "Johnny will love it, later on."

Walter's first dinner invitation of the autumn season arrived by post eight days after the Osborns had gone. In the same mail were three letters, each addressed by his sister. Eve thanked him for his great kindness; he would never know what it had meant, the holiday it had been. They were in a hotel, and it was a great change from the south. In a P.S. she said they were moving to the new farm soon. The children were their great worry. She went on about schools. The postscript was longer than the body of the letter.

The other two envelopes, although addressed by Eve, contained letters from Mary and Johnny. The boy spelled difficult words correctly, simple words hopelessly, and got his own name wrong.

"Dear Uncle Walter," he wrote. "Thank you for letting us stay at your house." A row of dots led out to the margin, where he had added, "and for Kim." The text of the letter went on, "It was the most exciting, and enjoyable time I have ever had. Please tell Angelo on the way back we were fined for overtaking in a village, but we got safley out of France. I hope the hamster is well and happy. Tell Angelo there are two very small kittens down in the kitchin of the hotel where we now rent two rooms. They are sweat, white, snowballs, also there is a huge golden labridore, he is very stuppid. Love from Johny."

The girl's letter had been written on a line guide. Her hand was firm. "Dear Uncle Walter," she said. "Thank you for letting us sleep in your house and for everything too. We had a lovely time. Will you please tell Angelo that on the way to Paris Daddy was fined 900 francs for overtaking in a village. He was livid. On Monday I had two teeth out, one on each side. I hope the hamster is healthy. Will you please tell Angelo that our trunks have arrived with my books and he can have one as a present from me, if he will tell me which one he likes best.

> Successful Show Jumping
> Bridle Wise
> Pink and Scarlet
> The Young Rider

"These are my favorites and so I would like him to have one. Also, here is a poem I have copied out for him from a book.

FROM THE DREAM OF AN OLD MELTONIAN
by W. Bromley Davenport

Though a rough-riding world may bespatter your breeches
Though sorrow may cross you, or slander revile,
Though you plunge overhead in misfortune's blind ditches,
Shun the gap of deception – the hand gate of guile.

"Tell Angelo we miss him, and William of Orange, and the hamster too. Thank you again for everything. Your affectionate niece, Mary."

Walking to the kitchen with the letters in his hand, he tried to see the passionate child – dancer, he had thought – on the summer beach. But although eight days had passed, no more, he had forgotten what she was like. He tried to think of England then. Someone had told him the elms were going, because of an American disease. He knew that all this thinking and drifting was covering one displeasure, one blister on his pride: it was Mary's letter he had been waiting for.

"These letters are intended for you," he said, and put them in

Angelo's hands. "They were addressed to me by mistake. Or perhaps the family didn't know your full name. I didn't know you were
interested in horses, by the way."

Angelo sat at the kitchen table, cleaning the hamster's cage.
Mme. Rossi sat facing him. Neither of them rose. "Master-
servant," Eve had said. She ought to have seen Angelo's casual
manner now, the way he accepted his morning's post—as though
Walter were the servant. The boy's secretive face bent over the
letters. Already Angelo's tears were falling. Walter watched, exasperated, as the ink dissolved.

"You can't keep on crying every time I mention the children," he
said. "Look at the letters now. You won't be able to read them."

"He is missing the family," Mme. Rossi said. "Even though they
made more work for him. He cries the whole day."

Of course he was missing the family. He was missing the
family, the children were missing him. Walter looked at the boy's
face, which seemed as close and vain as a cat's. "They meant
more work for you," he said. "Did you hear that?"

"We could have kept the children," Angelo mumbled. His lips
hung open. His face was Negroid, plump. One day he would
certainly be fat.

"What, brought them up?"

"Only for one week," said Angelo, wiping his eyes.

"It seems to me you overheard rather a good deal." Another
thought came to him: it would have been a great responsibility.
He felt aggrieved that Angelo did not take into consideration the
responsibilities Walter already had—for instance, he was responsible for Angelo's being in France. If Angelo were to steal a car
and smash it, Walter would have to make good the loss. He was
responsible for the house, which was not his, and for William of
Orange, who was no better and no worse, but lay nearly paralyzed in a cardboard box, demanding much of Angelo's attention.
Now he was responsible for a hamster in a cage.

"They would have taken me on the farm," Angelo said.

"Nonsense." Walter remembered how Eve avoided a brawl,
and he imitated her deliberately mild manner. He understood
now that they had been plotting behind his back. He had raised
Angelo in cotton wool, taught him Kipling and gardening and
how to wash the car, fed him the best food . . . "My brother-
in-law is Irish," he said. "You mustn't think his promises are
real."

The boy sat without moving, expressionless, sly. He was waiting for Walter to leave the room so that he could have the letters
to himself.

"Would you like to go home, Angelo?" Walter said. "Would you like to go back and live in Italy, back with your family?" Angelo shook his head. Of course he would say no to that; for one thing, they relied on his pocket money – on the postal orders he sent them. An idea came to Walter. "We shall send for your mother," he said. The idea was radiant now. "We shall bring your old mother here for a visit. Why not? That's what we shall do. Bring your mother here. She can talk to you. I'm sure that is all you need."

"Can you imagine that lazy boy on an English farm?" said Walter to Mrs. Wiggott. "That is what I said to him: "Have you ever worked as a farmer? Do you know what it means?' " He blotted imaginary tears with his sleeve to show how Angelo had listened. His face was swollen, limp.

"Stop it, Walter," said Mrs. Wiggott. "I shall *perish.*"

"And so now the mother is coming said Walter. "That is where the situation has got to. They will all sit in the kitchen eating my food, gossiping in Calabrian. I say 'all' because of course she is bound to come with a *covey* of cousins. But I am hoping that when I have explained the situation to the old woman she can reason with Angelo and make him see the light."

"Darling Walter," said Mrs. Wiggott. "This could only happen to you."

"If only I could explain things to Angelo in *our* terms," said Walter. "How to be a good friend, a decent host, all the rest. Not to expect too much. How to make the best of life, as we do."

"As we do," said Mrs. Wiggott, solemn now.

"Live for the minute, I would like to tell him. Look at the things I put up with, without complaint. The summer I've had! Children everywhere. Eggs and bacon in the hottest weather. High tea – my brother-in-law's influence, of course. Look at the house I live in. Ugly box, really. I never complain."

"That is true," said his old friend.

"No heat in winter. Not an anemone in the garden. Les Anémones, they called it, and not an anemone on the place. Nothing but a lot of iris, and I put those in myself."

The End of the World

I never like to leave Canada, because I'm disappointed every time. I've felt disappointed about places I haven't even seen. My wife went to Florida with her mother once. When they arrived there, they met some neighbors from home who told them about a sign saying "No Canadians." They never saw this sign anywhere, but they kept hearing about others who did, or whose friends had seen it, always in different places, and it spoiled their trip for them. Many people, like them, have never come across it but have heard about it, so it must be there somewhere. Another time I had to go and look after my brother Kenny in Buffalo. He had stolen a credit card and was being deported on that account. I went down to vouch for him and pay up for him and bring him home. Neither of us cared for Buffalo.

"What have they got here that's so marvellous?" I said.

"Proust," said Kenny.

"What?"

"Memorabilia," he said. He was reading it off a piece of paper.

"Why does a guy with your education do a dumb thing like swiping a credit card?" I said.

"Does Mother know?" said Kenny.

"Mum knows, and Lou knows, and I know, and Beryl knows. It was in the papers, 'Kenneth Apostolesco, of this city . . .' "

"I'd better stay away," my brother said.

"No, you'd better not, for Mum's sake. We've only got one mother."

"Thank God," he said. "Only one of each. One mother and one father. If I had more than one of each, I think I'd still be running."

It was our father who ran, actually. He deserted us during the last war. He joined the Queen's Own Rifles, which wasn't a Montreal regiment – he couldn't do anything like other people, couldn't even join up like anyone else – and after the war he just chose to go his own way. I saw him downtown in Montreal one time after the war. I was around twelve, delivering prescriptions for a drugstore. I knew him before he knew me. He looked the way he had always managed to look, as if he had all the time in the world. His mouth was drawn in, like an old woman's, but he still had his coal black hair. I wish we had his looks. I leaned my bike with one foot on the curb and he came down and stood by me, rocking on his feet, like a dancer, and looking off over my head. He said he was night watchman at a bank and that he was waiting for the Army to fix him up with some teeth. He'd had all his teeth out, though there wasn't anything wrong with them. He was eligible for new ones provided he put in a claim that year, so he thought he might as well. He was a bartender by profession, but he wasn't applying for anything till he'd got his new teeth. "I've told them to hurry it up," he said. "I can't go round to good places all gummy." He didn't ask how anyone was at home.

I had to leave Canada to be with my father when he died. I was the person they sent for, though I was the youngest. My name was on the back page of his passport: "In case of accident or death notify WILLIAM APOSTOLESCO. Relationship: Son." I was the one he picked. He'd been barman on a ship for years by then, earning good money, but he had nothing put by. I guess he never expected his life would be finished. He collapsed with a lung hemorrhage, as far as I could make out, and they put him off at a port in France. I went there. That was where I saw him. This town had been shelled twenty years ago and a lot of it looked bare and new. I wouldn't say I hated it exactly, but I would never have come here of my own accord. It was worse than Buffalo in some ways. I didn't like the food or the coffee, and they never gave you anything you needed in the hotels – I had to go out and buy some decent towels. It didn't matter, because I had to buy everything for my father anyway – soap and towels and Kleenex. The hospital didn't provide a thing except the bedsheets, and when a pair of those was put on the bed it seemed to be put there once and for all. I was there twenty-three days and I think I saw the sheets changed once. Our grandfathers had been glad to get out of Europe. It took my father to go back. The hospital he was in was an old convent or monastery. The beds were so close together you could hardly get a chair between them. Women patients were always wandering around the men's wards, and although I wouldn't swear to it, I think some of them had their beds there, at the far end. The patients were given crocks of tepid water to wash in, not by their beds but on a long table in the middle of the ward. Anyone too sick to get up was just out of luck unless, like my father, he had someone to look after him. I saw beetles and cockroaches, and I said to myself, This is what a person gets for leaving home.

My father accepted my presence as if it were his right – as if he hadn't lost his claim to any consideration years ago. So as not to scare him, I pretended my wife's father had sent me here on business, but he hardly listened, so I didn't insist.

"Didn't you drive a cab one time or other?" he said. "What else have you done?"

I wanted to answer, "You know what I've been doing? I've been supporting your wife and educating your other children, practically singlehanded, since I was twelve."

I had expected to get here in time for his last words, which ought to have been "I'm sorry." I thought he would tell me where he wanted to be buried, how much money he owed, how many bastards he was leaving behind, and who was looking out for them. I imagined them in ports like this, with no-good mothers. *Somebody* should have been told – telling me didn't mean telling the whole world. One of the advantages of having an Old Country in the family is you can always say the relations that give you trouble have gone there. You just say, "He went back to the Old Country," and nobody asks any questions. So he could have told me the truth, and I'd have known and still not let the family down. But my father never confided anything. The trouble was he didn't know he was dying – he'd been told, in fact, he was getting better – so he didn't act like a dying man. He used what breath he had to say things like "I always liked old Lou," and you would have thought she was someone else's daughter, a girl he had hardly known. Another time he said, "Did Kenny do well for himself? I heard he went to college."

"Don't talk," I said.

"No, I mean it. I'd like to know how Kenny made out."

He couldn't speak above a whisper some days, and he was careful how he pronounced words. It wasn't a snobbish or an English accent – nothing that would make you grit your teeth. He just sounded like a stranger. When I was sent for, my mother said, "He's dying a pauper, after all his ideas. I hope he's satisfied." I didn't answer, but I said to myself, This isn't a question of satisfaction. I wanted to ask her, "Since you didn't get along with him and he didn't get along with you, what did you go and have three children for?" But those are the questions you keep to yourself.

"What's your wife like?" my father croaked. His eyes were interested. I hadn't been prepared for this, for how long the mind stayed alive and how frivolous it went on being. I thought he should be more serious. "*Wife*," my father insisted. "What about her?"

"Obedient" came into my head, I don't know why; it isn't important. "Older than me," I said, quite easily, at last. "Better educated. She was a kindergarten teacher. She knows a lot about art." Now, why that, of all the side issues? She doesn't like a bare wall, that's all. "She prefers the Old Masters," I said. I was thinking about the Scotch landscape we've got over the mantelpiece.

"Good, good. Name?"

"You know – *Beryl*. We sent you an announcement, to that place in Mexico where you were then."

"That's right. Beryl." "Burrull" was what he actually said.

I felt reassured, because my father until now had sounded like a strange person. To have "Beryl" pronounced as I was used to hearing it made up for being alone here and the smell of the ward and the coffee made of iodine. I remembered what the Old Master had cost – one hundred and eighty dollars in 1962. It must be worth more now. Beryl said it would be an investment. Her family paid for half. She said once, about my father, "One day he'll be sick; we'll have to look after him." "We can sell the painting," I said. "I guess I can take care of my own father."

It happened – I was here, taking care of him; but he spoiled it now by saying, "You look like you'd done pretty well. That's not a bad suit you've got on."

"Actually," I said, "I had to borrow from Beryl's father so as to get here."

I thought he would say, "Oh, I'm sorry," and I had my next answer ready about not begrudging a cent of it. But my father closed his eyes, smiling, saving up more breath to talk about nothing.

"I liked old Lou," he said distinctly. I was afraid he would ask, "Why doesn't she write to me?" and I would have to say, "Because she never forgave you," and he was perfectly capable of saying then, "Never forgave me for what?" But instead of that he laughed, which was the worst of the choking and wheezing noises he made now, and when he had recovered he said, "Took her to Eaton's to choose a toy village. Had this shipment in, last one in before the war. Summer '39. The old man saw the ad, wanted to get one for the kid. Old man came – each of us had her by the hand. Lou looked round, but every village had something the matter, as far as Her Royal Highness was concerned. The old man said, 'Come on, Princess, hurry it up,' but no, she'd of seen a scratch, or a bad paint job, or a chimney too big for a cottage. The old man said, 'Can't this kid make up her mind about anything? She's going to do a lot more crying than laughing,' he said, 'and that goes for you, too.' He was wrong about me. Don't know about Lou. But she was smart that time – not to want something that wasn't perfect."

He shut his eyes again and breathed desperately through his mouth. The old man in the story was his father, my grandfather.

"Nothing is perfect," I said. I felt like standing up so everyone could hear. It wasn't sourness but just the way I felt like reacting to my father's optimism.

Some days he seemed to be getting better. After two weeks I was starting to wonder if they hadn't brought me all this way for nothing. I couldn't go home and come back later, it had to be now; but I couldn't stay on and on. I had already moved to a cheaper hotel room. I dreamed I asked him, "How much longer?" but luckily the dream was in a foreign language – so foreign I don't think it was French, even. It was a language no one on earth had ever heard of. I wouldn't have wanted him to understand it, even in a dream. The nurses couldn't say anything. Sometimes I wondered if they knew who he was – if they could tell one patient from another. It was a big place, and poor. These nurses didn't seem to have much equipment. When they needed sterile water for anything, they had to boil it in an old saucepan. I got to the doctor one day, but he didn't like it. He had told my father he was fine, and that I could go back to Canada any time – the old boy must have been starting to wonder why I was staying so long. The doctor just said to me, "Family business is of no interest to me. You look after your duty and I'll look after mine." I was afraid that my dream showed on my face and that was what made them all so indifferent. I didn't know how much time there was. I wanted to ask my father why he thought everything had to be perfect, and if he still stood by it as a way of living. Whenever he was reproached about something – by my mother, for instance – he just said, "Don't make my life dark for me." What could you do? He certainly made her life dark for her. One year when we had a summer cottage, he took a girl from the village, the village tramp, out to an island in the middle of the lake. They got caught in a storm coming back, and around fifty people stood on shore waiting to see the canoe capsize and the sinners drown. My mother had told us to stay in the house, but when Kenny said, to scare me, "I guess the way things are, Mum's gone down there to drown herself," I ran after her. She didn't say anything to me, but took her raincoat off and draped it over my head. It would have been fine if my father had died then – if lightning had struck him, or the canoe gone down like a stone. But no, he waded ashore – the slut, too – and someone even gave her a blanket. It was my mother that was blamed, in a funny way. "Can't you keep your husband home?" this girl's father said. I remember that same summer some other woman saying to her, "You'd better keep your husband away from my daughter. I'm telling you for your own good, because my husband's got a gun in the house." Someone did say, "Oh, poor

Mrs. Apostolesco!" but my mother only answered, "If you think that, then I'm poor for life." That was only one of the things he did to her. I'm not sure if it was even the worst.

It was hard to say how long he had been looking at me. His lips were trying to form a word. I bent close and heard, "Sponge."

"Did you say 'sponge'? Is 'sponge' what you said?"

"Sponge," he agreed. He made an effort: "Bad night last night. Awful. Wiped everything with my sponge – blood, spit. Need new sponge."

There wasn't a bed table, just a plastic bag that hung on the bedrail with his personal things in it. I got out the sponge. It needed to be thrown away, all right. I said, "What color?"

"Eh?"

"This," I said, and held it up in front of him. "The new one. Any special color?"

"Blue." His voice broke out of a whisper all at once. His eyes were mocking me, like a kid seeing how far he can go. I thought he would thank me now, but then I said to myself, You can't expect anything; he's a sick man, and he was always like this.

"Most people think it was pretty good of me to have come here," I wanted to explain – not to boast or anything, but just for the sake of conversation. I was lonely there, and I had so much trouble understanding what anybody was saying.

"Bad night," my father whispered. "Need sedation."

"I know. I tried to tell the doctor. I guess he doesn't understand my French."

He moved his head. "Tip the nurses."

"You don't mean it!"

"Don't make me talk." He seemed to be using a reserve of breath. "At least twenty dollars. The ward girls less."

I said, "Jesus God!" because this was new to me and I felt out of my depth. "They don't bother much with you," I said, talking myself into doing it. "Maybe you're right. If I gave them a present, they'd look after you more. Wash you. Maybe they'd put a screen around you – you'd be more private then."

"No, thanks," my father said. "No screen. Thanks all the same."

We had one more conversation after that. I've already said there were always women slopping around in the ward, in felt slippers, and bathrobes stained with medicine and tea. I came in and found one – quite young, this one was – combing my father's hair. He could hardly lift his head from the pillow, and still she thought he was interesting. I thought, Kenny should see this.

"She's been telling me," my father gasped when the woman had left. "About herself. Three children by different men. Met a North African. He adopts the children, all three. Gives them his name. She has two more by him, boys. But he won't put up with a sick woman. One day he just doesn't come. She's been a month in another place; now they've brought her here. Man's gone. Left the children. They've been put in all different homes, she doesn't know where. Five kids. Imagine."

I thought, You left *us*. He had forgotten; he had just simply forgotten that he'd left his own.

"Well, we can't do anything about her, can we?" I said. "She'll collect them when she gets out of here."

"If she gets out."

"That's no way to talk," I said. "Look at the way she was talking and walking around ... " I could not bring myself to say, "and combing your hair." "Look at how *you* are," I said. "You've just told me this long story."

"She'll seem better, but she'll get worse," my father said. "She's like me, getting worse. Do you think I don't know what kind of ward I'm in? Every time they put the screen around a patient, it's because he's dying. If I had t.b., like they tried to make me believe, I'd be in a t.b. hospital."

"That just isn't true," I said.

"Can you swear I've got t.b.? You can't."

I said without hesitating, "You've got a violent kind of t.b. They had no place else to put you except here. The ward might be crummy, but the medicine ... the medical care ... " He closed his eyes. "I'm looking you straight in the face," I said, "and I swear you have this unusual kind of t.b., and you're almost cured." I watched, without minding it now, a new kind of bug crawling along the base of the wall.

"Thanks, Billy," said my father.

I really was scared. I had been waiting for something without knowing what it would mean. I can tell you how it was: it was like the end of the world. "I didn't realize you were worried," I said. "You should of asked me right away."

"I knew you wouldn't lie to me," my father said. "That's why I wanted you, not the others."

That was all. Not long after that he couldn't talk. He had deserted the whole family once, but I was the one he abandoned twice. When he died, a nurse said to me, "I am sorry." It had no meaning, from her, yet only a few days before it was all I thought I wanted to hear.

The Accident

I was tired and did not always understand what they were asking me. I borrowed a pencil and wrote:

PETER HIGGINS
CALGARY 1935 – ITALY 1956

But there was room for more on the stone, and the English clergyman in this Italian town who was doing all he could for me said, "Is there nothing else, child?" Hadn't Pete been my husband, somebody's son? That was what he was asking. It seemed enough. Pete had renounced us, left us behind. His life-span might matter, if anyone cared, but I must have sensed even then that no one would ever ask me what he had been like. His father once asked me to write down what I remembered. He wanted to compose a memorial booklet and distribute it at Christmas, but then his wife died, too, and he became prudent about recollections. Even if I had wanted to, I couldn't have told much – just one or two things about the way Pete died. His mother had some information about him, and I had some, but never enough to describe a life. She had the complete knowledge that puts parents at a loss, finally: she knew all about him except his opinion of her and how he was with me. They were never equals. She was a grown person with part of a life lived and the habit of secrets before he was conscious of her. She said, later, that she and Pete had been friends. How can you be someone's friend if you have had twenty years' authority over him and he has never had one second's authority over you?

He didn't look like his mother. He looked like me. In Italy, on our wedding trip, we were often taken for brother and sister. Our height, our glasses, our soft myopic stares, our assurance, our sloppy comfortable clothes made us seem to the Italians related and somehow unplaceable. Only a North American could have guessed what our families were, what our education amounted to, and where we had got the money to spend on travelling. Most of the time we were just pie-faces, like the tourists in ads – though we were not as clean as those couples, and not quite as grown-up. We didn't seem to be married: the honeymoon in hotels, in strange beds, the meals we shared in cheap, bright little restaurants, prolonged the clandestine quality of love before. It was still a game, but now we had infinite time. I became bold, and I dismissed the universe: "It was a rotten little experiment," I said,

95

"and we were given up long ago." I had been brought up by a forcible, pessimistic, widowed mother, and to be able to say aloud "we were given up" shows how far I had come. Pete's assurance was natural, but mine was fragile, and recent, and had grown out of love. Travelling from another direction, he was much more interested in his parents than in God. There was a glorious treason in all our conversations now. Pete wondered about his parents, but I felt safer belittling Creation. My mother had let me know about the strength of the righteous; I still thought the skies would fall if I said too much.

What struck me about these secret exchanges was how we judged our parents from a distance now, as if they were people we had known on a visit. The idea that he and I could be natural siblings crossed my mind. What if I, or Pete, or both, had been adopted? We had been raised in different parts of Canada, but we were only children, and neither of us resembled our supposed parents. Watching him, trapping him almost in mannerisms I could claim, I saw my habit of sprawling, of spreading maps and newspapers on the ground. He had a vast appetite for bread and pastries and sweet desserts. He was easily drunk and easily sick. Yes, we were alike. We talked in hotel rooms, while we drank the drink of the place, the *grappa* or wine or whatever we were given, prone across the bed, the bottle and glasses and the ashtray on the floor. We agreed to live openly, without secrets, though neither of us knew what a secret was. I admired him as I could never have admired myself. I remembered how my mother, the keeper of the castle until now, had said that one day – one treeless, sunless day – real life would overtake me, and then I would realize how spoiled and silly I had always been.

The longest time he and I spent together in one place was three days, in a village up behind the Ligurian coast. I thought that the only success of my life, my sole achievement, would be this marriage. In a dream he came to me with the plans for a house. I saw the white lines on the blue paper, and he showed me the sunny Italian-style loggia that would be built. "It is not quite what we want," he said, "but better than anything we have now." "But we can't afford it, we haven't got the capital," I cried, and I panicked, and woke: woke safe, in a room of which the details were dawn, window, sky, first birds of morning, and Pete still sleeping, still in the dark.

The last Italian town of our journey was nothing – just a black beach with sand like soot, and houses shut and dormant because it was the middle of the afternoon. We had come here from our village only to change trains. We were on our way to Nice, then

Paris, then home. We left our luggage at the station, with a porter looking after it, and we drifted through empty, baking streets, using up the rest of a roll of film. By now we must have had hundreds of pictures of each other in market squares, next to oleanders, cut in two by broomstick shade, or backed up, squinting, against scaly noonday shutters. Pete now chose to photograph a hotel with a cat on the step, a policeman, and a souvenir stand, as if he had never seen such things in Canada – as if they were monuments. I never once heard him say anything. was ugly or dull; for if it was, what were we doing with it? We were often stared at, for we were out of our own background and did not fit into the new. That day, I was eyed more than he was. I was watched by men talking in dark doorways, leaning against the façades of inhospitable shops. I was travelling in shorts and a shirt and rope-soled shoes. I know now that this costume was resented, but I don't know why. There was nothing indecent about my clothes. They were very like Pete's.

He may not have noticed the men. He was always on the lookout for something to photograph, or something to do, and sometimes he missed people's faces. On the steep street that led back to the railway station, he took a careful picture of a bakery, and he bought crescent-shaped bread with a soft, pale crust, and ate it there, on the street. He wasn't hungry; it was a question of using time. Now the closed shutters broke out in the afternoon, and girls appeared – girls with thick hair, smelling of jasmine and honeysuckle. They strolled hand in hand, in light stockings and clean white shoes. Their dresses – blue, lemon, the palest peach – bloomed over rustling petticoats. At home I'd have called them cheap, and made a face at their cheap perfume, but here, in their own place, they were enravishing, and I thought Pete would look at them and at me and compare; but all he remarked was "How do they stand those clothes on a day like this?" So real life, the grey noon with no limits, had not yet begun. I distrusted real life, for I knew nothing about it. It was the middle-aged world without feeling, where no one was loved.

Bored with his bread, he tossed it away and laid his hands on a white Lambretta propped against the curb. He pulled it upright, examining it. He committed two crimes in a second: wasted bread and touched an adored mechanical object belonging to someone else. I knew these were crimes later, when it was no use knowing, no good to either of us. The steering of the Lambretta was locked. He saw a bicycle then, belonging, he thought, to an old man who was sitting in a kitchen chair out on the pavement. "This all right with you?" Pete pointed to the bike, then himself, then down the hill. With a swoop of his hand he tried to show he would come straight back. His pantomime also meant that there was still time before we had to be on the train, that up at the station there was nothing to do, that eating bread, taking pictures of shops, riding a bike downhill and walking it back were all doing, using up your life; yes, it was a matter of living.

The idling old man Pete had spoken to bared his gums. Pete must have taken this for a smile. Later, the old man, who was not the owner of the bike or of anything except the fat sick dog at his feet, said he had cried "Thief!" but I never heard him. Pete tossed me his camera and I saw him glide, then rush away, past the girls who smelled of jasmine, past the bakery, down to the corner, where a policeman in white, under a parasol, spread out one arm and flexed the other and blew hard on a whistle. Pete was standing, as if he were trying to coast to a stop. I saw things meaningless now – for instance that the sun was sifted through leaves. There were trees we hadn't noticed. Under the leaves he seemed under water. A black car, a submarine with Belgian plates, parked at an angle, stirred to life. I saw sunlight deflected from six points on the paint. My view became discomposed, as if the sea were suddenly black and opaque and had splashed up over the policeman and the road, and I screamed, "He's going to open the door!" Everyone said later that I was mistaken, for why would the Belgian have started the motor, pulled out, and *then* flung open the door? He had stopped near a change office; perhaps he had forgotten his sunglasses, or a receipt. He started, stopped abruptly, hurled back the door. I saw that, and then I saw him driving away. No one had taken his number.

Strangers made Pete kneel and then stand, and they dusted the bicycle. They forced him to walk – where? Nobody wanted him. Into a pharmacy, finally. In a parrot's voice he said to the policeman, "Don't touch my elbow." The pharmacist said, "He can't stay here," for Pete was vomiting, but weakly – a weak coughing, like an infant's. I was in a crowd of about twenty people, a spectator with two cameras round my neck. In kind somebody's living room, Pete was placed on a couch with a cushion under his head and another under his dangling arm. The toothless old man turned up now, panting, with his waddling dog, and cried that we had a common thief there before us, and everyone listened and marvelled until the old man spat on the carpet and was turned out.

When I timidly touched Pete, trying to wipe his face with a crumpled Kleenex (all I had), he thought I was one of the strangers. His mouth was a purple color, as if he had been in icy water. His eyes looked at me, but he was not looking out.

"Ambulance," said a doctor who had been fetched by the policeman. He spoke loudly and slowly, dealing with idiots.

"Yes," I heard, in English. "We must have an ambulance."

Everyone now inspected me. I was, plainly, responsible for something. For walking around the streets in shorts? Wasting bread? Conscious of my sweaty hair, my bare legs, my lack of Italian – my nakedness – I began explaining the true error of the day: "The train has gone, and all our things are on it. Our luggage. We've been staying up in that village – oh, what's the name of it, now? Where they make the white wine. I can't remember, no, I can't remember where we've been. I could find it, I could take you there; I've just forgotten what it's called. We were down here waiting for the train. To Nice. We had lots of time. The porter took our things and said he'd put them on the train for us. He said the train would wait here, at the border, that it waited a long time. He was supposed to meet us at the place where you show your ticket. I guess for an extra tip. The train must have gone now. My purse is in the duffelbag up at the the ... I'll look in my husband's wallet. Of course that is my husband! Our passports must be on the train, too. Our traveller's checks are in our luggage, his and mine. We were just walking round taking pictures instead of sitting up there in the station. Anyway, there was no place to sit – only the bar, and it was smelly and dark."

No one believed a word of this, of course. Would you give your clothes, your passport, your traveller's checks to a porter? A man you had never seen in your life before? A bandit disguised as a porter, with a stolen cap on his head?

"You could not have taken that train without showing your passport," a careful foreign voice objected.

"What are you two, anyway?" said the man from the change office. His was a tough, old-fashioned movie-American accent. He was puffy-eyed and small, but he seemed superior to us, for he wore an impeccable shirt. Pete, on the sofa, looked as if he had been poisoned, or stepped on. "What are you?" the man from the change office said again. "Students? Americans? No? What, then? Swedes?"

I saw what the doctor had been trying to screen from me: a statue's marble eye.

The tourist who spoke the careful foreign English said, "Be careful of the pillows."

"What? What?" screamed the put-upon person who owned them.

"Blood is coming out of his ears," said the tourist, halting between words. "That is a bad sign." He seemed to search his memory for a better English word. "An *unfortunate* sign," he said, and put his hand over his mouth.

Pete's father and mother flew from Calgary when they had my cable. They made flawless arrangements by telephone, and knew exactly what to bring. They had a sunny room looking onto rusty palms and a strip of beach about a mile from where the accident had been. I sat against one of the windows and told them what I thought I remembered. I looked at the white walls, the white satin bedspreads, at Mrs. Higgins' spotless dressing case, and finally down at my hands.

His parents had not understood, until now, that ten days had gone by since Pete's death.

"What have you been doing, dear, all alone?" said Mrs. Higgins, gently.

"Just waiting, after I cabled you." They seemed to be expecting more. "I've been to the movies," I said.

From this room we could hear the shrieks of children playing on the sand.

"Are they orphans?" asked Mrs. Higgins, for they were little girls, dressed alike, with soft pink sun hats covering their heads.

"It seems to be a kind of summer camp," I said. "I was wondering about them, too."

"It would make an attractive picture," said Pete's mother, after a pause. "The blue sea, and the nuns, and all those bright hats. It would look nice in a dining room."

They were too sick to reproach me. My excuse for not having told them sooner was that I hadn't been thinking, and they didn't ask me for it. I could only repeat what seemed important now. "I don't want to go back home just yet" was an example. I was already in the future, which must have hurt them. "I have a girl friend in the Embassy in Paris. I can stay with her." I scarcely moved my lips. They had to strain to hear. I held still, looking down at my fingers. I was very brown, sun streaks in my hair, more graceful than at my wedding, where I knew they had found me maladroit – a great lump of a. Camp Fire Girl. That was how I had seen myself in my father-in-law's eyes. Extremes of shock had brought me near some ideal they had of prettiness. I appeared now much more the kind of girl they'd have wanted as Pete's wife.

So they had come for nothing. They were not to see him, or bury him, or fetch home his bride. All I had to show them was a still unlabelled grave.

When I dared look at them, I saw their way of being was not Pete's. Neither had his soft selective stare. Mr. Higgins' eyes were a fanatic blue. He was thin and sunburned and unused to nonsense. Summer and winter he travelled with his wife in climates that were bad for her skin. She had the fair, papery coloring that requires constant vigilance. All this I knew because of Pete.

They saw his grave at the best time of day, in the late afternoon, with the light at a slant. The cemetery was in a valley between two plaster towns. A flash of the sea was visible, a corner of ultramarine. They saw a stone wall covered with roses, pink and white and near-white, open, without secrets. The hiss of traffic on the road came to us, softer than rain; then true rain came down, and we ran to our waiting taxi through a summer storm. Later they saw the station where Pete had left our luggage but never come back. Like Pete – as Pete had intended to – they were travelling to Nice. Under a glass shelter before the station I paused and said, "That was where it happed, down there." I pointed with my white glove. I was not as elegant as Mrs. Higgins, but I was not a source of embarrassment. I wore gloves, stockings, shoes.

The steep street under rain was black as oil. Everything was reflected upside down. The neon signs of the change office and the pharmacy swam deeply in the pavement.

"I'd like to thank the people who were so kind," said Mrs. Higgins. "Is there time? Shirley, I suppose you got their names?"

"Nobody was kind," I said.

"Shirley! We've met the doctor, and the minister, but you said there was a policeman, and a Dutch gentleman, and a lady – you were in this lady's living room."

"They were all there, but no one was kind."

"The bike's paid for?" asked Mr. Higgins suddenly.

"Yes, I paid. And I paid for having the sofa cushions cleaned."

What sofa cushions? What was I talking about? They seemed petrified, under the glass shelter, out of the rain. They could not take their eyes away from the place I had said was *there*. They never blamed me, never by a word or a hidden meaning. I had explained, more than once, how the porter that day had not put our bags on the train after all but had stood waiting at the customs barrier, wondering what had become of us. I told them how I had found everything intact – passports and checks and maps and sweaters and shoes . . . They could not grasp the importance of it. They knew that Pete had chosen me, and gone away with me, and they never saw him again. An unreliable guide had taken them to a foreign graveyard and told them, without evidence, that now he was there.

"I still don't see how anyone could have thought Pete was stealing," said his mother. "What would Pete have wanted with someone's old bike?"

They were flying home from Nice. They loathed Italy now, and they had a special aversion to the sunny room where I had described Pete's death. We three sat in the restaurant at the airport, and they spoke quietly, considerately, because the people at the table next to ours were listening to a football match on a portable radio.

I closed my hand into a fist and let it rest on the table. I imagined myself at home, saying to my mother, "All right, real life has begun. What's your next prophecy?"

I was not flying with them. I was seeing them off. Mrs. Higgins sat poised and prepared in her linen coat, with her large handbag, and her cosmetics and airsickness tablets in her dressing case, and her diamond maple leaf so she wouldn't be mistaken for an American, and her passport ready to be shown to anyone. Pale gloves lay folded over the clasp of the dressing case. "You'll want to go to your own people, I know," she said. "But you have a home with us. You mustn't forget it." She paused. I said nothing, and so she continued, "What are you going to do, dear? I mean, after you have visited your friend. You mustn't be lonely."

I muttered whatever seemed sensible. "I'll have to get a job. I've never had one and I don't know anything much. I can't even type – not properly." Again they gave me this queer impression of expecting something more. What did they want? "Pete said it was no good learning anything if you couldn't type. He said it was the only useful thing he could do."

In the eyes of his parents was the same wound. I had told them something about him they hadn't known.

"Well, I understand," said his mother, presently. "At least, I think I do."

They imagine I want to be near the grave, I supposed. They think that's why I'm staying on the same side of the world. Pete and I had been waiting for a train; now I had taken it without him. I was waiting again. Even if I were to visit the cemetery every day, he would never speak. His last words had not been for me but to a policeman. He would have said something to me, surely, if everyone hadn't been in such a hurry to get him out of the way. His mind was quenched, and his body out of sight. "You don't love with your soul," I had cried to the old clergyman at the funeral – an offensive remark, judging from the look on his face as he turned it aside. Now I was careful. The destination of a soul was of no interest. The death of a voice – now, that was real. The Dutchman suddenly covering his mouth was horror, and a broken elbow was true pain. But I was careful; I kept this to myself.

"You're our daughter now," Pete's father said. "I don't think I want you to have to worry about a job. Not yet." Mr. Higgins happened to know my family's exact status. My father had not left us well off, and my mother had given everything she owned to a sect that did not believe in blood transfusions. She expected the end of the world, and would not eat an egg unless she had first met the hen. That was Mr. Higgins' view. "Shirley must work if that's what she wants to do," Mrs. Higgins said softly.

"I do want to!" I imagined myself, that day, in a river of people pouring into subways.

"I'm fixing something up for you, just the same," said Mr. Higgins hurriedly, as if he would not be interrupted by women.

Mrs. Higgins allowed her pale forehead to wrinkle, under her beige veil. Was it not better to struggle and to work, she asked. Wasn't that real life? Would it not keep Shirley busy, take her mind off her loss, her disappointment, her tragedy, if you like (though "tragedy" was not an acceptable way of looking at fate), if she had to think about her daily bread?

"The allowance I'm going to make her won't stop her from working," he said. "I was going to set something up for the kids anyway."

She seemed to approve; she had questioned him only out of some prudent system of ethics.

He said to me, "I always have to remember I could go any minute, just like that. I've got a heart." He tapped it – tapped his light suit. "Meantime you better start with this." He gave me the envelope that had been close to his heart until now. He seemed diffident, made ashamed by money, and by death, but it was he and not his wife who had asked if there was a hope that Pete had left a child. No, I had told him. I had wondered, too, but now I was sure. "Then Shirley is all we've got left," he had said to his wife, and I thought they seemed bankrupt, having nothing but me.

"If that's a check on a bank at home, it might take too long to clear," said his wife. "After all Shirley's been through, she needs a fair-sized sum right away."

"She's had that, Betty," said Mr. Higgins, smiling.

I had lived this: three round a table, the smiling parents. Pete had said, "They smile, they go on talking. You wonder what goes on."

"How you manage everything you do without a secretary with you all the time I just don't know," said his wife, all at once admiring him.

"You've been saying that for twenty-two years," he said.

"Twenty-three, now."

With this the conversation came to an end and they sat staring, puzzled, not overcome by life but suddenly lost to it, out of touch. The photograph Pete carried of his mother, that was in his wallet when he died, had been taken before her marriage, with a felt hat all to one side, and an organdie collar, and Ginger Rogers hair. It was easier to imagine Mr. Higgins young – a young Gary Cooper. My father-in-law's blue gaze rested on me now. Never in a million years would he have picked me as a daughter-in-law. I knew that; I understood. Pete was part of him, and Pete, with all the girls he had to choose from, had chosen me. When Mr. Higgins met my mother at the wedding, he thanked God, and was overheard being thankful, that the wedding was not in Calgary. Remembering my mother that day, with her glasses on her nose and a strange borrowed hat on her head, and recalling Mr. Higgins' face, I thought of words that would keep me from laughing. I found, at random, "threesome," "smother," "gambling," "habeas corpus," "sibling." . . .

"How is your mother, Shirley?" said Mrs. Higgins.

"I had a letter . . . She's working with a pendulum now."

"A pendulum?"

"Yes. A weight on a string, sort of. It makes a diagnosis – whether you've got something wrong with your stomach, if it's an ulcer, or what. She can use it to tell when you're pregnant and if the baby will be a girl or a boy. It depends whether it swings north-south or east-west."

"Can the pendulum tell who the father is?" said Mr. Higgins.

"They are useful for people who are afraid of doctors," said Mrs. Higgins, and she fingered her neat gloves, and smiled to herself. "Someone who won't hear the truth from a doctor will listen to any story from a woman with a pendulum or a piece of crystal."

"Or a stone that changes color," I said. "My mother had one of those. When our spaniel had mastoids it turned violet."

She glanced at me then, and caught in her breath, but her husband, by a certain amount of angry fidgeting, made us change the subject. That was the one moment she and I were close to each other – something to do with quirky female humor.

Mr. Higgins did not die of a heart attack, as he had confidently expected, but a few months after this Mrs. Higgins said to her maid in the kitchen, "I've got a terrible pain in my head. I'd better lie down." Pete's father wrote, "She knew what the matter was, but she never said. Typical." I inherited a legacy and some jewelry from her, and wondered why. I had been careless about writing. I could not write the kind of letters she seemed to want. How could I write to someone I hardly knew about someone else who did not exist? Mr. Higgins married the widow of one of his closest friends – a woman six years older than he. They travelled to Europe for their wedding trip. I had a temporary job as an interpreter in a department store. When my father-in-law saw me in a neat suit, with his name, HIGGINS fastened to my jacket, he seemed to approve. He was the only person then who did not say that I was wasting my life and my youth and ought to go home. The new Mrs. Higgins asked to be taken to an English-speaking hairdresser, and there, under the roaring dryer, she yelled that Mr. Higgins may not have been Pete's father. Perhaps he had been, perhaps he hadn't, but one thing he was, and that was a saint. She came out from under the helmet and said in a normal voice, "Martin doesn't know I dye my hair." I wondered if he had always wanted this short, fox-colored woman. The new marriage might for years have been in the maquis of his mind, and of Mrs. Higgins' life. She may have known it as she sat in the airport that day, smiling to herself, touching her unstained gloves. Mr. Higgins had drawn up a new way of life, like a clean will with everyone he loved cut out. I was trying to draw up a will, too, but I was patient, waiting, waiting for someone to tell me what to write. He spoke of Pete conventionally, in a senti-mental way that forbade any feeling. Talking that way was easier for both of us. We were both responsible for something – for surviving, perhaps. Once he turned to me and said defiantly, "Well, she and Pete are together now, aren't they? And didn't they leave us here?"

Malcolm and Bea

Walking diagonally over the sacred grass on his way up from the parking lot, Malcolm Armitage hears first the *gardien's* whistle, then children shooting. To oblige the children, he doubles over his bent arm, wounded. Death, in children's wars, arrives by way of the stomach. Malcolm does not have to turn to know the children are Americans, just as the *gardien,* though he may not place Malcolm accurately, can tell he is not French. He can tell because Malcolm is walking on the grass between the apartment blocks, and because he is in his shirtsleeves, carrying his jacket. This is the only warm day in a cold spring. Nato is leaving, and by the time school has ended Malcolm and the embattled children will have disappeared. The children, talked of as rough, destructive, loud, laughed at for the boys' cropped heads and girls' strange clothes, are identifiable because they play. They play without admonitions and good advice. They tear over the grass shooting and killing. They shoot their mothers dead through picture windows, and each of them has died over and over, a hundred times. The *gardien* is not a real policeman, just a bad-tempered old man in a dirty collar, with a whistle and a caved-in cap. In the late warm afternoon the thinned army retreats in the direction of the wading pool, which is full of last year's leaves and fenced in, but this particular army knows how to get over a fence. The new children gradually replacing them do not mix and do not play. White net curtains cover their windows, and at night double curtains are drawn. The new children attend school on Saturdays, and when they come home they go indoors at once. They do their lessons; then the blue light of television flashes in the chink of the curtains. When they walk, it is in a reasonable manner, keeping to the paths. They seem foreign, but of course they are not: they are French, and Résidence Diane, six miles west of Versailles, is part of France.

As he reaches the brick path edged with ornamental willows and one spared lime tree, Malcolm, unseen, comes upon his family. Bea has her back to him. Her bright-yellow dress is splashed with light. She carries the folding stool she takes to the playground and, tucked high under one arm, "Montcalm and Wolfe," which she has been reading for weeks and weeks. When Malcolm asks how far along she is, she says, "Up to where it says Canada was the prey of jackals." Then she looks as if *he* were the jackal, because he was born in England. She looks as if she had access to historical information Malcolm will never understand. Only once he said, "Who do you hate most, Bea? The English, the French, or the Americans?" He has had to learn not to tease.

Behind her, for the moment abandoned, is the old blue stroller they bought after some other international baby had grown out of it. Ruth, Malcolm's child, is asleep in it, slumped to one side. Roy, astride his tricycle, faces Bea. Malcolm imagines himself as two miniatures – two perspiring stepfathers – on the child's eyes. Roy's eyes are mirrors. He never looks at you: there is no you. "Look at me," you say, and Roy looks over there.

The family scene set up and waiting for Malcolm consists of a fight for life. Roy, who is afraid of mosquitoes, has refused to ride his tricycle through a swarm of gnats. He is at a dead stop, with a foot on the path. His dark curls stick to his forehead. His resistance to Bea lies in his silence and stubbornness, or in sudden vandalism. Last weekend he snapped the head off every spaced, prized, counted, daffodil in reach of the playground. Malcolm heard Bea say, "I'll kill you!" He walked up to them – as he is doing now – trying to show the neighbors nothing was wrong. Bea is moved by an audience; Malcolm would like to be invisible. He drew Bea's arms back and Roy fell like a sack. She was crying. "Ah, he's not mine," she said. "He can't be. They made a mistake in the hospital." Only then did she notice Roy had been biting. She showed Malcolm her arm, mutely. He looked at the small oval, her stigmata. "He can't be mine," she said. "I had a lovely boy but some other mother got him. They gave me Roy by mistake."

"Listen," said Malcolm. "Never say that again."

Bea, suddenly cheerful, said, "But Roy's said worse than that to *me!*"

"Say right now, so he can hear you, that he's yours and there was no mistake."

Of course Roy was hers! She said so, laughing. He was hers like the crickets she kept in plastic cages and fed on scraps of lettuce the size of Ruth's fingernails; like the hedgehog she raised and trained to drink milk out of a wineglass; like the birds she buys on the Quai de la Corse in Paris and turns out to freeze or starve or be pecked to death. It is always after she has said something harebrained, on the very limit of reason, that she seems most appealing. Her outrageousness is part of the coloration of their marriage, their substitute for a plot. "Poor kid," Malcolm will suddenly say, not about the wronged child but of Bea. It is easy for Bea to crave this pity of his, to feel unloved, bullied, to turn to him, though she thinks he is a bully too.

A rotary sprinkler now pivots on its stem. Roy is protected from Bea by rainbows. Bea, waiting for Roy to surrender, heaves her slight weight onto one foot. Her dress follows the line of her spine. "Honestly, Roy, you're just a coward, you know," she says. Accustomed to making animals trust her, she advances now almost without seeming to move. "Afraid of some old bugs! When I was your age I wasn't scared of anything." Bea has passed the lime tree. Her dress is in full sun. She will drop the stool and the book and shoot through rainbows. She will suddenly shove Roy off his tricycle and slap him twice, coming and going. She will drag the tricycle away and leave him there to mull over his defeat. No, none of it happens: Roy suddenly comes to life, pushes forward to meet her. When she turns back with him, she sees Malcolm. His whole family comes toward him now, and Bea is smiling.

A grievance overtakes her welcoming look. Something has come up. What now? On the way indoors she tells him: Leonard and Verna Baum, their closest friends, the only Canadians they know here, are not going to Belgium. Leonard is going to Germany, with the Army. Her interest in having Canadian friends, like her interest in history, is new. She does not always recognize a Canadian when she hears one.

"What's your father?" she said to a stray little boy who, like a puppy, followed Roy home one day. Just like that: not even "What's your name?"

"He's an Ayer Force Mayn," said the innocent, in syllables that should have rung like gongs to Bea.

"Well, Roy happens to be Canadian," said Bea haughtily, demonstrating how you put down any American aged about five.

By mistake, Bea has packed and shipped to Belgium pots and pans that belong to their landlord. She forgot to send their trunk of winter clothes. Ruth is back to baby food, and Roy (when he will eat, lives on marmalade sandwiches. Malcolm and Bea will have their dinner at the local bric-a-brac snack bar called Drug Diane. He knows, because she seems so comfortable in this ramshackle way of living, that she must have had something like it when she was a child. As if he had never seen her house, never known her father, she sometimes describes a house and a garden and a set of parents. "I liked it when we first came over to France and lived right in Versailles," she will say. "It was more like home."

The desire to be rid of Bea overtakes Malcolm at hopeless times, when he can do nothing about it. If she left him now, this second, it would settle every problem he ever has had in his life — even the problem of the winter clothes left behind. Bea, questioned about it, says she has never wanted to leave *him*. Sometimes she says, "All right, you take Roy, I'll keep Ruth." She forgets Roy isn't his. She thinks her difficulties would be resolved if she just knew something more about men. All she knows is Malcolm. The father of Roy hardly counted. She slept with him "only the once," as she puts it, and hated it. She warned Malcolm the other day: she would have an affair. If she waits too long, no one will want her. When Malcolm said, "With Leonard?" she burst out laughing. A few seconds later, evidently thinking of herself in bed with Leonard, she laughed again. "*Him*," she said. "It's too easy. Anybody can have him. They say any girl that ever worked in his office ..." But her interest dies quickly. Malcolm has seldom heard her gossiping. Gossip implies at least a theory about behavior, and Bea has none. "Anyway, Leonard's losing his hair and all," she said, seriously.

So, she has an idea about a lover, Malcolm can see that, but it is still someone unreal.

Bea hasn't asked what Malcolm and Leonard were doing in Paris today, Saturday. She knows that Leonard rang just after lunch and said, "Can you come in and get me? I can't drive my car." He gave the address of a hospital.

"I think Leonard's had a heart attack," he said to Bea. "Don't say anything to Verna yet."

But when Malcolm found Leonard he discovered that Leonard's Danish girl, Karin, had cut her wrists with a fruit knife – one of those shallow cuts, with the knife held the wrong way. She isn't dead, but her stomach has been pumped out for good measure, and she is tied to her hospital bed. The police have Leonard's name.

Bea hasn't even said, "What was wrong with Leonard?" or "what did he want?" – which means she knows. If she knows, then Verna knows. Leonard is at this moment telling a carefully invented story to Verna, who may pretend to be taken in.

Bea sits very calmly on the balcony of the apartment, with Ruth in a pen at her feet, and waits for Malcolm to bring her a drink.

"Leonard's done a lot of lying to Verna," she says, out of the blue. "But I'm the sort of person no man would ever lie to."

She sits in a deck chair, serene, hair pulled into a dark ponytail so tense her black eyes look Asian. She means raw lying, such as a man's saying he is going out to buy cigarettes when he really wants to send a telegram. She would never think of a more subtle form, and might not consider it lying. She truly thinks that her face, her way of being invite the truth.

Malcolm is convinced he will never have an idea about Bea
until he understands her idea of herself. Of course Bea has an
idea; what woman hasn't? In her mind's eye she is always advanc-
ing, she is walking between lanes of trees on a June day. She is
small and slight in her dreams, as she is in life. She advances
toward herself, as if half of her were a mirror. In the vision she
carries Ruth, her prettiest baby, newly born, or a glass goblet, or
a bunch of roses. Whatever she holds must be untouched, fresh,
scarcely breathed on.

What is her destination in this dream? Is it Malcolm?

She looks taken aback. It is herself. She *is* final. She can't go
farther than herself, and Malcolm can't go any farther than Bea.

Malcolm, pouring straight gin, thinks "infantile" and then
"conceited." Having her entire attention, he sits on the balcony
railing and tries to tell her that no one is a destination, and no
marriage simply endures: it is difficult to begin, and difficult to
end. (Her dark eyes are full of love. She takes this for a declaration.)
The only question, the correct question, about any marriage – the
Baums', for instance – would be "What is it about?" Every marriage
is about something. It must have a plot. Sometimes it has a puzzling
or incoherent plot. If you saw it acted out, it would bore you. "Turn
it off," you would say. "No one *I* know lives that way." It has a
mood, a setting, a vocabulary, bone structure, a climate.

All Bea says to that is "Well, no man would ever lie to me."

It is not true that Bea put pressure on me to marry her, Malcolm
decides. In her cloudiest rages she says, "You were maneuvered!
I lied to you from the beginning! If that's what you think, why
don't you come out with it?" But I have never thought it. There
was no beginning. There were springs, and sources, but miles
apart, uncharted. It would be like crossing a continent on foot to
find them all. I would find some of them long before I knew she
existed. The beginning, to her, would need a date to it – the day
we met. I had been in Canada four months then, and was still
without friends or money, waiting for a job I had been promised
in London. Friends and money – I thought I was coming to a
place where it would be easy to find both. One afternoon – a
Saturday? – I was picked up in a movie by two giggling girls.
Outside, I saw they were dumpy, narrow-eyed. They were twins,
they told me, named Pattie and Claire. In that Western city every
face bore a racial stamp, and because this was new to me I kept
asking people what they were. The girls shrugged. They were
called Griffith, whatever that was worth. Their father had come
out here from Cape Breton Island after their mother died. I
understood they might be blueberry blondes – Indians. I was still

so ignorant then that I thought you could say this. The poisonous hate in their eyes lasted two or three seconds. My accent saved me. My English accent, so loathed, so resented out here, seemed hilarious to Pattie and Claire. I was hardly a generation away from signs reading, "Men Wanted. No British Need Apply," but the girls didn't know that. They must have been fifteen, sixteen. They wanted me to take them somewhere, but on a Saturday afternoon there was nowhere to go, nowhere I could take them, except my one-room flat ("suite" the girls called it). They drank rye and tap water, and told dirty stories, and laughed, and opened all the drawers and cupboards. They weren't tarts. They didn't want money. It was their idea of a normal afternoon. They wanted me to ring up some bachelor friend, but I didn't know anyone well enough. The upshot of the day was that they took me home with them. It was about eight o'clock; the sun was still high and hot.

"When you meet our Dad, just say you've always known us," said Pattie.

"No, say we went to see you for a summer job," said Claire. "Anyway, he won't ask."

They lived in a dark-green painted house behind a dried-up garden. Nearly blocking the entrance was a pram with a sleeping baby in it. His lips were slightly parted, his face flushed and mosquito-bitten. The baby's rasped thighs, his dark damp curls, the curdled-milk stain on the pillow had the print of that moment, as if I had already left Canada (I was, already, trying to do just that) and was getting ready to remember Bea, whom I hadn't met. I memorized the bright hot summer night, the stunning season that was new to me, a kind of endless afternoon, the street that seemed neither town nor country, the curtain at the window perfectly still behind a screen. The pram, the baby, and, once we were indoors, even the Seven Dwarfs on the fake chimneypiece, displayed like offerings in a museum, seemed reality, something important, from which my upbringing had protected me. I understood I had met the right people too late, for Canada had been a mistake, and it was already part of the past in my mind. The living room was spotless and cool; the linoleum on the floor gleamed pink and green. Upon it two dark-red carpets lay at pointless but evidently carefully chosen angles. Plants – dark furry begonias and a number of climbers – grew on the windowsill. A cat lay curled before the logs of the fire, exactly as if there were a real blaze. We did not stop here; the girls led me down a passage and into the kitchen. I remember a television set with the sound turned off. On the screen a man wearing a Stetson leaned against a fence, telling us to fly, fly, because the skies were falling

– if the sound had been on, he would merely have been singing a song. On one wall was a row of cages with canaries, and there were still more green plants. We had walked into a quarrel. When two people are at right angles to each other they can only be quarrelling. I saw for the first time Bea's profile, and then heard her voice. The voices of most Canadian girls grated on me; they talked from a space between the teeth and the lips, as if breath had no part in speech. But the voices of all three Griffith girls were low-pitched and warm. The girls' father sat at the table drinking beer, leaning on a spread-out newspaper. Behind him was the photograph of a good-looking young man in Army uniform. At first I thought it must be his son.

"All Cath'lic girls are called Pat and Claire" was one of the first things Bea ever said to me. "I got my mother's name. *Beetriss.*" She mocked me, looking at me, gently exaggerating the way she and her sisters sounded, so as to make slight fun of me.

What did I fall in love with? A taciturn man who was anchored in the last war; two silly girls; quiet Bea. We ate quantities of toast and pickles and drank beer. "Come back any time," said Mr. Griffith, without smiling. Bea saw me out.

"I like it here," I said carefully, for I had learned something about the touchiness of Canadians, "but I may be going over to Nato. Somebody's pulling strings for me." I was diffident, in case she thought I thought I was being clever.

"That's like the Army, isn't it?"

"Not for me. I'm a civilian."

"I hope we'll see something of you before you go," she said. "But we're not very interesting for you."

"I love your family," I think I said. I said something else about "kitchen warmth."

"You like that, do you? I'd like to get out of it. But I'm stuck, and no one can help me. Well, I've got used to it. I mean, I guess I've got used to kitchens."

I wasn't the first person in her life. There was the father of Roy. What about him? "Oh, he was scared," she said. "Scared of what he'd done." She seemed curiously innocent – did not understand her sisters' jokes, or the words that sounded like other words and made them laugh. When I knew I was leaving, a few months after that, I felt I had no right to leave her behind. Even so, there was no beginning. Talking about her mother one day, we came close to talking about a common future.

"She died," Bea said, "but not at home. After the twins were born she thought everyone had it in for her, that Dad was getting secret messages over the radio, all that. She thought the cushions on the back of the sofa were watching her. She tried to drown the twins. Dad thinks we'll be like her. He thinks we already are."

"He's wrong," I said. "No one knows much about that kind of illness, but it isn't inherited." I went on – cautiously now, "Was your mother Indian? Indians are often paranoid, for some reason."

"No. Would you mind if she was?"

Nothing would have let her believe how interesting, how exotic I would have found it. "I'd mind other things more," I said. "Hemophilia, for instance."

It was exactly as if I were asking her to marry me. She looked at me, and decided not to trust me. "My mother was French-Canadian," she said. "Dad's Irish and Welsh."

I may have gone on talking then; I may have compressed my feelings about leaving her into a question. We were in a restaurant. She was a slow eater, never ate much, left half of everything on her plate. Now she stopped altogether and said quietly, "All right. I mean, yes, I want to. More than anything. But do something for me. Write it down."

"What do you want me to write? A proposal?"

"Yes. Say it in writing."

"Why?" I said. "Do you think I'm going to take it back?"

"No. I want it for Dad. Date it from three months back, so he won't be able to say I held a gun at your head."

"What is this?" I said. What's it about?"

"Well, I'm pregnant," said Bea. "I was afraid if I told you you'd say it wasn't yours. Anyway there's nothing I could force you to do. There's no way of forcing a man to do anything. I could only wait for you to make up your mind about me. Dad thinks we're already engaged. I told him that to keep him quiet. I didn't want him to go down to your office and that."

The thought of what had been going on made my blood stop. I had never seen a change in him; there were always the same meals in the kitchen, the early supper, the noiseless television, the twins' laughter. Then Bea said, "I'll get rid of this one if you want, because of your new job and all. I suppose I can't keep my cat?"

I had expected "Can I keep Roy?"

"You can have another," I said. We seemed to be talking about the same thing.

Mr. Griffith asked me a few questions. One was "Been married before?" and another "What about the boy?"

"I'm adopting Roy," I said. This had not come up, except in my mind. Bea must have been waiting, once again, for me to decide. I remember that she looked completely astonished as I said it; not grateful, not even relieved. When she gave my written proposal to her father, her remark was "Don't say I never gave you anything for your old age."

It was nearly our farewell evening. We were around the kitchen table drinking wine I had brought. He read the proposal, made a ball of it, and threw it in the sink. Bea's face went dark, as if a curtain had been blown across the light. It was a dark look I saw later on Roy when he was learning to stand up to her. Mr. Griffith said, "Let's get back to something serious," and hoisted the bottle before him. His hand shook, and that made Bea smile. When she saw she had made him tremble, she smiled. That is all I know about her father and Bea.

Before we left she took her cat away to be destroyed. She had already stopped watering the plants, and the birdcages were empty. By the time we were married and she went away to start a new life with me, the household, the life in it, had been killed, or had committed suicide; anyway, it was dead.

Earlier today, in the tunnel of Saint-Cloud, between the western limit of Paris and the autoroute, stalled in Saturday traffic, Leonard Baum talked about his wife. The Nato removal coincides, for the Baums, with a fresh start. They have come to a "When all's said and done" stage of marriage. When all's said and done, it hasn't worked out too badly. When all's said and done, we did a good job with the children. We see absolutely eye to eye where the children are concerned. There's always that.

They are a raggle-taggle international family. They have been in Denmark, and in the Congo. Unless you know many varieties of North American accent (Bea knows none, as Malcolm can easily prove), they could be from anywhere. The girls, with their perpetual sniffles, their droopy skirts, their washed-out slacks, and their wide backsides, seem reasonably Canadian to Malcolm, though Bea says she has never seen anything like them in her life before.

"I feel like hell about Karin," Leonard said, "but that's what she wants me to feel. Suicide is always against somebody. She knew I wasn't responsible for her. I couldn't be. I am responsible for Martha and Susan and ..." He forgot his wife's name. So did Malcolm. Both men searched for her name. Malcolm tried to pretend he was looking at her, straight across a room. She was tall and fair, her hair was pinned up, she looked like Malcolm's idea of a transfigured horse and like his idea of a missionary. *"Verna!"* said Leonard. "I'm responsible for Verna." Leonard now spoke so plainly that he must be suffering from shock.

"When Verna turned Catholic, she said she didn't want any more sex. She didn't want any more children, and she had this new religion. Once there was no more of that to argue about, we got on better than before. I never missed a weekend at home and I never missed a meal. I didn't want my home to fall apart. I gave Karin as much time as I could. She poured all her life into the time I gave her. My life today makes no more sense than a sweeper's in India. I've been writing my own obituary: 'He left two young daughters and a hard-up wife.' 'His many friends were unanimous – the guy was a bastard.' 'All his life he thought he was going to Pichipoi.' You know what Pichipoi means?"

He's going to talk like this all the way home, Malcolm thought. He has talked about himself before now, but himself thirty years ago. We know about his mother and his father and his mother's cherry jam. He never talked about Verna, any more than I would talk about Bea. I know about Pichipoi. It was the name of an unknown place. The Jews in Paris invented it. It was their destination, but it was a place that might not be any worse than the present. Some of them thought it might even be better, because no one had come back yet to say it was worse. They couldn't imagine it. It was half magic. Sometimes in their transit camps they'd say, "Let's get to Pichipoi and get it over with." Leonard wasn't here. He must have been in Canada, in college. I was what – four, five? Roy's age? Leonard is still in control of his life. He was in control when he chose Verna over Karin. There is no more terror and mystery in Leonard's life than in mine. Now he thinks he has no control. His life is running away with him, because the girl tried to kill herself, the French have kicked us out and they hate us, the police have his name, he has to face Verna, and the future can't be worse than the way he feels now, stalled in the tunnel of Saint-Cloud. He shouldn't say "Pichipoi." It was a word that children invented. That makes it entirely magic. It is a sacred word. But it was such a long time ago, as long ago as the Children's Crusade. Leonard is generous; he knows he is presuming. He is on sacred ground, with his shoes on. *They* were on their way to dying. If every person thought his life was a deportation, that he had no say in where he was going, or what would happen once he got there, the air would be filled with invisible trains and we would collide in our dreams.

Leonard said, "I feel vindictive, now we're leaving. This is a private conversation, so I don't mind telling you. I get pleasure knowing a recession is on the way. When I see the sports cars with '*À Vendre*' in the windshield and I hear that cleaning women are coming round now and asking for work, I think of how we were gouged. Four hundred a month we paid for that dump. The phone never worked. We paid extra for hot water and heating and for using the elevator. Verna keeps asking, 'What's going to happen now?' Verna's very intelligent, but she asks me these questions, like 'Why are there wars?' She said, 'Leonard, explain to Martha and Susan about the new patterns of history. The girls are very interested in current affairs.' 'It's easy,' I said. 'Say Uganda has a project. They want to put a man on the moon. They'll apply to France.' 'Leonard, are you being serious?' Verna says.''

Leonard knew he didn't have to say, "Don't repeat anything I've told you." He simply said, "Thanks a lot, I've talked your ear off." The shopping center of Résidence Diane looked like a giant motel. Where the lawns began, midges danced under the trees. Three American wives, in bare feet, holding mugs of coffee, stood on the holy grass. The *gardien* was furiously whistling, like a lifeguard who for some reason was unable to launch a boat. He stood at the edge of the grass and the three wives did not look at him; they stood laughing together with their mugs of coffee. Malcolm and Leonard saw something Malcolm, at least, had never seen before: a grown person dancing with rage. The *gardien* could not stop blowing his whistle; it seemed to be part of his breath. His arms were stiff with temper and he danced, there, on the path. Leonard raised his shoulders. He looked at Malcolm, and all at once seemed slightly foreign and droll.

In the midst of her packing and sorting and of Leonard's explanation, Verna Baum has remembered Malcolm and Bea. The ring at the door now is Verna, pushing a waterproof shopping cart. In it is an electric iron than cannot be plugged in anywhere except Hamilton, Ontario, two pairs of hand-painted porcelain doorknobs bought in the Paris Flea Market, a souvenir chessboard from Florence and about thirteen chessmen, a shoebox filled with old Christmas cards and Kodachrome holiday memories – these are for Roy. Roy will sit on the floor peering at them and sorting them over and over.

Bea, who has rubbish problems too, looks out of the corner of her eye and says, "Just leave it all in the hall."

Verna has also come because she wants to tell Bea exactly what her mistakes are as a mother. She may never see Bea and Malcolm again. They will exchange a letter or two, then Christmas greetings, then nothing at all. She sits down in the kitchen. Her long missionary horseface blocks Malcolm's view of Bea. Verna accepts sherry (half a tumbler), which she thinks has less alcohol in it than beer. Does she know that Leonard's girl tried to kill herself, that Leonard was too scared afterward to drive his own car? All she chooses to say is that she studied psychology in an American university and is in a position to analyze Roy, pass censure on Bea, and caution Malcolm. He understands her to say "I was a Syke-Major" and for a moment takes it to mean her maiden name. Bea is making the children passive, Verna says. Roy will be a homosexual and Ruth will be sucking her thumb at thirty-five unless Malcolm at once confiscates the stroller and the tricycle. Verna's words are "I want you to hear this, Mac. It's time somebody around here spoke up. Those two little kids should be walking on their own four feet. Roy doesn't trust you. He never asks a question. When Martha was hardly older than Roy I told her about you-know and she said, 'How long does it take?' She trusted me then and she trusts me now."

"If Ruth ever asks me anything like that, I'll belt her one," says Bea. "It's none of her damned business."

"It will have to be her business at some point," says Verna.

"Well, her business is none of mine. I don't want my own daughter coming round telling me it's too much or not enough."

"Your reactions are so aggressive, Bea," says Verna. "I wish you'd have someone take a look at Roy. I'm glad Mac's here, because I want him to hear this. Mac, Leonard is very worried about Roy. He's a very sick child. He's an autistic child. You know that, don't you?"

"Autistic my foot," says Bea. "He's bone lazy, that's all. He talks when he wants to."

Malcolm, standing with his back to the sink, half sitting on the edge of it, slides along to where he has a better view of Bea. Verna has a red sherry flush right up to the edge of her eyes. "Mac never looks at Ruthie," she says. "You wouldn't know she had a father. If intelligent parents like you two can't do the right things, what can you expect from people like the Congolese? I don't mean that racially. They make mistakes over weaning and that, but they have every excuse. Even our parents had an excuse. They didn't know anything."

"Mine did," says Bea. "My mother was a saint and my father worshipped her. We were very, very happy. Three girls. When I was thirteen my mother said to me, 'All men are filth.'" Bea laughs.

Verna swings round to Malcolm as if to say, "Now do you see what's wrong with Bea as a mother?"

Bea, glancing at Malcolm, says, "I can't talk openly if somebody thinks I'm telling lies."

"Oh, Bea, I don't!" This is Verna, but who cares what Verna says? The play is back to Malcolm and Bea.

Purified, exalted, because she has just realized what a good mother she is; sensing that Malcolm at this moment either wants to leave her or know something more about her, so that the marriage is at extremes of tension again, Bea calls happily, "Roy, there's a whole box of pictures for you in the hall."

She cuts the crusts off Roy's sandwiches and carries the plate to the living room. A puppet show is adjusted for him on the hired television and he is told to turn the sound off the instant it ends. Bea comes back and sits on a kitchen stool with her skirt at the top of her thighs. She grows excited, delaying Verna, keeping her because Malcolm wants her to go.

To say she had not wanted her children, as Verna sometimes hints, is a lie, Bea argues. She wanted a boy, then a girl – just what she was given. You have to take into account how Roy was conceived. She hardly knew the man. She never tried to hide Roy, or pretend he wasn't hers, though under the circumstances she might have been pardoned. She read Spock and gave Roy calcium and Vitamin D. "Mystery" had been her word for Roy unborn. But why hadn't anyone warned her the Mystery was so very ugly? Birth was ugly. Death was another ugly mystery. Her mother, dying . . .

"Now, Bea, that's just brooding over the past." Verna again.

But most of everything is just dirt and pain, says Bea. When she was pregnant with Ruth, she knew there was no mystery, she knew what to expect. She knew Malcolm wanted a child just to satisfy his ego, and because he felt guilty over something, and she woke him up in the night to say, "Look at how ugly you've made me."

Their lives are spread out for Verna like the wet tea leaves in the sink; like debris after a crash. No secret, dreaded destination could be worse than this. He leaves the room, walking between the two women, who seem too rapt to notice him. In the living room Roy is playing with Kodachromes, squinting, holding them up to the light. Malcolm bends down, as if helping the child. He sees the Baums' holiday in Spain, the Baums around a Christmas tree. Roy does not seem to notice Malcolm, but then he seldom does.

Neither Malcolm nor Roy heard the music rise and become poignant.

"Oh, *damn!*" Bea darts into the room. Roy kneels, staring at the screen. A woman lies on a large old-fashioned bed, surrounded by weeping children. Bea says, "The goddam mother's died. Roy shouldn't be looking at that."

Roy will speak now that Bea is here: "It's sad."

She raises her hand. "You know you're only supposed to

watch the kids' programs." Her hand changes direction. She snaps off the sound.

Verna, looking as unhappy as Malcolm has ever seen any woman in his life, trails after Bea. In snatches, sometimes drowned in Ruth's bath water, he hears from sad Verna that it is depressing to live in rooms where half the furniture is gone. It reduces the feeling of stability. Tomorrow we'll be gone from here. No one will miss us. There will be homes for twelve hundred people now on a waiting list. As if a rich country could not house its people any other way. They will pay half the rents we are paying now. The landlords will paint and clean as they never had to for us. I'm not sad to be leaving.

A door is slammed. Behind the door, Verna whispers. Leonard's story is being retold.

Malcolm stood up as Bea came into the room. He said, "Don't come to Belgium." A blind movement of Roy at his feet drew his attention. "All right," he said. "I know you're there. Where do *you* want to go? Who do you want to go with, I mean?"

The child formed "Her" with his lips.

"You're sure? It beats me, but we won't discuss it now."

As if looking for help, Bea turned to the screen. Silently, washed by a driving rain (a defect of transmission), the President of the Republic's long bald head floated up the steps of a war memorial. The frames shot up wildly, spinning, like a window shade. Bea stood staring at the mute news, which seemed to be about stalled cars and middle-aged faces. Roy looked at his mother. His brow was furrowed, like an old man's.

I should have told Leonard, Malcolm thought: The real meaning of Pichipoi is being alone. It means each of us flung separately – Roy, Ruth, Bea – into a room without windows. It can't be done. It can't be permitted, I mean. No jumping off the train. I nearly made it, he said to himself. And then what?

"No," he said aloud.

A sigh escaped the child, as if he knew the denial was an affirmation, that it meant "Yes, I am still here, we are all of us together."

Breathing again, the child began his mindless sorting of old pictures and Christmas cards.

"Well, Roy," said Malcolm, as if answering some comment, "half the people in the world don't even get as far as I did just now."

That was the end of it – the end of the incident. It turned into a happy evening, one of their last in France.

The Prodigal Parent

We sat on the screened porch of Rhoda's new house, which was close to the beach on the ocean side of Vancouver Island. I had come here in a straight line, from the East, and now that I could not go any farther without running my car into the sea, any consideration of wreckage and loss, or elegance of behavior, or debts owed (not of money, of my person) came to a halt. A conqueror in a worn blazer and a regimental tie, I sat facing my daughter, listening to her voice – now describing, now complaining – as if I had all the time in the world. Her glance drifted round the porch, which still contained packing cases. She could not do, or take in, a great deal at once. I have light eyes, like Rhoda's, but mine have been used for summing up.

Rhoda had bought this house and the cabins round it and a strip of maimed landscape with her divorce settlement. She hoped to make something out of the cabins, renting them weekends to respectable people who wanted a quiet place to drink. "Dune Vista" said a sign, waiting for someone to nail it to a tree. I wondered how I would fit in here – what she expected me to do. She still hadn't said. After the first formal Martinis she had made to mark my arrival, she began drinking rye, which she preferred. It was sweeter, less biting than the whiskey I remembered in my youth, and I wondered if my palate or its composition had changed. I started to say so, and my daughter said, "Oh, God, your accent again! You know what I thought you said now? 'Oxbow was a Cheswick charmer.' "

"No, no. Nothing like that."

"Try not sounding so British," she said.

"I don't, you know."

"Well, you don't sound Canadian."

The day ended suddenly, as if there had been a partial eclipse. In the new light I could see my daughter's face and hands.

"I guess I'm different from all my female relatives," she said. She had been comparing herself with her mother, and with half sisters she hardly knew. "I don't despise men, like Joanne does. There's always somebody. There's one now, in fact. I'll tell you about him. I'll tell you the whole thing, and you say what you think. It's a real mess. He's Irish, he's married, and he's got no money. Four children. He doesn't sleep with his wife."

"Surely there's an age limit for this?" I said. "By my count, you must be twenty-eight or -nine now."

"Don't I know it." She looked into the dark trees, darkened still more by the screens, and said without rancor, "It's not my fault. I wouldn't keep on falling for lushes and phonies if you hadn't been that way."

I put my glass down on the packing case she had pushed before me, and said, "I am not, I never was, and I never could be an alcoholic."

Rhoda seemed genuinely shocked. "I never said *that*. I never heard you had to be put in a hospital or anything, like my stepdaddy. But you used to stand me on a table when you had parties, Mother told me, and I used to dance to 'Piccolo Pete.' What happened to that record, I wonder? One of your wives most likely got it in lieu of alimony. But may God strike us both dead here and now if I ever said you were alcoholic." It must have been to her a harsh, clinical word, associated with straitjackets. "I'd like you to meet him," she said. "But I never know when he'll turn up. He's Harry Pay. The writer," she said, rather primly. "Somebody said he was a new-type Renaissance Man – I mean, he doesn't just sit around, he's a judo expert. He could throw *you* down in a second."

"Is he Japanese?"

"God, no. What makes you say that? I already told you what he is. He's white. Quite white, *entirely* white I mean."

"Well – I could hardly have guessed."

"You shouldn't have to guess," she said. "The name should be enough. He's famous. Round here, anyway."

"I'm sorry," I said. "I've been away so many years. Would you write the name down for me? So I can see how it's spelled?"

"I'll do better than that." It touched me to see the large girl she was suddenly moving so lightly. I heard her slamming doors in the living room behind me. She had been clumsy as a child, in every gesture like a wild creature caught. She came back to me with a dun folder out of which spilled loose pages, yellow and smudged. She thrust it at me and, as I groped for my spectacles, turned on an overhead light. "You read this," she said, "and I'll go make us some sandwiches, while I still can. Otherwise we'll break into another bottle and never eat anything. This is something he never shows *anyone*."

"It is my own life exactly," I said when she returned with the sandwiches, which she set awkwardly down. "At least, so far as school in England is concerned. Cold beds, cold food, cold lavatories. Odd that anyone still finds it interesting. There must be twenty written like it every year. The revolting school, the homosexual master, then a girl—saved!"

"Homo *what*?" said Rhoda, clawing the pages. "It's possible. He has a dirty mind, actually."

"Really? Has he ever asked you to do anything unpleasant, such as type his manuscripts?"

"Certainly not. He's got a perfectly good wife for that."

When I laughed, she looked indignant. She had given a serious answer to what she thought was a serious question. Our conversations were always like this – collisions.

"Well?" she said.

"Get rid of him."

She looked at me and sank down on the arm of my chair. I felt her breath on my face, light as a child's. She said, "I was waiting for something. I was waiting all day for you to say something personal, but I didn't think it would be that. Get rid of him? He's all I've got."

"All the more reason. You can do better."

"Who, for instance?" she said. "You? You're no use to me."

She had sent for me. I had come to Rhoda from her half sister Joanne, in Montreal. Joanne had repatriated me from Europe, with an air passage to back the claim. In a new bare apartment, she played severe sad music that was like herself. We ate at a scrubbed table the sort of food that can be picked up in the hand. She was the richest of my children, through her mother, but I recognized in her guarded, slanting looks the sort of avarice and fear I think of as a specific of women. One look seemed meant to tell me, "You waltzed off, old boy, but look at me now," though I could not believe she had wanted me only for that. "I'll never get married" was a remark that might have given me a lead. "I won't have anyone to lie to me, or make a fool of me, or spend my money for me." She waited to see what I would say. She had just come into this money.

"Feeling as you do, you probably shouldn't marry," I said. She looked at me as Rhoda was looking now. "Don't expect too much from men," I said.

"Oh, I don't!" she cried, so eagerly I knew she always would. The cheap sweet Ontario wine she favored and the smell of paint in her new rooms and the raw meals and incessant music combined to give me a violent attack of claustrophobia. It was probably the most important conversation we had.

"We can't have any more conversation now," said Rhoda. "Not after that. It's the end. You've queered it. I should have known. Well, eat your sandwiches now that I've made them."

"Would it seem petulant if, at this point, I did not eat a tomato sandwich?" I said.

"Don't be funny. I can't understand what you're saying anyway."

"If you don't mind, my dear," I said, "I'd rather be on my way."

"What do you mean, on your way? For one thing, you're in no condition to drive. Where d'you think you're going?"

"I can't very well go that way," I said, indicating the ocean I could not see. "I can't go back as I've come."

"It was a nutty thing, to come by car," she said. "It's not even all that cheap."

"As I can't go any farther," I said, "I shall stay. Not here, but perhaps not far."

"Doing what? What *can* you do? We've never been sure."

"I can get a white cane and walk the streets of towns. I can ask people to help me over busy intersections and then beg for money."

"You're kidding."

"I'm not. I shall say – let me think – I shall say I've had a mishap, lost my wallet, pension check not due for another week, postal strike delaying it even more – "

"That won't work. They'll send you to the welfare. You should see how we hand out welfare around here."

"I'm counting on seeing it," I said.

"You can't. It would look – " She narrowed her eyes and said, "If you're trying to shame me, forget it. Someone comes and says, 'That poor old blind bum says he's your father,' I'll just answer, 'Yes, what about it?'"

"My sight *is* failing, actually."

"There's welfare for that, too."

"We're at cross-purposes," I said. "I'm not looking for money."

"Then waja come here for?"

"Because Regan sent me on to Goneril, I suppose."

"That's a lie. Don't try to make yourself big. Nothing's ever happened to you."

"Well, in my uneventful life," I began, but my mind answered for me, "No, nothing." There are substitutes for incest but none whatever for love. What I needed now was someone who knew nothing about me and would never measure me against a promise or a past. I blamed myself, not for anything I had said but for having remembered too late what Rhoda was like. She was positively savage as an infant, though her school tamed her later on. I remember sitting opposite her when she was nine – she in an unbecoming tartan coat – while she slowly and seriously ate a large plate of ice cream. She was in London on a holiday with her mother, and as I happened to be there with my new family I gave her a day.

"Every Monday we have Thinking Day," she had said, of her school. "We think about the Brownies and the Baden-Powells and sometimes Jesus and all."

"Do you, really?"

"I can't *really*," Rhoda had said. "I never met any of them."

"Are you happy, at least?" I said, to justify my belief that no one was ever needed. But the savage little girl had become an extremely careful one.

That afternoon, at a matinée performance of "Peter Pan," I went to sleep. The slaughter of the pirates woke me, and as I turned, confident, expecting her to be rapt, I encountered a face of refusal. She tucked her lips in, folded her hands, and shrugged away when I helped her into a taxi.

"I'm sorry, I should not have slept in your company," I said. "It was impolite."

"It wasn't that," she burst out. "It was 'Peter Pan.' I hated it. It wasn't what I expected. You could see the wires. Mrs. Darling didn't look right. She didn't have a lovely dress on – only an old pink thing like a nightgown. Nana wasn't a real dog, it was a lady. I couldn't understand anything they said. Peter Pan wasn't a boy, he had bosoms."

"I noticed that, too," I said. "There must be a sound traditional reason for it. Perhaps Peter is really a mother figure."

"No, he's a *boy*."

I intercepted, again, a glance of stony denial – of me? We had scarcely met.

"I couldn't understand. They all had English accents," she complained.

For some reason that irritated me. "What the hell did you expect them to have?" I said.

"When I was little," said the nine-year-old, close to tears now, "I thought they were all Canadian."

The old car Joanne had given me was down on the beach, on the hard sand, with ribbons of tire tracks behind it as a sign of life, and my luggage locked inside. It had been there a few hours and already it looked abandoned – an old heap someone had left to rust among the lava rock. The sky was lighter than it had seemed from the porch. I picked up a sand dollar, chalky and white, with the tree of life on its underside, and as I slid it in my pocket, for luck, I felt between my fingers a rush of sand. I had spoken the truth, in part; the landscape through which I had recently travelled still shuddered before my eyes and I would not go back. I heard, then saw, Rhoda running down to where I stood. Her hair, which she wore gathered up in a bun, was half down, and she breathed,

running, with her lips apart. For the first time I remembered something of the way she had seemed as a child, something more than an
anecdote. She clutched my arm and said, "Why did you say I should
ditch him? *Why*?"

I disengaged my arm, because she was hurting me, and said,
"He can only give you bad habits."

"At my age?"

"Any age. Dissimulation. Voluntary barrenness – someone else
has had his children. Playing house, a Peter-and-Wendy game, a life
he would never dare try at home. There's the real meaning of Peter,
by the way." But she had forgotten.

She clutched me again, to steady herself, and said, "I'm old
enough to know everything. I'll soon be in my thirties. That's all
I care to say."

It seemed to me I had only recently begun making grave
mistakes. I had until now accepted all my children, regardless of
who their mothers were. The immortality I had imagined had not
been in them but on the faces of women in love. I saw, on the
dark beach, Rhoda's mother, the soft hysterical girl whose fatal
"I am pregnant" might have enmeshed me for life.

I said, "I wish they would find a substitute for immortality."

"I'm working on it," said Rhoda, grimly, seeming herself
again. She let go my arm and watched me unlock the car door.
"You'd have hated it here," she said, then, pleading, "You
wouldn't want to live here like some charity case – have me
support you?"

"I'd be enchanted," I said.

"No, no, you'd hate it," she said. "I couldn't look after you. I
haven't got time. And you'd keep thinking I should do better
than *him*, and the truth is I can't. You wouldn't want to end up
like some old relation, fed in the kitchen and all."

"I don't know," I said. "It would be new."

"Oh," she cried, with what seemed unnecessary despair, "what
did you come for? All right," she said. "I give up. You asked for
it. You can stay. I mean, I'm inviting you. You can sit around
and say, 'Oxbow was a Cheswick charmer,' all day and when
someone says to me, 'Where jer father get his accent?' I'll say, 'It
was a whole way of life.' But remember, you're not a prisoner or
anything, around here. You can go whenever you don't like the
food. I mean, if you don't like it, don't come to me and say, 'I don't
like the food.' You're not my prisoner," she yelled, though her face
was only a few inches from mine. "You're only my father. That's all
you are."

The Wedding Ring

On my windowsill is a pack of cards, a bell, a dog's brush, a book about a girl named Jewel who is a Christian Scientist and won't let anyone take her temperature, and a white jug holding field flowers. The water in the jug has evaporated; the sand-and-amber flowers seem made of paper. The weather bulletin for the day can be one of several: No sun. A high arched yellow sky. Or, creamy clouds, stillness. Long motionless grass. The earth soaks up the sun. Or, the sky is higher than it ever will seem again, and the sun far away and small.

From the window, a field full of goldenrod, then woods; to the left as you stand at the front door of the cottage, the mountains of Vermont.

The screen door slams and shakes my bed. That was my cousin. The couch with the India print spread in the next room has been made up for him. He is the only boy cousin I have, and the only American relation my age. We expected him to be homesick for Boston. When he disappeared the first day, we thought we would find him crying with his head in the wild cucumber vine; but all he was doing was making the outhouse tidy, dragging out of it last year's magazines. He discovers a towel abandoned under his bed by another guest, and shows it to each of us. He has unpacked a trumpet, a hatchet, a pistol, and a water bottle. He is ready for anything except my mother, who scares him to death.

My mother is a vixen. Everyone who sees her that summer will remember, later, the gold of her eyes and the lovely movement of her head. Her hair is true russet. She has the bloom women have sometimes when they are pregnant or when they have fallen in love. She can be wild, bitter, complaining, and ugly as a witch, but that summer is her peak. She has fallen in love.

My father is – I suppose – in Montreal. The guest who seems to have replaced him except in authority over me (he is still careful, still courts my favor) drives us to a movie. It is a musical full of monstrously large people. My cousin sits intent, bites his nails, chews a slingshot during the love scenes. He suddenly dives down in the dark to look for lost, mysterious objects. He has seen so many movies that this one is nearly over before he can be certain he has seen it before. He always knows what is going to happen and what they are going to say next.

At night we hear the radio – disembodied voices in a competition, identifying tunes. My mother, in the living room, seen from my bed, plays solitaire and says from time to time, "That's an old song I like," and "When you play solitaire, do you turn out two cards or three?" My cousin is not asleep either; he stirs on his couch. He shares his room with the guest. Years later we will be astonished to realize how young the guest must have been – twenty-three, perhaps twenty-four. My cousin, in his memories, shared a room with a middle-aged man. My mother and I, for the first and last time, ever, sleep in the same bed. I see her turning out the cards, smoking, drinking cold coffee from a breakfast cup. The single light on the table throws the room against the black window. My cousin and I each have an extra blanket. We forget how the evening sun blinded us at suppertime – how we gasped for breath.

My mother remarks on my hair, my height, my teeth, my French, and what I like to eat, as if she had never seen me before. Together, we wash our hair in the stream. The stones at the bottom are the color of trout. There is a smell of fish and wildness as I kneel on a rock, as she does, and plunge my head in the water. Bubbles of soap dance in place, as if rooted, then the roots stretch and break. In a delirium of happiness I memorize ferns, moss, grass, seedpods. We sunbathe on camp cots dragged out in the long grass. The strands of wet hair on my neck are like melting icicles. Her "Never look straight at the sun" seems extravagantly concerned with my welfare. Through eyelashes I peep at the milky-blue sky. The sounds of this blissful moment are the radio from the house; my cousin opening a ginger-ale bottle; the stream, persistent as machinery. My mother, still taking extraordinary notice of me, says that while the sun bleaches her hair and makes it light and fine, dark hair (mine) turns ugly – "like a rusty old stove lid" – and should be covered up. I dart into the cottage and find a hat: a wide straw hat, belonging to an unknown summer. It is so large I have to hold it with a hand flat upon the crown. I may look funny with this hat on, but at least I shall never be like a rusty old stove lid. The cots are empty; my mother has gone. By mistake, she is walking away through the goldenrod with the guest, turned up from God knows where. They are walking as if they wish they were invisible, of course, but to me it is only a mistake, and I call and run and push my way between them. He would like to take my hand, or pretends he would like to, but I need my hand for the hat.

My mother is developing one of her favorite themes – her lack of roots. To give the story greater power, or because she really believes what she is saying at that moment, she gets rid of an extra parent: "I never felt I had any stake anywhere until my parents died and I had their graves. The graves were my only property. I felt I belonged somewhere."

Graves? What does she mean? My grandmother is still alive.

"That's so sad," he says.

"Don't you ever feel that way?"

He tries to match her tone. "Oh, I wouldn't care. I think everything was meant to be given away. Even a grave would be a tie. I'd pretend not to know where it was."

"My father and mother didn't get along, and that prevented me feeling close to any country," says my mother. This may be new to him, but, like my cousin at a musical comedy, I know it by heart, or something near it. "I was divorced from the land-scape, as they were from each other. I was too taken up wondering what was going to happen next. The first country I loved was somewhere in the north of Germany. I went there with my mother. My father was dead and my mother was less tense and I was free of their troubles. That is the truth," she says, with some astonishment.

The sun drops, the surface of the leaves turns deep blue. My father lets a parcel fall on the kitchen table, for at the end of one of her long, shattering, analytical letters she has put "P.S. Please bring a four-pound roast and some sausages." Did the guest depart? He must have dissolved; he is no longer visible. To show that she is loyal, has no secrets, she will repeat every word that was said. But my father, now endlessly insomniac and vigilant, looks as if it were he who had secrets, who is keeping something back.

The children – hostages released – are no longer required. In any case, their beds are needed for Labor Day weekend. I am to spend six days with my cousin in Boston – a stay that will, in fact, be prolonged many months. My mother stands at the door of the cottage in nightgown and sweater, brown-faced, smiling. The tall field grass is grey with cold dew. The windows of the car are frosted with it. My father will put us on a train, in care of a conductor. Both my cousin and I are used to this.

"He and Jane are like sister and brother," she says – this of my cousin and me, who do not care for each other.

Uncut grass. I saw the ring fall into it, but I am told I did not – I was already in Boston. The weekend party, her chosen audi-ence, watched her rise, without warning, from the wicker chair on the porch. An admirer of Russian novels, she would love to make an immediate, Russian gesture, but cannot. The porch is screened, so, to throw her wedding ring away, she must have walked a few steps to the door and *then* made her speech, and flung the ring into the twilight, in a great spinning arc. The others looked for it next day, discreetly, but it had disappeared. First it slipped under one of those sharp bluish stones, then a beetle moved it. It left its print on a cushion of moss after the first winter. No one else could have worn it. My mother's hands were small, like mine.

New Year's Eve

On New Year's Eve the Plummers took Amabel to the opera.

"Whatever happens tonight happens every day for a year," said Amabel, feeling secure because she had a Plummer on either side.

Colonel Plummer's car had broken down that afternoon; he had got his wife and their guest punctually to the Bolshoi Theatre, through a storm, in a bootleg taxi. Now he discovered from his program that the opera announced was neither of those they had been promised.

His wife leaned across Amabel and said, "Well, which is it?" She could not read any Russian and would not try.

She must have known it would take him minutes to answer, for she sat back, settled a width of gauzy old shawl on her neck, and began telling Amabel the relative sizes of the Bolshoi and some concert hall in Vancouver the girl had never heard of. Then, because it was the Colonel's turn to speak, she shut her eyes and waited for the overture.

The Colonel was gazing at the program and putting off the moment when he would have to say that it was "Ivan Susanin," a third choice no one had so much as hinted at. He wanted to convey that he was sorry and that the change was not his fault. He took bearings: he was surrounded by women. To his left sat the guest, who mewed like a kitten, who had been a friend of his daughter's, and whose name he could not remember. On the right, near the aisle, two quiet unknown girls were eating fruit and chocolates. These two smelled of oranges; of clothes worn a long time in winter; of light recent sweat; of women's hair. Their arms were large and bare. When the girl closest to him moved slightly, he saw a man's foreign wristwatch. He wondered who she was, and how the watch had come to her, but he had been here two years now – long enough to know he would never be answered. He also wondered if the girls were as shabby as his guest found everyone in Moscow. His way of seeing women was not concerned with that sort of evidence: shoes were shoes, a frock was a frock.

The girls took no notice of the Colonel. He was invisible to them, wiped out of being by a curtain pulled over the inner eye.

He felt his guest's silence, then his wife's. The visitor's profile was a kitten's, to match her voice. She was twenty-two, which his Catherine would never be. Her gold dress, packed for improbable

130

gala evenings, seemed the size of a bathing suit. She was divorcing someone, or someone in Canada had left her – he remembered that, but not her name.

He moved an inch or two to the left and muttered, "It's Ivan."

"What?" cried his wife. "What did you say?"

In the old days, before their Catherine had died, when the Colonel's wife was still talking to him, he had tried to hush her in public places sometimes, and so the habit of loudness had taken hold.

"It isn't Boris. It isn't Igor. It's Ivan. They must both have had sore throats."

"Oh, well, bugger it," said his wife.

Amabel supposed that the Colonel's wife had grown peculiar through having lived so many years in foreign parts. Having no one to speak to, she conversed alone. Half of Mrs. Plummer's character was quite coarse, though a finer Mrs. Plummer somehow kept order. Low-minded Mrs. Plummer chatted amiably and aloud with her high-minded twin – far more pleasantly than the whole of Mrs. Plummer ever talked to anybody.

"Serves you right," she said.

Amabel gave a little jump. She wondered if Mrs. Plummer's remark had anything to do with the opera. She turned her head cautiously. Mrs. Plummer had again closed her eyes.

The persistence of memory determines what each day of the year will be like, the Colonel's wife decided. Not what happens on New Year's Eve. This morning I was in Moscow; between the curtains snow was falling. The day had no color. It might have been late afternoon. Then the smell of toast came into my room and I was back in my mother's dining room in Victoria, with the gros-point chairs and the framed embroidered grace on the wall. A little girl I had been ordered to play with kicked the baseboard, waiting for us to finish our breakfast. A devilish little boy, Hume something, was on my mind. I was already attracted to devils, I believed in their powers. My mother's incompetence about choosing friends for me shaped my life, because that child, who kicked the baseboard and left marks on the paint . . .

When she and her husband had still been speaking, this was how Frances Plummer had talked. She had offered him hours of reminiscence, and the long personal thoughts that lead to quarrels. In those days red wine had made her aggressive, whiskey made him vague.

Not only vague, she corrected: stubborn too. *Speak?* said one half of Mrs. Plummer to the other. Did we speak? We yelled!

The quiet twin demanded a fairer portrait of the past, for she had no memory.

Oh, he was a shuffler, back and forth between wife and mistress, said the virago, who had forgotten nothing. He'd desert one and then leave the other – flag to flag, false convert, double agent, reason why a number of women had long, hilly conversations, like the view from a train – monotonous, finally. That was the view a minute ago, you'd say. Yes, but look now.

The virago declared him incompetent; said he had shuffled from embassy to embassy as well, pushed along by a staunch ability to retain languages, an untiring recollection of military history and wars nobody cared about. What did he take with him? His wife, for one thing. At least she was here, tonight, at the opera. Each time they changed countries he supervised the packing of a portrait of his mother, wearing white, painted when she was seventeen. He had nothing of Catherine's: when Catherine died, Mrs. Plummer gave away her clothes and her books, and had her little dog put to sleep.

How did it happen? In what order? said calm Mrs. Plummer. Try and think it in order. He shuffled away one Easter; came shuffling back; and Catherine died. It is useless to say, "Serves you right," for whatever served him served you.

The overture told Amabel nothing, and by the end of the first act she still did not know the name of the opera or understand what it was about. Earlier in the day the Colonel had said, "There is some uncertainty – sore throats here and there. The car, now – you can see what has happened. It doesn't start. If our taxi should fail us, and isn't really a taxi, we might arrive at the Bolshoi too late for me to do anything much in the way of explaining. But you can easily figure it out for yourself." His mind cleared; his face lightened. "If you happen to see Tartar dances, then you will know it is Igor. Otherwise it is Boris."

The instant the lights rose, Amabel thrust her program at him and said, "What does that mean?"

"Why, Ivan. It's Ivan."

"There are two words, aren't there?"

"Yes. What's-His-Name had a sore throat, d'you see? We knew it might all be changed at any moment. It was clever of them to get these printed in time."

Mrs. Plummer, who looked like the Red Queen sometimes, said, "A life for the tsar," meanwhile staring straight ahead of her.

"Used to be, used to be," said the Colonel, and he smiled at Amabel, as if to say to her, Now you know.

The Plummers did not go out between acts. They never smoked, were seldom thirsty or hungry, and they hated crowds. Amabel stood and stretched so that the Russians could appreciate her hair, her waist, her thin arms, and, for those lucky enough to glimpse them, her thighs. After a moment or two Mrs. Plummer thought the Russians had appreciated Amabel enough, and she said very loudly, "You might be more comfortable sitting down."

"Lakmé is coming," said the Colonel, for it was his turn to speak. "It's far and away my favorite opera. It makes an awful fool of the officer caste." This was said with ambiguous satisfaction. He was not really disowning himself.

"How does it do that?" said Amabel, who was not more comfortable sitting down.

"Why, an officer runs off with the daughter of a temple priest. No one would ever have got away with that. Though the military are awful fools most of the time."

"You're that class – caste, I mean – aren't you?"

The Colonel supposed that like most people he belonged to the same caste as his father and mother. His father had worn a wig and been photographed wearing it just before he died. His mother, still living, rising eighty, was given to choked melancholy laughter over nothing, a habit carried over from a girlhood of Anglican giggling. It was his mother the Colonel had wanted in Moscow this Christmas – not Amabel. He had wanted to bring her even if it killed her; even if she choked to death on her own laughter as she shook tea out of a cup because her hand trembled, or if she laughed and said, "My dear boy, nobody forced you to marry Frances." The Colonel saw himself serene, immune to reminders; observed a new Colonel Plummer crowned with a wig, staring out of a photograph, in the uniform his father had worn at Vimy Ridge; sure of himself and still, faded to a plain soft neutral color; unhearing, at peace – dead, in short. He had dreamed of sending the plane ticket, of meeting his mother at the airport with a fur coat over his arm in case she had come dressed for the wrong winter; had imagined giving her tea and watching her drink it out of a glass set in a metal base decorated all over with Soviet cosmonauts; had sat beside her here, at the Bolshoi, at a performance of "Eugene Onegin," which she once had loved. It seemed fitting that he now do some tactful, unneeded, appreciated thing for her, at last – she who had never done anything for him.

One evening his wife had looked up from the paperback spy novel she was reading at dinner and – having waited for him to notice she was neither eating nor turning pages – remarked that

Amabel Bacon, who had been Amabel Fisher, that pretty child Catherine roomed with in school, had asked if she might come to them for ten days at Christmas.

"Nothing for children here," he said. "And not much space."

"She must be twenty-two," said his wife, "and can stay in a hotel."

They stared at each other, as if they were strangers in a crush somewhere and her earring had caught on his coat. Their looks disentangled. That night Mrs. Plummer wrote to Amabel saying that they did not know any young people; that Mrs. Plummer played bridge from three to six every afternoon; that the Colonel was busy at the embassy; that it was difficult to find seats at the ballet; that it was too cold for sightseeing; Lenin's tomb was temporarily closed; there was nothing in the way of shopping; the Plummers, not being great mixers, avoided parties; they planned to spend a quiet Christmas and New Year's; and Amabel was welcome.

Amabel seemed to have forgotten her question about the officer caste. " . . . hissing and whispering behind us the whole time" was what she was saying now. "I could hardly hear the music." She had a smile ready, so that if the Colonel did look at her he would realize she was pleased to be at the Bolshoi and not really complaining. "I suppose you know every note by heart, so you aren't bothered by extra noise." She paused, wondering if the Colonel was hard of hearing. "I hate whispering. It's more bothersome than something loud. It's like that hissing you get on stereo sometimes, like water running."

"Water running?" said the Colonel, not deafly but patiently.

"I mean the people behind us."

"A mother explaining to a child," he said, without looking.

Amabel turned, pretending she was only lifting her long, soft hair away from her neck. She saw a little girl, wearing a white hair ribbon the size of a melon, leaning against, and somehow folded into, a seal-shaped mother. The two shared a pear, bite for bite. Everyone around them was feeding, in fact. It's a zoo, Amabel thought. On the far side of the Colonel, two girls munched on chocolates. They unwrapped each slowly, and dropped the paper back in the box. Amabel sighed and said, "Are they happy? Cheap entertainment isn't everything. Once you've seen 'Swan Lake' a hundred times, what is there to do here?"

Mrs. Plummer slapped at her bangles and said, "We were told when we were in Morocco that children with filthy eye diseases and begging their food were perfectly happy."

"Well, at least they have the sun in those places," said Amabel. She had asked the unanswerable only because she herself was so unhappy. It was true that she had left her husband – it was not the other way around – but he had done nothing to keep her. She had imagined pouring all this out to dead Catherine's mother, who had always been so kind on school holidays because Amabel's parents were divorced; who had invited her to Italy once, and another time to Morocco. Why else had Amabel come all this way at Christmastime, if not to be adopted? She had fancied herself curled at the foot of Mrs. Plummer's bed, Mrs. Plummer with a grey braid down on one shoulder, her reading spectacles held between finger and thumb, her book – one of the thick accounts of somebody's life at Cambridge, the reading of the elderly – slipping off the counterpane as she became more and more engrossed in Amabel's story. She had seen Mrs. Plummer handing her a deep-blue leather case stamped with dead Catherine's initials. The lid, held back by Mrs. Plummer, was lined with sky-blue moire; the case contained Catherine's first coral bracelet, her gold sleeper rings, her first locket, her chains and charm bracelets, a string of pearls, her childless godmother's engagement ring . . . . "I have no one to leave these to, and Catherine was so fond of you," said a fantastic Mrs. Plummer.

None of it could happen, of course: from⁾ a chance phrase Amabel learned that the Plummers had given everything belonging to Catherine to the gardener's children of that house in Italy where Catherine caught spinal meningitis and died. Moreover, Amabel never saw so much as the wallpaper of Mrs. Plummer's bedroom. When she hinted at her troubles, said something about a wasted life, Mrs. Plummer cut her off with "Most lives are wasted. All are shortchanged. A few are tragic."

The Plummers lived in a dark, drab, high-ceilinged flat. They had somehow escaped the foreigners' compound, but their isolation was deeper, as though they were embedded in a large block of ice, Amabel had been put in a new hotel, to which the Colonel conducted her each night astonishingly early. They ate their dinner at a nursery hour, and as soon as Amabel had drunk the last of the decaffeinated coffee the Plummers served, the Colonel guided her over the pavement to where his Rover was waiting and freezing, then drove her along streets nearly empty of traffic, but where lights signalled and were obeyed, so that it was like driving in a dream. The sidewalks were dark with crowds. She wiped the mist away from the window with her glove, and saw people dragging Christmas trees along – not for Christmas, for the New Year, Colonel Plummer told her. When he left her in the hotel lobby it was barely half past eight. She felt as if her visit were a film seen in fragments, with someone's head moving back and forth in front of her face; or as if someone had been describing a story while a blind flapped and a window banged. In the end she would recall nothing except shabby strangers dragging fir trees through the dark.

"Are you enjoying it?" said Mrs. Plummer, snatching away from the Colonel a last-ditch possibility. He had certainly intended to ask this question next time his turn came round.

"Yes, though I'd appreciate it more if I understood," said Amabel. "Probably."

"Don't you care for music?"

"I love music. Understood Russian, I meant."

Mrs. Plummer did not understand Russian, did not need it, and did not miss it. She had not heard a thing said to her in French, or in Spanish, let alone any of the Hamitic tongues, when she and the Colonel were in Morocco; and she had not cared to learn any Italian in Italy. She went to bed early every night and read detective novels. She was in bed before nine unless an official reason kept her from going. She would not buy new clothes now; would not trouble about her hair, except for cutting it. She played bridge every afternoon for money. When she had enough, she intended to leave him. Dollars, pounds, francs, crowns, lire, deutsche marks, and guldens were rolled up in nylon stockings and held fast with elastic bands.

But of course she would never be able to leave him: she would never have enough money, though she had been saving, and rehearsing her farewell, for years. She had memorized every word and seen each stroke of punctuation, so that when the moment arrived she would not be at a loss. The parting speech would spring from her like a separate Frances. Sentences streamed across a swept sky. They were pure, white, unblemished by love or compassion. She felt a complicity with her victim. She leaned past their guest and spoke to him and drew his attention to something by touching his hand. He immediately placed his right hand, the hand holding the program, over hers, so that the clasp, the loving conspiracy, was kept hidden.

So it appeared to Amabel – a loving conspiracy. She was embarrassed, because they were too old for this; then she was envious, then jealous. She hated them for flaunting their long understanding, making her seem discarded, left out of a universal game. No one would love her the way the Colonel loved his wife. Mrs. Plummer finished whatever trivial remark she had considered urgent and sat back, very straight, and shook down her Moroccan bangles, and touched each of her long earrings to see if it was still in place – as if the exchange of words with the Colonel had in fact been a passionate embrace.

Amabel pretended to read the program, but it was all in Russian; there wasn't a word of translation. She wished she had never come.

The kinder half of Mrs. Plummer said aloud to her darker twin, "Oh, well, she is less trouble than that damned military-cultural mission last summer."

Tears stood in Amabel's eyes and she had to hold her head as stiffly as Mrs. Plummer did; otherwise the tears might have spilled on her program and thousands of people would have heard them fall. Later, the Plummers would drop her at her hotel, which could have been in Toronto, in Caracas, or in Amsterdam; where there was no one to talk to, and where she was not loved. In her room was a tapped cream-colored telephone with framed instructions in a secret alphabet, and an oil painting of peonies concealing a microphone to which a Russian had his ear glued the clock around. There were three thousand rooms in the hotel, which meant three thousand microphones and an army of three thousand listeners. Amabel kept her coat, snow boots, and traveller's checks on a chair drawn up to the bedside, and she slept in her bra and panties in case they came to arrest her during the night.

"My bath runs sand," she said. Mrs. Plummer merely looked with one eye, like a canary.

"In my hotel," said Amabel. "Sand comes out of the tap. It's in the bath water."

"Speak to the manager," said Mrs. Plummer, who would not put up with complaints from newcomers. She paused, conceding that what she had just advised was surrealistic. "I've found the local water clean. I drink quarts of it."

"But to bathe in . . . and when I wash my stockings . . ."

"One thing you will never hear of is typhoid here," said the Colonel, kindly, to prevent his wife from saying, "Don't wash your damned stockings." He took the girl's program and looked at it, as if it were in some way unlike his own. He turned to the season's events on the back page and said, "Oh, it isn't Lakmé after all," meanwhile wondering if that was what had upset her.

Amabel saw that she would never attract a man again; she would never be loved, for she had not held even the Colonel's attention. First he sat humming the music they had just heard, then he was hypnotized by the program, then he looked straight up at the ceiling and brought his gaze down to the girls sitting next to the aisle. What was so special about them? Amabel leaned forward, as if looking for a dropped glove. She saw two heads, bare round arms, a pink slip strap dropped on the curve of a shoulder. One of the girls divided an orange, holding it out so the juice would not drip on her knees.

They all look like servants, thought the unhappy guest. I can't help it. That's what they look like. They dress like maids. I'm having a rotten time. She glanced at the Colonel and thought, They're his type. But he must have been good-looking once.

The Colonel was able to learn the structure of any language, given a few pages of colloquial prose and a dictionary. His wife was deaf to strangers, and she barely noticed the people she could not understand. As a result, the Colonel had grown accustomed to being alone among hordes of ghosts. With Amabel still mewing beside him, he heard in the ghost language only he could capture, "Yes, but are you happy?"

His look went across the ceiling and came down to the girls. The one who had whispered the question was rapt; she held a section of orange suspended a few inches from her lips as she waited. But the lights dimmed. "Cht," her friend cautioned. She gathered up the peelings on her lap in a paper bag.

Mrs. Plummer suddenly said clearly to herself or to Amabel, "My mother used to make her children sing. If you sing, you must be happy. That was another idea of happiness."

Amabel thought, Every day of the year will be like tonight.

He doesn't look at women now, said Mrs. Plummer silently. Doesn't dare. Every girl is a wife screaming for justice and revenge; a mistress deserted, her life shrunk down to a postage stamp; a daughter dead.

He walked away in Italy, after a violent drinking quarrel, with Catherine there in the house. Instead of calling after him, Mrs. Plummer sat still for an hour, then remembered she had forgotten to leave some money for the postman for Easter. It was early morning; she was dressed; neither of them had been to bed. She found an envelope, the kind she used for messages to servants and the local tradesmen, and crammed a thousand-lire note inside. She was sober and cursing. She scribbled the postman's name. Catherine, in the garden, on her knees, tore out the pansy plants she had put in the little crevices between paving stones the day before. She looked up at her mother.

"Have you had your breakfast?" her mother said.

"It's no use chasing *them*," Catherine answered. "They've gone."

That was how he had done it – the old shuffler: chosen the Easter holiday, when his daughter was home from school, down in Italy, to creep away. And Catherine understood, for she said "them," though she had never known that the other person existed. Well, of course he came shuffling back, because of Catherine. All was safe: wife was there, home safe, daughter safe, books in place, wine cellar intact, career unchipped. He came out of it scot-free, except that Catherine died. Was it accurate to say, "Serves you right?" Was it fair?

Yes! Yes! "Serves you right!"

Amabel heard, and supposed it could only have to do with the plot of the opera. She said to herself, It will soon be over.

The thing he was most afraid of now was losing his memory. Sometimes he came to breakfast wearing two kinds of shoes. He could go five times to a window to see if snow was falling and forget each time why he was standing there. He had thrown three hundred dollars in a wastepaper basket and carefully kept an elastic band. It was of extreme importance that he remember his guest's name. The name was royal, or imperial, he seemed to recall. Straight down an imperial tree he climbed, counting off leaves: Julia, Octavia, Livia, Cleopatra – not likely – Messalina, Claudia, Domitia. Antonia? It was a name with two "a"s but with an "m" and not an "n."

"Marcia," he said in the dark, half turning to her.

"It's Amabel, actually," she said. "I don't even know a Marcia." Like a child picking up a piece of glass and innocently throwing it, she said, "I don't think Catherine knew any Marcias either."

The woman behind them hissed for silence. Amabel swung round, abruptly this time, and saw that the little girl had fallen asleep. Her ribbon was askew, like a frayed birthday wrapping.

The Colonel slept for a minute and dreamed that his mother was a reed, or a flower. "If only you had always been like that!" he cried, in the dream.

Amabel thought that the scene of the jewel case still might take place: a tap at the hotel-room door tomorrow morning, and there would be Mrs. Plummer, tall and stormy, in her rusty-orange ancient mink, with her square fur bonnet, first visitor of the year, starting the new cycle with a noble gesture. She undid a hastily wrapped parcel, saying, "Nothing really valuable – Catherine was too young." But no, for everything of Catherine's belonged to the gardener's children in Italy now. Amabel rearranged tomorrow morning: Mrs. Plummer brought *her own case* and said, "I have no one to leave anything to except a dog hospital," and there was Amabel, sitting up in bed, hugging her knees, loved at last, looking at emeralds.

Without speaking, Colonel Plummer and his wife each understood what the other had thought of the opera, the staging, and the musical quality of the evening; they also knew where Mrs.

Plummer would wait with Amabel while he struggled to the cloakroom to fetch their wraps.

He had taken great care to stay close behind the two girls. For one thing, he had not yet had the answer to "Are you happy?" He heard now, "I am twenty-one years old and I have not succeeded . . ." and then he was wrenched out of the queue. Pushing back, pretending to be armored against unknown forces, like his wife, he heard someone insult him and smiled uncomprehendingly. No one knew how much he understood – except for his wife. It was as though he listened to stones, or snow, or trees speaking. " . . . even though we went to a restaurant and I paid for his dinner," said the same girl, who had not even looked round, and for whom the Colonel had no existence. "The next night he came to the door very late. My parents were in bed. He had come from some stuffy place – his coat stank. But he looked clean and important. He always does. We went into the kitchen. He said he had come up because he cared and could not spend an evening without seeing me, and then he said he had no money, or had lost his money somewhere. I did not want my mother to hear. I said, 'Now I know why you came to see me.' I gave him money – how could I refuse? He knows we keep it in the same drawer as the knives and forks. He could have helped himself, but instead he was careful not to look at the drawer at all. When he wants to show tenderness, he presses his face to my cheek, his lips as quiet as his forehead – it is like being embraced by a dead animal. I was ashamed to think he knew I would always be there waiting. He thinks he can come in whenever he sees a light from the street. I have no advantage from my loyalty, only disadvantages."

Her friend seemed to be meditating deeply. "If you are not happy, it might be your fault," she said.

The cloakroom attendant flung first the girls' coats and woollen caps on the counter, and then their boots, which had been stored in numbered cubby-holes underneath, and it was the Colonel's turn to give up plastic tokens in exchange for his wife's old fur-lined cloak, Amabel's inadequate jacket, his own overcoat – but of course the girls were lost, and he would never see them again. What nagged at him was that disgraceful man. Oh, he could imagine him well enough: an elegant black-marketeer, speaking five languages, wearing a sable hat, following tourists in the snow, offering icons in exchange for hard currency. It would explain the watch and perhaps even the chocolates and oranges. "His coat stank" and "he looked clean and important" were typically feminine contradictions, of unequal value. He thought he saw the girls a moment later, but they may have been two like them, leaning on a wall, holding each other's coats as they tugged their boots on; then he saw them laughing, collapsed in each other's arms. This is unusual, he told himself, for when do people laugh in public anywhere in the north – not only in this sullen city? He thought, as though suddenly superior to the person he had been only a minute ago, what an iron thing it would be never to regret one's losses.

His wife and Amabel looked too alert, as if they had been discussing him and would now pretend to talk about something else.

"That didn't take long," remarked Mrs. Plummer, meaning to say that it had. With overwhelming directness she said, "The year still has an hour to run, so Amabel tells me, and so we had better take her home with us for a drink."

"Only an hour left to change the year ahead," said Amabel without tact.

The Colonel knew that the city was swept by a Siberian blizzard and that their taxi would be nowhere in sight. But outside he saw only the dust of snow sifting past street lights. The wind had fallen; and their driver was waiting exactly where he had promised. Colonel Plummer helped Amabel down the icy steps of the opera house, then went back for his wife. Cutting off a possible question, she said, "I can make a bed for her somewhere."

Wait, he said silently, looking at all the strangers disappearing in the last hour of the year. Come back, he said to the girls. Who are you? Who was the man?

Amabel's little nose was white with cold. Though this was not her turn to speak, Mrs. Plummer glanced down at her guest, who could not yet hear, saying, "'He is not glad that he is going home, nor sorry that he has not had time to see the city . . .'"

"It's the *sights* of the city,' I think," said the Colonel. "I'll look it up." He realized he was not losing his memory after all. His breath came and went as if he were still very young. He took Amabel's arm and felt her shiver, though she did not complain about the weather and had her usual hopeful smile ready in case he chose to look. Hilarity is happiness, he thought, sadly, remembering those two others. Is it?

Mrs. Plummer took her turn by remarking, "Used to read the same books," to no one in particular.

Without another word, the Plummers climbed into the taxi and drove with Amabel back to the heart of their isolation, where there was no room for a third person; but the third person knew nothing about this, and so for Amabel the year was saved.

In the Tunnel

Sarah's father was a born widower. As she had no memory of a mother, it was as though Mr. Holmes had none of a wife and had been created perpetually bereaved and knowing best. His conviction that he must act for two gave him a jocular heaviness that made the girl react for a dozen, but his jokes rode a limitless tide of concern. He thought Sarah was subjective and passionate, as small children are. She knew she was detached and could prove it. A certain kind of conversation between them was bound to run down, wind up, run down again: you are, I'm not, yes, no, you should, I won't, you'll be sorry. Between eighteen and twenty, Sarah kept meaning to become a psychosociologist. Life would then be a tribal village through which she would stalk soft-footed and disguised: that would show him who was subjective. But she was also a natural *amoureuse*, as some girls were natural actresses, and she soon discovered that love refused all forms of fancy dress. In love she had to show her own face, and speak in a true voice, and she was visible from all directions.

One summer, after a particularly stormy spring, her father sent her to Grenoble to learn about French civilization – actually, to get her away from a man he always pretended to think was called Professor Downcast. Sarah raged mostly over the harm her father had brought to Professor Downcast's career, for she had been helping with his "Urban and Regional Studies of the Less Privileged in British Columbia," and she knew he could not manage without her. She did not stay long in Grenoble; she had never intended to. She had decided beforehand that the Alps were shabby, the cultural atmosphere in France was morbid and stifling, and that every girl she met would be taking the civilization course for the wrong reason. She packed and caught a bus down the Napoleon Route to the Mediterranean.

Professor Downcast had been forced to promise he would not write, and so, of course, Sarah would not write her father. She wanted to have new friends and a life that was none of his business. The word "Riviera" had predicted yellow mornings and snowy boats, and crowds filling the streets in the way dancers fill a stage. Her mind's eye had kept them at a distance so that they shimmered and might have been plumed, like peacocks. Up close, her moralist's eye selected whatever was bound to disappoint: a stone beach skirted with sewage, a promenade that was really a through speedway, an eerie bar. For the first time she recognized prostitutes; they clustered outside her hotel, gossiping, with faces like dead letters. For friends she had a pair of middle-aged tourists who took her sightseeing and warned her not to go out at night by herself. Grenoble had been better after all. Who was to blame? She sent her father a letter of reproach, of abuse, of cold reason, and also of apology – the postmark was bound to be a shock. She then began waiting round American Express for an answer. She was hoping it would be a cable saying "Come on home."

His feelings, when he got round to describing them, filled no more than one flimsy typewritten page. She thought she was worth more than that. What now? She walked out of American Express, still reading her letter. A shadow fell over the page. At the same time a man's soft voice said, "Don't be frightened."

She looked up, not frightened – appraising. The man was about twice her age, and not very tall. He was dressed in clean, not too new summer whites, perhaps the remains of a naval officer's uniform. His accent was English. His eyes were light brown. Once he had Sarah's attention, and had given her time to decide what her attention would be, he said his name was Roy Cooper and asked if she wouldn't like to have lunch with him somewhere along the port.

Of course, she answered: it was broad daylight and there were policemen everywhere – polite, old-fashioned, and wearing white, just like Roy Cooper. She was always hungry, and out of laziness had been living on pizzas and ice cream. Her father had never told her to keep experience at bay. For mystery and horror he had tried to substitute common sense, which may have been why Sarah did not always understand him. She and Roy Cooper crossed the promenade together. He held her arm to guide her through traffic, but let go the minute they reached the curb. "I've been trying to talk to you for days now," he said. "I was hoping you might know someone I knew, who could introduce us."

"Oh, I don't know anyone *here*," said Sarah. "I met a couple of Americans in my hotel. We went to see this sort of abandoned chapel. It has frescoes of Jesus and Judas and . . . " He was silent. "Their name was Hayes?"

He answered that his car was parked over near the port in the shade. It was faster to walk than drive, down here. He was staying outside Nice; otherwise he wouldn't bother driving at all.

They moved slowly along to the port, dragging this shapeless conversation between them, and Sarah was just beginning to wonder if he wasn't a friend of her father's, and if this might be one of her father's large concrete jokes, when he took her bare arm in a way no family friend would have dared and said look here, what about this restaurant? Again he quickly dropped her arm before she could tug away. They sat down under an awning with a blue tablecloth between them. Sarah frowned, lowered her eyes, and muttered something. It might have been a grace before eating had she not seemed so determined; but her words were completely muffled by the traffic grinding by. She leaned forward and repeated, "I'd like to know what your motives are, exactly." She did not mean anything like "What do you want?" but "What is it? Why Roy Cooper? Why me?" At the back of her mind was the idea that he deserved a lesson: she would eat her lunch, get up, coolly stroll away.

His answer, again miles away from Sarah's question, was that he knew where Sarah was staying and had twice followed her to the door of the hotel. He hadn't dared to speak up.

"Well, it's a good thing you finally did," she said. "I was only waiting for a letter, and now I'm going back to Grenoble. I don't like it here."

"Don't do that, don't leave." He had a quiet voice for a man, and he knew how to slide it under another level of sound and make himself plain. He broke off to order their meal. He seemed so at ease, so certain of other people and their reactions – at any moment he would say he was the ambassador of a place where nothing mattered but charm and freedom. Sarah was not used to cold wine at noon. She touched the misty decanter with her fingertips and wet her forehead with the drops. She wanted to ask his motives again but found he was questioning hers – laughing at Sarah, in fact. Who was she to frown and cross-examine, she who wandered around eating pizzas alone? She told him about Professor Downcast and her father – she had to, to explain what she was going here – and even let him look at her father's letter. Part of it said, "My poor Sarah, no one ever seems to interest you unless he is

no good at his job
small in stature, I wonder why?

'Marxist-Leninist' (since you sneer at 'Communist' and will not allow its use around the house)

married or just about to be
in debt to God and humanity.

I am not saying you should look for the opposite in every case, only for some person who doesn't combine all these qualities at one time."

"I'm your father's man," said Roy Cooper, and he might well have been, except for the problem of height. He was a bachelor, and certainly the opposite of a Marxist-Leninist: he was a former prison inspector whose career had been spent in an Asian colony. He had been retired early when the Empire faded out and the New Democracy that followed no longer required inspection. As for "debt to God and humanity," he said he had his own religion, which made Sarah stare sharply at him, wondering if his idea of being funny was the same as her father's. Their conversation suddenly became locked; an effort would be needed to pull it in two, almost a tug-of-war. I could stay a couple of days or so, she said to herself. She saw the south that day as she would see it finally, as if she had picked up an old dress and first wondered, then knew, how it could be changed to suit her.

They spent that night talking on a stony beach. Sarah half lay, propped on an elbow. He sat with his arms around his knees. Behind him, a party of boys had made a bonfire. By its light Sarah told him all her life, every season of it, and he listened with the silent attention that honored her newness. She had scarcely reached the end when a fresh day opened, streaky and white. She could see him clearly: even unshaven and dying for sleep he was the ambassador from that easy place. She tossed a stone, a puppy asking for a game. He smiled, but still kept space between them, about the distance of the blue tablecloth.

They began meeting every day. They seemed to Sarah to be moving toward each other without ever quite touching; then she thought they were travelling in the same direction, but still apart. They could not turn back, for there was nothing to go back to. She felt a pause, a hesitation. The conversation began to unlock; once Sarah had told all her life she could not think of anything to say. One afternoon he came to the beach nearly two hours late. She sensed he had something to tell her, and waited to hear that he had a wife, or was engaged, or on drugs, or had no money. In the most casual voice imaginable he asked Sarah if she would spend the rest of her holiday with him. He had rented a place up behind Nice. She would know all his friends, quite openly; he did not want to let her in for anything squalid or mean. She could come for a weekend. If she hated it, no hard feelings. It was up to her.

This was new, for of course she had never *lived* with anyone. Well, why not? In her mind she told her father, After all, it was a bachelor you wanted for me. She abandoned her textbooks and packed instead four wooden bowls she had bought for her father's sister and an out-of-print Matisse poster intended for Professor Downcast. Now it would be Roy's. He came to fetch her that day in the car that was always parked somewhere in shade – it was a small open thing, a bachelor's car. They rolled out of Nice with an escort of trucks and buses. She thought there should have been carnival floats spilling yellow roses. Until now, this was her most important decision, for it supposed a way of living, a style. She reflected on how no girl she knew had ever done quite this, and on what her father would say. He might not hear of it; at least not right away. Meanwhile, they made a triumphant passage through blank white suburbs. Their witnesses were souvenir shops, a village or two, a bright solitary supermarket, the walls and hedges of villas. Along one of these flowering barriers they came to a stop and got out of the car. The fence wire looked tense and new; the plumbago it supported leaned every way, as if its life had been spared but only barely. It was late evening. She heard the squeaky barking of small dogs, and glimpsed, through an iron gate, one of those stucco bungalows that seem to beget their own palm trees. They went straight past it, down four shallow garden steps, and came upon a low building that Sarah thought looked like an Indian lodge. It was half under a plane tree. Perhaps it was the tree, whose leaves were like plates, that made the house and its terrace seem microscopic. One table and four thin chairs was all the terrace would hold. A lavender hedge surrounded it.

"They call this place The Tunnel," Roy said. She wondered if he was already regretting their adventure; if so, all he had to do was drive her back at once, or even let her down at a bus stop. But then he lit a candle on the table, which at once made everything dark, and she could see he was smiling as if in wonder at himself. The Tunnel was a long windowless room with an arched whitewashed ceiling. In daytime the light must have come in from the door, which was protected by a soft white curtain of mosquito netting. He groped for a switch on the wall, and she saw there was next to no furniture. "It used to be a storage place for wine and olives," he said. "The Reeves fixed it up. They let it to friends."

"What are Reeves?"

"People – nice people. They live in the bungalow."

She was now in this man's house. She wondered about procedure: whether to unpack or wait until she was asked, and whether she had any domestic duties and was expected to cook. Concealed by a screen was a shower bath; the stove was in a cupboard. The lavatory, he told her, was behind the house in a garden shed. She would find it full of pictures of Labour leaders. The only Socialist the Reeves could bear was Hugh Dalton (Sarah had never heard of him, or most of the others, either), because Dalton had paid for the Queen's wedding out of his own pocket when she was a slip of a girl without a bean of her own. Sarah said, "What did he want to do that for?" She saw, too late, that he meant to be funny.

He sat down on the bed and looked at her. "The Reeves versus Labour," he said. "Why should you care? You weren't even born." She was used to hearing that every interesting thing had taken place before her birth. She had a deadly serious question waiting: "What shall I do if you feel remorseful?"

"If I am," he said, "you'll never know. That's a promise."

It was not remorse that overcame him but respectability: first thing next day, Sarah was taken to meet his friends, landlords, and neighbors, Tim and Meg Reeve. "I want them to like you," he said. Wishing to be liked by total strangers was outside anything that mattered to Sarah; all the same, quickened by the new situation and its demands, she dressed and brushed her hair and took the path between the two cottages. The garden seemed a dry, cracked sort of place. The remains of daffodils lay in brown ribbons on the soil. She looked all round her, at an olive tree, and yesterday's iron gate, and at the sky, which was fiercely azure. She was not as innocent as her father still hoped she might turn out to be, but not as experienced as Roy thought, either. There was a world of knowledge between last night and what had gone before. She wondered, already, if violent feelings were going to define the rest of her life, or simply limit it. Roy gathered her long hair in his hand and turned her head around. They'd had other nights, or attempts at nights, but this was their first morning. Whatever he read on her face made him say, "You know, it won't always be as lovely as this." She nodded. Professor Downcast had a wife and children, and she was used to fair warnings. Roy could not guess how sturdy her emotions were. Her only antagonist had been her father, who had not touched her self-confidence. She accepted Roy's caution as a tribute: *he*, at least, could see that Sarah was objective.

Roy rang the doorbell, which set off a gunburst of barking. The Reeves' hall smelled of toast, carpets, and insect spray. She wanted southern houses to smell of jasmine. "Here, Roy," someone called, and Roy led her by the hand into a small sitting room where two people, an old man and an old woman, sat in armchairs eating breakfast. The man removed a tray from his knees and stood up. He was gaunt and tall, and looked oddly starched, like a nurse coming on duty. "Jack Sprat could eat no fat" came to Sarah's mind. Mrs. Reeve was – she supposed – obese. Sarah stared at her; she did not know how to be furtive. Was the poor woman ill? *No*, answered the judge who was part of Sarah too.

Mrs. Reeve is just greedy. Look at the jam she's shovelled on her plate.

"Well, this is Sarah Holmes," said Roy, stroking her hair, as if he was proving at the outset there was to be no hypocrisy. "We'd adore coffee."

"You'd better do something about it, then," said the fat woman. "We've got tea here. You know where the kitchen is, Roy." She had a deep voice, like a moo. "You, Sarah Holmes, sit down. Find a pew with no dog hair, if you can. Of course, if you're going to be fussy, you won't last long around *here* – eh, boys? You can make toast if you like. No, never mind. I'll make it for you."

It seemed to Sarah a pretty casual way for people their age to behave. Roy was older by a long start, but the Reeves were *old*. They seemed to find it natural to have Roy and Sarah drift over for breakfast after a night in the guesthouse. Mr. Reeve even asked quite kindly, "Did you sleep well? The plane tree draws mosquitoes, I'm afraid."

"I'll have that tree down yet," said Mrs. Reeve. "Oh, I'll have it down one of these days. I can promise you that." She was dressed in a bathrobe that looked like a dark parachute. "We decided not to have eggs," she said, as though Sarah had asked. "Have 'em later. You and Roy must come back for lunch. We'll have a good old fry-up." Here she attended to toast, which meant shaking and tapping an antique wire toaster set on the table before her. "When Tim's gone – bless him – I shall never cook a meal again," she said. "Just bits and pieces on a tray for the boys and me." The boys were dogs, Sarah guessed – two little yappers up on the sofa, the color of Teddy-bear stuffing.

"I make a lot of work for Meg," Mr. Reeve said to Sarah. "The breakfasts – breakfast every day, you know – and she is the one who looks after the Christmas cards. Marriage has been a bind for her. She did a marvellous job with evacuees in the war. And poor old Meg loathed kids, still does. You'll never hear her say so. I've never known Meg to complain."

Mrs. Reeve had not waited for her husband to die before starting her widow's diet of tea and toast and jam and gin (the bottle was there, by the toaster, along with a can of orange juice). Sarah knew about this, for not only was her father a widower but they had often spent summers with a widowed aunt. The Reeves seemed like her father and her aunt grown elderly and distorted. Mrs. Reeve now unwrapped a chocolate bar, which caused a fit of snorting and jostling on the sofa. "No chockie bits for boys with bad manners," she said, feeding them just the same. Yes, there she sat, a widow with two dogs for company. Mr. Reeve, delicately buttering and eating the toast meant for Sarah, murmured that when he *did* go he did not want poor Meg to have any fuss. He seemed to be planning his own modest gravestone; in a heightened moment of telepathy Sarah was sure she could see it too. To Sarah, the tall old man had already ceased to be. He was not Mr. Reeve, Roy's friend and landlord, but an ectoplasmic impression of somebody like him, leaning forward, lips slightly parted, lifting a piece of toast that was caving in like a hammock with a weight of strawberry jam. Panic was in the room, but only Sarah felt it. She had been better off, safer, perhaps happier even, up in Grenoble, trying not to yawn over "*Tout m'afflige, et me nuit, et conspire à me nuire.*" What was she doing here, indoors, on this glowing day, with these two snivelly dogs and these gluttonous old persons? She turned swiftly, hearing Roy, and in her heart she said, in a quavering spoiled child's voice, "I want to go home." (How many outings had she ruined for her father. How many picnics, circuses, puppet shows, boat rides. From how many attempted holidays had he been fetched back with a telegram from whichever relation had been trying to hold Sarah down for a week. The strong brass chords of "I want my own life" had always been followed by this dismal piping.)

Roy poured their coffee into pottery mugs and his eyes met Sarah's. His said, Yes, these are the Reeves. They don't matter. I only want one thing, and that's to get back to where we were a few hours ago.

So they were to be conspirators: she liked that.

The Reeves had now done with chewing, feeding, swallowing, and brushing crumbs, and began placing Sarah. Who was she? Sarah Holmes, a little transatlantic pickup, a student slumming round for a summer? What had she studied? Sociology, psychology, and some economics, she told them.

"Sounds Labour" was Mr. Reeve's comment.

She simplified her story and mentioned the thesis. "Urban and Regional Studies of the Less Privileged in British Columbia," as far as Mr. Reeve was concerned, contained only one reassuring word, and that was "British." Being the youngest in the room, Sarah felt like the daughter of the house. She piled cups and plates on one of the trays and took them out to the kitchen. The Reeves were not the sort of people who would ever bother to whisper: she heard that she was "a little on the tall side" and that her proportions made Roy seem slight and small, "like a bloody dago." Her hair was too long; the fringe on her forehead looked sparse and pasted down with soap. She also heard that she had a cast in one eye, which she did not believe.

"One can't accuse her of oversmartness," said Mrs. Reeve.

Roy, whose low voice had carrying qualities, said, "No, Meg. Sarah's jeans are as faded, as baggy, as those brown corduroys of yours. However, owing to Sarah's splendid and enviable shape, hers are not nearly so large across the beam end." This provoked two laughs – a cackle from Jack Sprat and a long three-note moo from his wife.

"Well, Roy," said Tim Reeve, "all I can say is, you amaze me. How do you bring it off?"

"What about me?" said Sarah to herself. "How do *I* bring it off?"

"At least she's had sense enough not to come tramping around in high-heeled shoes, like some of our visitors," said Mrs. Reeve – her last word for the moment.

Roy warned Sarah what lunch – the good old fry-up – would be. A large black pan the Reeves had brought to France from England when they emigrated because of taxes and Labour would be dragged out of the oven; its partner, a jam jar of bacon fat, stratified in a wide extent of suety whites, had its permanent place on top of the stove. The lowest, or Ur, line of fat marked the very first fry-up in France. A few spoonfuls of this grease, releasing blue smoke, received tomatoes, more bacon, eggs, sausages, cold boiled potatoes. To get the proper sausages they had to go to a shop that imported them, in Monte Carlo. This was no distance, but the Reeves' car had been paid for by Tim, and he was mean about it. He belonged to a generation that had been in awe of batteries: each time the ignition was turned on, he thought the car's lifeblood was seeping away. When he became too stingy with the car, then Meg would not let him look at television: the set was hers. She would push it on its wheeled table over bumpy rugs into their bedroom and put a chair against the door.

Roy was a sharp mimic and he took a slightly feminine pleasure in mocking his closest friends. Sarah lay on her elbow on the bed as she had lain on the beach and thought that if he was disloyal to the Reeves then he was all the more loyal to her. They had been told to come back for lunch around three; this long day was in itself like a whole summer. She said, "It sounds like a movie. Are they happy?"

"Oh, blissful," he answered, surprised, and perhaps with a trace of reproval. It was as if he were very young and she had asked an intimate question about his father and mother.

The lunch Roy had described was exactly the meal they were given. She watched him stolidly eating eggs fried to a kind of plastic lace, and covering everything with mustard to damp out

the taste of grease. When Meg opened the door to the kitchen
she was followed by a blue haze. Tim noticed Sarah's look – she
had wondered if something was burning – and said, "Next time
you're here that's where we'll eat. It's what we like. We like our
kitchen."

"Today we are honoring Sarah," said Meg Reeve, as though
baiting Roy.

"So you should," he said. It was the only attempt at sparring;
they were all much too fed and comfortable. Tim, who had been
to Monte Carlo, had brought back another symbol of their roots,
the Hovis loaf. They talked about his shopping, and the things
they liked doing – gambling a little, smuggling from Italy for
sport. One thing they never did was look at the Mediterranean. It
was not an interesting sea. It had no tides. "I do hope you aren't
going to bother with it," said Tim to Sarah. It seemed to be their
private measure for a guest – that and coming round in the wrong
clothes.

The temperature in full sun outside the sitting-room window
was thirty-three degrees centigrade. "What does it mean?" said
Sarah. Nobody knew. Tim said that 16°C. was the same thing as
61°F. but that nothing else corresponded. For instance, 33°C.
could not possibly be 33°F. – No, it felt like a lot more.

After the trial weekend Sarah wrote to her father, "I am in this
interesting old one-room guest-house that belongs to an elderly
couple here. It is in their garden. They only let reliable people
stay in it." She added, "Don't worry, I'm working." If she
concealed information she did not exactly lie: she thought she *was*
working. Instead of French civilization taught in airless class-
rooms she would study expatriates at first hand. She decided to
record the trivia first – how visitors of any sort were a catastrophe, how a message from old friends staying at Nice brought Tim
back from the telephone wearing the look of someone whose
deepest feelings have been raked over.

"Come on, Tim, what was it?" his wife would call. "The who?
What did they want? An invitation to their hotel? Damned cheek.
More likely a lot of free drinks here, that's what they want."
They lived next to gas fires with all the windows shut, yelling
from room to room. Their kitchen was comfortable providing one
imagined it was the depth of January in England and that sleet
was battering at the garden. She wanted to record that Mr. Reeve
said "heith" and "strenth" and that they used a baby language
with each other – walkies, tummy, spend-a-penny. When Sarah
said "cookie" it made them laugh: a minute later, feeding the
dogs a chocolate cookie, Meg said, "Here, have a chockie bicky."

If Tim tried to explain anything, his wife interrupted with "Come on, get to Friday." Nobody could remember the origin of the phrase; it served merely to rattle him.

Sarah meant to record this, but Professor Downcast's useful language had left her. The only words in her head were so homespun and plain she was ashamed to set them down. The heat must have flattened her brain, she thought. The Reeves, who never lowered their voices for anyone, bawled one night that "old Roy was doting and indulgent" and "the wretched girl is in love." That was the answer. She had already discovered that she could live twenty-four hours on end just with the idea that she was in love; she also knew that a man could think about love for a while but then he would start to think about something else. What if Roy never did? Sarah Cooper didn't sound bad; Mrs. R. Cooper was better. But Sarah was not that foolish. She was looking ahead only because she and Roy had no past. She did say to him, "What do you do when you aren't having a vacation?"

"You mean in winter? I go to Marbella. Sometimes Kenya. Where my friends are."

`"Don't you work?"

"I did work. They retired me."

"You're too young to be retired. My father isn't even retired. You should write your memoirs – all that colonial stuff."

He laughed at her. She was never more endearing to him than when she was most serious; that was not her fault. She abandoned the future and rearranged their short history to suit herself. Every word was recollected later in primrose light. Did it rain every Sunday? Was there an invasion of red ants? She refused the memory. The Reeves' garden incinerator, which was never cleaned out, set oily smoke to sit at their table like a third person. She drank her coffee unaware of this guest, seeing nothing but butterflies dancing over the lavender hedge. Sarah, who would not make her own bed at home, insisted now on washing everything by hand, though there was a laundry in the village. Love compelled her to buy enough food for a family of seven. The refrigerator was a wheezy old thing, and sometimes Roy got up and turned it off in the night because he could not sleep for its sighing. In the morning Sarah piled the incinerator with spoiled meat, cheese, and peaches, and went out at six o'clock to buy more and more. She was never so bathed in love as when she stood among a little crowd of villagers at a bus stop – the point of creation, it seemed – with her empty baskets; she desperately hoped to be taken for what the Reeves called "part of the local populace." The market she liked was two villages over; the buses were tumbrils. She could easily have driven Roy's car or had everything sent from shops, but she was inventing fidelities. Once, she saw Meg Reeve, wearing a floral cotton that compressed her figure and gave her a stylized dolphin shape, like an ornament on a fountain. On her head was a straw hat with a polka-dot ribbon. She found a place one down and across the aisle from Sarah, who shrank from her notice for fear of that deep voice letting the world know Sarah was not a peasant. Meg unfolded a paper that looked like a prescription; slid her glasses along her nose; held them with one finger. She always sat with her knees spread largely. In order not to have Meg's thigh crushing his, her neighbor, a priest in a dirty cassock, had to squeeze against the window.

"She doesn't care," Sarah said to herself. "She hasn't even looked to see who is there." When she got down at the next village Meg was still rereading the scrap of paper, and the bus rattled on to Nice.

Sarah never mentioned having seen her; Meg was such a cranky, unpredictable old lady. One night she remarked, "Sarah's going to have trouble landing Roy," there, in front of him, on his own terrace. "He'll never marry." Roy was a bachelor owing to the fact he had too many rich friends, and because men were selfish.... Here Meg paused, conceding that this might sound wrong. No, it sounded right; Roy was a bachelor because of the selfishness of men, and the looseness and availability of young women.

"True enough, they'll do it for a ham sandwich," said Tim, as if a supply of sandwiches had given him the pick of a beach any day.

His wife stared at him but changed her mind. She plucked at her fork and said, "When Tim's gone – bless him – I shall have all my meals out. Why bother cooking?" She then looked at her plate as if she had seen a mouse on it.

"It's all right, Meg," said Roy. "Sarah favors the cooking of the underdeveloped countries. All our meals are raw and drowned in yogurt." He said it so kindly Sarah had to laugh. For a time she had tried to make them all eat out of her aunt's bowls, but the untreated wood became stained and Roy found it disgusting. The sight of Sarah scouring them out with ashes did not make him less squeamish. He was, in fact, surprisingly finicky for someone who had spent a lifetime around colonial prisons. A dead mosquito made him sick —even the mention of one.

"It is true that Roy has never lacked for pretty girls," said Tim. "We should know, eh, Roy?" Roy and the Reeves talked quite a lot about his personal affairs, as if a barrier of discretion had long ago been breached. They were uncomfortable stories, a little harsh sometimes for Sarah's taste. Roy now suddenly chose to tell about how he had met his own future brother-in-law in a brothel in Hong Kong – by accident, of course. They became the best of friends and remained so, even after Roy's engagement was broken off.

"Why'd she dump you?" Sarah said. "She found out?"

Her way of asking plain questions froze the others. They looked as if winter had swept over the little terrace and caught them. Then Roy took Sarah's hand and said, "I'm ashamed to say I wasn't gallant – I dumped the lady."

"Old Roy probably thought, um, matrimony," said Tim. "Eh, Meg?" This was because marriage was supposed to be splendid for Tim but somehow confining for his wife.

"She said I was venomous," said Roy, looking at Sarah, who knew he was not.

"She surely didn't mean venomous," said Tim. "She meant something more like, moody." Here he lapsed into a mood of his own, staring at the candles on the table, and Sarah remembered her shared vision of his unassuming gravestone; she said to Roy in an undertone, "Is anything wrong with him?"

"Wrong with him? Wrong with old Tim? Tim!" Roy called, as if he were out of sight instead of across the table. "When was the last time you ever had a day's illness?"

"I was sick on a Channel crossing – I might have been ten," said Tim.

"Nothing's the matter with Tim, I can promise you that," said his wife. "Never a headache, never a cold, no flu, no rheumatism, no gout, nothing."

"Doesn't feel the amount he drinks," said Roy.

"Are you ever sick, Mrs. Reeve?" Sarah asked.

"Oh, poor Meg," said Tim immediately. "You won't get a word out of her. Never speaks of herself."

"The ailments of old parties can't possibly interest Sarah," said Meg. "Here, Roy, give Sarah something to drink," meaning that her own glass was empty. "My niece Lisbet will be here for a weekend. Now, *that's* an interesting girl. She interviews people for jobs. She can see straight through them, mentally speaking. She had stiff training – had to see a trick cyclist for a year."

"I abhor that subject," said Roy. "No sensible prison governor ever allowed a trick cyclist anywhere near. The good were good and the bad were bad and everyone knew it."

"Psycho-whatnot does no harm if the person is sound," said Meg. "Lisbet just went week after week and had a jolly old giggle with the chap. The firm was paying."

"A didactic analysis is a waste of time," said Sarah, chilling them all once more.

"I didn't say that or anything like it," said Meg. "I said the firm was paying. But you're a bit out of it, Roy," turning to him and heaving her vast garments so Sarah was cut out. "Lisbet said it did help her. You wouldn't believe the number of people she turns away, whatever their education. She can tell if they are likely to have asthma. She saves the firm thousands of pounds every year."

"Lisbet can see when they're queer," said Tim.

"What the hell do you mean?" said Roy.

"What did she tell you?" said Meg, now extremely annoyed. "Come on, Tim, get to Friday."

But Tim had gone back to contemplating his life on the Other Side, and they could obtain nothing further.

Sarah forgot all about Mrs. Reeve's niece until Lisbet turned up, wearing a poncho, black pants, and bracelets. She was about Roy's age. All over her head was a froth of kinky yellow hair – a sort of Little Orphan Annie wig. She stared with small blue eyes and gave Sarah a boy's handshake. She said, "So you're the famous one!"

Sarah had come back from the market to find them all drinking beer in The Tunnel. Her shirt stuck to her back. She pulled it away and said, "Famous one what?" From the way Lisbet laughed she guessed she had been described as a famous comic turn. Roy handed Sarah a glass without looking at her. Roy and Tim were talking about how to keep Lisbet amused for the weekend. Everything was displayed – the night racing at Cagnes, the gambling, the smuggling from Italy, which bored Sarah but which even Roy did for amusement. "A picnic," Sarah said, getting in something she liked. Also, it sounded cool. The Hayeses, those anxious tourists at her hotel in Nice, suddenly rose up in her mind offering advice. "There's this chapel," she said, feeling a spiky nostalgia, as if she were describing something from home. "Remember, Roy, I mentioned it? Nobody goes there . . . you have to get the keys from a café in the village. You can picnic in the churchyard; it has a gate and a wall. There's a river where we washed our hands. The book said it used to be a pagan place. It has these paintings now, of the Last Judgment, and Jesus, naturally, and one of Judas after he hung himself."

"Hanged," said Roy and Lisbet together.

"Hanged. Well, somebody had really seen a hanging – the one who painted it, I mean."

"Have you?" said Roy, smiling.

"No, but I can imagine."

"No," he said, still smiling. "You can't. All right, I'm for the picnic. Sunday, then. We'll do Italy tomorrow."

His guests got up to leave. Tim suddenly said, for no reason Sarah could see, "I'm glad I'm not young."

As soon as the others were out of earshot Roy said, "God, what a cow! Planeloads of Lisbets used to come out to Asia looking for Civil Service husbands. Now they fly to Majorca and sleep with the waiters."

"Why do we have to be nice to her, if you feel like that?" said Sarah.

"Why don't you know about these things without asking?" said Roy.

My father didn't bring me up well, Sarah thought, and resolved to write and tell him so. Mr. Holmes would not have been nice to Lisbet and then called her a cow. He might have done one or the other, or neither. His dilemma as a widower was insoluble; he could never be too nice for fear of someone's taking it into her head that Sarah wanted a mother. Also, he was not violent about people, even those he had to eliminate. That was why he gave them comic names. "Perhaps you are right," she said to Roy, without being any more specific. He cared for praise, however ambiguous; and so they had a perfect day, and a perfect night, but those were the last: in the morning, as Sarah stood on the table to tie one end of a clothesline to the plane tree, she slipped, had to jump, landed badly, and sprained her ankle. By noon the skin was purple and she had to cut off her canvas shoe. The foot needed to be bandaged, but not by Roy: the very sight of it made him sick. He could not bear a speck of dust anywhere, or a chipped cup. She remembered the wooden bowls, and how he'd had to leave the table once because they looked a little doubtful, not too clean. Lisbet was summoned. Kneeling, she wrapped Sarah's foot and ankle in strips of a torn towel and fixed the strips with safety pins.

"It'll do till I see a doctor," Sarah said.

Lisbet looked up. How small her eyes were! "You don't want a doctor for that, surely?"

"Yes, I do. I think it should be X-rayed," Sarah said. "It hurts like anything."

"Of course she doesn't," said Roy.

Getting well with the greatest possible amount of suffering, and with your bones left crooked, was part of their code. It seemed to Sarah an unreasonable code, but she did not want to seem like someone making a fuss. All the same, she said, "I feel sick."

"Drink some brandy," said Lisbet.

"Lie down," said Roy. "We shan't be long." It would have been rude not to have taken Lisbet on the smuggling expedition just because Sarah couldn't go.

In the late afternoon Meg Reeve strolled down to see how Sarah was managing. She found her standing on one foot hanging washing on a line. The sight of Sarah's plaid slacks, bought on sale at Nice, caused Meg to remark, "My dear, are you a Scot? I've often wondered, seeing you wearing those." Sarah let a beach towel of Roy's fall to the ground.

"Damn, it'll have to be washed again," she said.

Meg had brought Roy's mail. She put the letters on the table, face down, as if Sarah were likely to go over the postmarks with a magnifying glass. The dogs snuffled and snapped at the ghosts of animal-haters. "What clan?" said Meg.

"Clan? Oh, you're still talking about my slacks. Clan *salade niçoise*, I guess."

"Well, you must not wear tartan," said Meg. "It is an insult to the family, d'you see? I'm surprised Roy hasn't . . . Ticky! Blue! Naughty boys!"

"Oh, the dogs come down here and pee all over the terrace every day," said Sarah.

"Roy used to give them chockie bits. They miss being spoiled. But now he hasn't time for them, has he?"

"I don't know. I can't answer for him. He has time for what interests him."

"Why do you hang your washing where you can see it?" said Meg. "Are you Italian?" Sarah made new plans; next time the Reeves were invited she would boil Ticky and Blue with a little sugar and suet and serve them up as pudding. I must look angelic at this moment, she thought.

She said, "No, I'm not Italian. I don't think so."

"There are things I could never bring myself to do," said Meg. "Not in my walk of life."

The sociologist snapped to attention. Easing her sore ankle, Sarah said, "Please, what is your walk of life, exactly?"

It was so dazzling, so magical, that Meg could not name it, but merely mouthed a word or two that Sarah was unable to lip-read. A gust of incinerator smoke stole between them and made them choke. "As for Tim," said Meg, getting her breath again, "you, with all your transatlantic money, couldn't buy what Tim has in his veins."

Sarah limped indoors and somehow found the forgotten language. "Necessity for imparting status information," she recorded, and added "erroneous" between "imparting" and "status." She was still, in a way, half in love with Professor Downcast.

She discovered this was a conversation neither Roy nor Lisbet could credit. They unpacked their loot from Italy on the wobbly terrace table – plastic table mats, plastic roses, a mermaid paper-weight, a bottle of apéritif that smelled like medicine, a Floren-tine stamp box . . . "Rubbish, garbage," Sarah said in her mind. "But Roy is happy." Also, he was drunk. So was Lisbet.

"Meg could not have said those things," said Roy, large-eyed.

"Meg doesn't always understand Sarah," said Lisbet. "The accent."

"Mrs. Reeve was doing the talking," said Sarah.

"She wouldn't have talked that way to an Englishwoman," said Roy, swinging round to Sarah's side.

"Wouldn't have dared," said Lisbet. She shouted, "Wouldn't have dared to me!"

"As for Tim, well, Tim really is the real thing," said Roy. "I mean to say that Tim really *is*."

"So is my aunt," said Lisbet, but Roy had disappeared behind the white net curtain, and they heard him fall on the bed. "He's had rather a lot," said Lisbet. Sarah felt anxiety for Roy, who had obviously had a lot of everything – perhaps of Lisbet too. And there was still the picnic next day, and no one had bought any food for it. Lisbet looked glowing and superb, as if she had been tramping in a clean wind instead of sitting crouched in a twilit bar somewhere on the Italian side. She should have been haggard and grey.

"Who was driving?" Sarah asked her.

"Took turns."

"What did you talk about?" She was remembering his "God, what a cow!"

"Capital punishment, apartheid, miscegenation, and my per-sonal problems with men. That I seem cold, but I'm not really."

"Boys, boys, boys!" That was Meg Reeve calling her dogs. They rolled out of the lavender hedge like a pair of chewed tennis balls. They might well have been eavesdropping. Sarah gave a shiver, and Lisbet laughed and said, "Someone's walking on your grave."

The sunlight on the terrace next morning hurt Roy's eyes; he made little flapping gestures, meaning Sarah was not to speak. "What were you drinking in Italy?" she said. He shook his head. Mutely, he took the dried laundry down and folded it. Probably, like Meg, he did not much care for the look of it. "I've made the picnic," Sarah next offered. "No reason why I can't come – we won't be doing much walking." She stood on one leg, like a stork. The picnic consisted of anything Sarah happened to find in the refrigerator. She included plums in brandy because she noticed a jar of them, and iced white wine in a thermos. At the last minute she packed olives, salted peanuts, and several pots of yogurt.

"Put those back," said Roy.

"Why? Do you think they'll melt?"

"Just do as I say, for once. Put them back."

"Do you know what I think? said Sarah after a moment. "I think we're starting out on something my father would call The Ill-Fated Excursion."

For the first time ever, she saw Roy looking angry. The vitality of the look made him younger, but not in a nice way. He became a young man, and ugly one. "Liz will have to drive," he said. "I've got a blinding headache, and you can't, not with *that*." He could not bring himself to name her affliction. "How do you know about this place?" he said. "Who took you there?"

"I told you. Some Americans in my hotel. Haynes – no, Hayes."

"Yes, I can imagine." He looked at her sidelong and said, "Just who were you sleeping with when I collected you?"

She felt what it was like to blush – like a rash of needles and pins. He knew every second of her life, because she had told it to him that night on the beach. What made her blush was that she sensed he was only pretending to be jealous. It offended her. She said, "Let's call the picnic off."

"I don't want to."

She was not used to quarrels, only to tidal waves. She did not understand that they were quarrelling now. She wondered again what he had been drinking over in Italy. Her ankle felt in a vise, but that was the least of it. They set off, all three together, and Lisbet drove straight up into the hills as if pursuing escaped prisoners. They shot past towns Sarah had visited with the Americans, who had been conscientious about churches; she saw, open-and-shut, views they had stopped to photograph. When she said "Look," nobody heard. She sat crumpled in the narrow back seat, with the picnic sliding all over as they rounded the mountain curves, quite often on the wrong side.

"That was the café, back there, where you get the key," Sarah had to say twice – once very loudly. Lisbet braked so they were thrown forward and then reversed like a bullet ricocheting. "Sarah knows about this," said Roy, as if it were a good thing to know about. That was encouraging. She gripped her ankle between her hands and set her foot down. She tested her weight and managed to walk and hop to the cool café, past the beaded curtain. She leaned on the marble counter; she had lost something. Was it her confidence? She wanted someone to come and take her home, but was too old to want that; she knew too many things. She said to the man standing behind the counter, "*J'ai mal*," to explain why she did not take the keys from him and at once go out. His reaction was to a confession of sorrow and grief; he poured out something to drink. It was clear as water, terribly strong, and smelled of warm fruit. When she gestured to show him she had no money, he said, "*Ça va.*" He was kind; the Hayeses, such an inadequate substitute for peacocks, had been kind too. She said to herself, "How awful if I should cry."

The slight inclination of Roy's head when she handed the keys to him meant he might be interested. She felt emboldened: "One's for the chapel, the other's the gate. There isn't a watchman or anything. It's too bad, because people write on the walls."

"Which way?" Lisbet interrupted. She chased her prisoners another mile or so.

Sarah had told them no one ever came here, but they were forced to park behind a car with Swiss license plates. Next to the gate sat a large party of picnickers squeezed round a card table. There was only one man among them, and Sarah thought it must be a harem and the man had been allowed several wives for having been reasonable and Swiss until he was fifty. She started to tell this to Roy, but he had gone blank as a monument; she felt overtaken by her father's humor, not her own. Roy gave the harem an empty look that reminded her of the prostitutes down in Nice, and now she knew what their faces had been saying. It was "I despise you." The chapel was an icebox; and she saw Roy and Lisbet glance with some consternation at the life of Jesus spread around for anyone to see. They would certainly have described themselves as Christians, but they were embarrassed by Christ. They went straight to Judas, who was more reassuring. Hanged, disembowelled, his stomach and liver exposed to ravens, Judas gave up his soul. His soul was a small naked creature. Perceiving Satan, the creature held out its arms.

"Now, *that* man must have eaten Sarah's cooking," said Roy, and such were their difficulties that she was grateful to hear him say anything. But he added, "A risk many have taken, I imagine." This was to Lisbet. Only Sarah knew what he meant. She fell back and pretended to be interested in a rack of postcards. The same person who trusted visitors not to write their names on paintings had left a coin box. Sarah had no money and did not want to ask Roy for any. She stole a reproduction of the Judas fresco and put it inside her shirt.

Roy and Lisbet ate some of the picnic. They sat where Sarah had sat with the Americans, but it was in no way the same. Of course, the season was later, the river lower, the grass drooping and dry. The shadows of clouds made them stare and comment, as if looking for something to say. Sarah was relieved when the two decided to climb up in the maquis, leaving her "to rest a bit" – this was Lisbet. "Watch out for snakes," Sarah said, and got from Roy one blurred, anxious, puzzled look, the last straight look he ever gave her. She sat down and drank all the brandy out of the jar of plums. Roy had an attitude to people she had never heard of: nothing must ever go wrong. An accident is degrading for the victim. She undid the towelling strips and looked at her bloated ankle and foot. Of course, it was ugly; but it was part of a living body, not a corpse, and it hurt Sarah, not Roy. She tipped out the plums so the ants could have a party, drank some of the white wine, and, falling asleep, thought she was engaged in an endless and heated discussion with some person who was in the wrong.

She woke up cramped and thirsty on the back seat of the car. They were stopped in front of the café and must have been parked for some time, for they were in an oblique shadow of late afternoon. Roy was telling Lisbet a lie: he said he had been a magistrate and was writing his memoirs. Next he told her of hangings he'd seen. He said in his soft voice, "Don't you think some people are better out of the way?" Sarah knew by heart the amber eyes and the pupils so small they seemed a mistake sometimes. She was not Sarah now but a prisoner impaled on a foreign language, seeing bright, light, foreign eyes offering something nobody wanted – death. "Flawed people, born rotten," Roy went on.

"Oh, everyone thinks that now," said Lisbet.

They were alike, with fortunes established in piracy. He liked executions; she broke people before they had a chance to break themselves. Lisbet stroked the back of her own neck. Sarah had noticed before that when Lisbet was feeling sure of herself she made certain her neck was in place. *Neurotic habit*, Sarah's memory asked her to believe; but no, it was only the gesture of someone at ease in a situation she recognized. Tranquil as to her neck, Lisbet now made sure of her hair. She patted the bright steel wool that must have been a comfort to her mother some thirty-five – no, forty – years before.

I am jealous, Sarah said to herself. How unwelcome. Jealousy is only . . . the jealous person is the one keeping something back and so . . .

"Oh, keys, always keys," said Roy, shaking them. He slammed out in a way that was surely rude to Lisbet. She rested her arm over the back of the seat and looked at Sarah. "You drank enough to stun a rhinoceros, little girl," she said. "We had to take you out behind the chapel and make you be sick before we could let you in the car." Sarah began to remember. She saw Roy's face, a grey flash in a cracked old film about a catastrophe. Lisbet said, "Look, Sarah, how old are you? Aren't you a bit out of your depth with Roy?" She might have said more, but a native spitefulness, or a native prudence, prevented her. She flew to Majorca the next day, as Roy had predicted, leaving everyone out of step.

Now Roy began hating; he hated the sea, the Reeves, the dogs, the blue of plumbago, the mention of Lisbet, and most of all he hated Sarah. The Reeves laughed and called it "old Roy being bloody-minded again," but Sarah was frightened. She had never known anyone who would simply refuse to speak, who would take no notice of a question. Meg said to her, "He misses that job of his. It came to nothing. He tried to give a lot of natives a sense of right and wrong, and then some Socialist let them vote."

"Yes, he liked that job," Sarah said slowly. "One day he'd watch a hanging, and the next he'd measure the exercise yard to see if it was up to standard." She said suddenly and for no reason she knew, "I've disappointed him."

Their meals were so silent that they could hear the swelling love songs from the Reeves' television, and the Reeves' voices bawling away at each other. Sarah's throat would go tight. In daytime the terrace was like an oven now, and her ankle kept her from sleeping at night. Then Roy gave up eating and lay on the bed looking up at the ceiling. She still went on shopping, but now it took hours. Mornings, before leaving, she would place a bowl of coffee for him, like an offering; it was still there, at the bedside, cold and oily-looking now, when she came back. She covered a tray with leaves from the plane tree – enormous powdery leaves, the size of her two hands – and she put cheese on the leaves, and white cheese covered with pepper, a Camembert, a salty goat cheese he had liked. He did not touch any. Out of a sort of desperate sentiment, she kept the tray for days, picking chalky pieces off as the goat cheese grew harder and harder and became a fossil. He must have eaten sometimes; she thought of him gobbling scraps straight from the refrigerator when her back was turned. She wrote a letter to her father that of course she did not send. It said, "I've been having headaches lately. I wind a thread around a finger until the blood can't get past and that starts a new pain. The headache is all down the back of my neck. I'm not sure what to do next. It will be terrible for you if I turn out to have a brain tumor. It will cost you a lot of money and you may lose your only child."

One dawn she knew by Roy's breathing that he was awake. Every muscle was taut as he pulled away, as if to touch her was defilement. No use saying what they had been like not long before, because he could not remember. She was a disgusting object because of a cracked ankle, because she had drunk too much and been sick behind a chapel, and because she had led an expedition to look at Jesus. She lay thinking it over until the dawn birds stopped and then she sat up on the edge of the bed, feeling absolutely out of place because she was undressed. She pulled clothes on as fast as she could and packed whatever seemed important. After she had pushed her suitcase out the door, she remembered the wooden bowls and the poster. These she took along the path and threw in the Reeves' foul incinerator, as if to get rid of all traces of witchery, goodness, and love. She realized she was leaving, a decision as final and as stunning as her having crossed the promenade in Nice with Roy's hand on her arm.

She said through the white netting over the door, "I'm sorry, Roy." It was not enough; she added, "I'm sorry I don't understand you more." The stillness worried her. She limped near and bent over him. He was holding his breath, like a child in temper. She said softly, "I could stay a bit longer." No answer. She said, "Of course, my foot will get better, but then you might find something else the matter with me." Still no answer, except that he began breathing. Nothing was wrong except that he was cruel, lunatic, Fascist – No, not even that. Nothing was wrong except that he did not love her. That was all.

She lugged her suitcase as far as the road and sat down beside it. Overnight a pocket of liquid the size of a lemon had formed near the anklebone. Her father would say it was all her own fault again. Why? Was it Sarah's fault that she had all this loving capital to invest? What was she supposed to do with it? Even if she always ended up sitting outside a gate somewhere, was she any the worse for it? The only thing wrong now was the pain she felt, not of her ankle but in her stomach. Her stomach felt as if it was filled up with old oyster shells. Yes, a load of old, ugly, used-up shells was what she had for stuffing. She had to take care not to breathe too deeply, because the shells scratched. In her research for Professor Downcast she had learned that one could be alcoholic, crippled, afraid of dying and of being poor, and she knew these things waited for everyone, even Sarah; but nothing had warned her that one day she would not be loved. That was the meaning of "less privileged." There was no other.

Now that she had vanished, Roy would probably get up, and shave, and stroll across to the Reeves, and share a good old fry-up. Then, his assurance regained, he would start prowling the bars and beaches, wearing worn immaculate whites, looking for a new, unblemished story. He would repeat the first soft words, "Don't be frightened," the charm, the gestures, the rituals, and the warning "It won't always be lovely." She saw him out in the open, in her remembered primrose light, before he was trapped in the tunnel again and had to play at death. "Roy's new pickup," the Reeves would bawl at each other. "I said, Roy's new one ... he hardly knows how to get rid of her."

At that, Sarah opened her mouth and gave a great sobbing cry; only one, but it must have carried, for next thing she heard was the Reeves' door, and, turning, she saw Tim in a dressing gown, followed by Meg in her parachute of a robe. Sarah stood up to face them. The sun was on her back. She clutched the iron bars of the gate because she had to stand like a stork again. From their side of it, Tim looked down at her suitcase. He said, "Do you want – are you waiting to be driven somewhere?"

"To the airport, if you feel like taking me. Otherwise I'll hitch."

"Oh, please don't do that!" He seemed afraid of another outburst from her – something low-pitched and insulting this time.

"Come in this minute," said Meg. "I don't know what you are up to, but we do have neighbors, you know."

"Why should I care?" said Sarah. "They aren't my neighbors."

"You *are* a little coward," said Meg. "Running away only because ... " There were so many reasons that of course she hesitated.

Without unkind intention Sarah said the worst thing: "It's just that I'm too young for all of you."

Meg's hand crept between the bars and around her wrist. "Somebody had to be born before you, Sarah," she said, and unlocked her hand and turned back to the house. "Yes, boys, dear boys, here I am," she called.

Tim said, "Would you like – let me see – would you like something to eat or drink?" It seemed natural for him to talk through bars.

"I can't stay in the same bed with someone who doesn't care," said Sarah, beginning to cry. "It isn't right."

"It is what most people do," said Tim. "Meg has the dogs, and her television. She has everything. We haven't often lived together. We gradually stopped. When did we last live together? When we went home once for the motor show." She finally grasped what he meant by "live together." Tim said kindly, "Look, I don't mean to pry, but you didn't take old Roy too much to heart, did you? He wasn't what you might call the love of your life?"

"I don't know yet."

"Dear, dear," said Tim, as if someone had been spreading bad news. He seemed so much more feminine than his wife; his hands were powdery – they seemed dipped in talcum. His eyes were embedded in a little volcano of wrinkles that gave him in full sunlight the look of a lizard. A white lizard, Sarah decided. "This has affected Meg," he said. "The violence of it. We shall talk it over for a long time. Well. You have so much more time. You will bury all of us." His last words were loud and sudden, almost a squawk, because Meg, light of tread and silent on her feet, had come up behind him. She wore her straw hat and carried her morning glass of gin and orange juice.

"Sarah? She'll bury *you*," said Meg. "Fetch the car, Tim, and take Sarah somewhere. Come along. Get to Friday. *Tim*." He turned, "Dress first," she said.

The sun which had turned Tim into a white lizard now revealed a glassy stain on Meg's cheek, half under her hair. Sarah's attention jumped like a child's. She said, "Something's bitten you. Look. Something poisonous."

Meg moved her head and the poisoned bite vanished under the shade of her hat. "Observant. Tim has never noticed. Neither has Roy. It is only a small malignant thing," she said indifferently. "I've been going to the hospital in Nice twice a week for treatment. They burned it – that's the reason for the scar."

"Oh, Meg," said Sarah, drawn round the gate. "Nobody knew. That was why you went to Nice. I saw you on the bus."

"I saw you," said Meg, "but why talk when you needn't? I get plenty of talk at home. May I ask where you are going?"

"I'm going to the airport, and I'll sit there till they get me on a plane."

"Well, Sarah, you may be sitting for some time, but I know you know what you are doing," said Meg. "I am minding the summer heat this year. I feel that soon I won't be able to stand it anymore. When Tim's gone I won't ever marry again. I'll look for some woman to share expenses. If you ever want to come back for a holiday, Sarah, you have only to let me know."

And so Tim, the battery of his car leaking its lifeblood all over French roads, drove Sarah down to Nice and along to the airport. Loyal to the Reeve standards, he did not once glance at the sea. As for Sarah, she sat beside him crying quietly, first over Meg, then over herself, because she thought she had spent all her capital on Roy and would never love anyone again. She looked for the restaurant with the blue tablecloths, and for the beach where they had sat talking for a night, but she could not find them; there were dozens of tables and awnings and beaches, all more or less alike.

"You'll be all right?" said Tim. He wanted her to say yes, of course.

She said, "Tim, Roy needs help."

He did not know her euphemisms any more than she understood his. He said, "Help to do what?"

"Roy is unhappy and he doesn't know what he wants. If you're over forty and you don't know what you want, well, I guess someone should tell you."

"My dear Sarah," said the old man, "that is an unkind thing to say about a friend we have confidence in."

She said quickly, "Don't you see, before he had a life that suited him, inspecting people in jails. They didn't seem like people *or* jails. It kept him happy, it balanced . . ." Suddenly she gave a great shiver in the heat of the morning and heard Lisbet laugh and say, "Someone's walking on your grave." She went on, "For example, he won't eat."

"Don't you worry about that," cried Tim, understanding something at last. "Meg will see that he eats." Right to the end, everyone was at cross-purposes. "Think of it this way," said Tim. "You had to go home sometime."

"Not till September."

"Well, look on the happy side. Old Roy . . . matrimony. You might not enjoy it, you know, unless you met someone like Meg." He obviously had no idea what he was saying anymore, and so she gave up talking until he set her down at the departures gate. Then he said, "Good luck to you, child," and drove away looking indescribably happy.

Sarah kept for a long time the picture of Judas with his guts spilling and with his soul (a shrimp of a man, a lesser Judas) reaching out for the Devil. It should have signified Roy, or even Lisbet, but oddly enough it was she, the victim, who felt guilty and maimed. Still, she was out of the tunnel. Unlike Judas she was alive, and that was something. She was so much younger than all those other people: as Tim had said, she would bury them all. She tacked the Judas card over a map of the world on a wall of her room. Plucked from its origins it began to flower from Sarah's; here was an image that might have followed her from the nursery. It was someone's photo, a family likeness, that could bear no taint of pain or disaster. One day she took the card down, turned it over, and addressed it to a man she was after. He was too poor to invite her anywhere and seemed too shy to make a move. He was also in terrible trouble – back taxes, ex-wife seizing his salary. He had been hounded from California to Canada for his political beliefs. She was in love with his mystery, his hardships, and the death of Trotsky. She wrote, "This person must have eaten my cooking. Others have risked it so please come to dinner on Friday, Sarah." She looked at the words for seconds before hearing another voice. Then she remembered where the card was from, and she understood what the entire message was about. She could have changed it, but it was too late to change anything much. She was more of an *amoureuse* than a psycho-anything, she would never use up her capital, and some summer or other would always be walking on her grave.

SELECTED NEW CANADIAN LIBRARY TITLES

Asterisks (*) denote titles of New Canadian Library Classics

McCLELLAND AND STEWART
publishers of The New Canadian Library
would like to keep you informed about
new additions to this unique series.

For a complete listing of titles and
current prices – or if you wish to be added
to our mailing list to receive future catalogues
and other new book information – write:

BOOKNEWS
McClelland and Stewart
481 University Avenue
Toronto, Canada M5G 2E9

McClelland and Stewart books are
available at all good bookstores.

Booksellers should be happy to order from our catalogues
any titles which they do not regularly stock.